Sign up for our newsletter to hear about
new and upcoming releases.

www.ylva-publishing.com

Other Books from Catherine Lane

The Set Piece

Heartwood

CATHERINE LANE

Acknowledgment

So many people to thank! Gill McKnight, who pushed me through two bad ideas into a good one. Susan X Meagher, who answered all my questions even when she was on vacation. Ann, Boz, and Liz—my awesome beta readers. Astrid Ohletz and her amazing team at Ylva, who really know how to support an author.

And then there is Sandra Gerth, my wonderful editor, who's been with me since the beginning and who is a fantastic teacher and mentor as well. Thank you for always going the extra mile. *Heartwood* wouldn't be half of what it is without you.

To Pat, who's always up for a walk and a laugh.

Chapter 1

NIKKA PUSHED THE FLOWERING CACTUS plant to the side of her engraved pencil holder and pulled the picture of her cats, Lucy and Desi, closer to her phone. There, that was better. No. She couldn't suppress the grin. It was perfect.

By big business standards, the small cubicle on the tenth floor was nothing special. Almost pathetic even. One hundred and twenty feet filled with a cheap melamine desk, an office chair with no arms, and a view of other lawyers bent over files and phones. But to Nikka it was the golden ring of the carousel of intellectual property law. For now, at least.

She had made the jump from the hinterland of the ninth floor to mid-level associate in just three years. A record at Truman and Steinbrecker. But after sitting at her new desk with new responsibilities for just ten minutes, wild aspirations rose up in her.

Nikka glanced down the windowed hallway that led to the partners' offices. Somewhere on that hallowed ground were breathtaking views of San Francisco Bay and Lea Truman's office. If she worked even harder, she, too, could make managing partner and have that million-dollar view. The to-do list materialized in her mind: *find her niche, take initiative, cultivate a mentor.* She would…

"Oh shit." A clerk's voice drifted across the low wall to her left.

Lea Truman strode down the hallway, a look of consternation plastered to her thin face. "All right, everyone. Stand up."

The whole cubicle farm rose as if they were in a flash mob dance. Nikka struggled to get up without sending her chair spinning into her file cabinet.

"Who here has a car?"

Half the people on their feet raised their hands.

Nikka looked around and slowly added hers to the raised arms.

"Who has it here in the parking lot downstairs?"

Several hands dropped back down.

Unbelievably, Nikka had braved the city traffic this morning since she had wanted to break in her brand-new Subaru Outback. Was this a good or bad thing?

"A GPS?"

Now only Nikka and an unfamiliar man with red hair and a trendy beard were still in the running. A small, triumphant smile played on his lips. His body tensed, ready to spring forward at the next question, like a contestant in a quiz show, poised to press the buzzer.

"And a full tank of gas?"

She had filled up just that morning, following her father's advice to never let the gas tank fall below the halfway mark.

The man's arm flopped to his side. Everyone in the cubicle farm swung to look at Nikka, some with envy, others with pity.

Her father's words rose in her mind. *Winners embrace opportunity, big or small.* She fought down the nausea rising in her stomach and turned to the managing partner with her head high.

Lea Truman met her gaze with a hard stare and waved her over. "Nikka, right?"

Nikka nodded vigorously.

"All right. Let's go."

Nikka grabbed her purse and her keys and tried to pump confidence into her reply. "Yes, Ms. Truman."

"Call me Lea. I'm your boss, not your headmistress."

"Yes…Lea." Nikka cringed. *Make a good impression* should have been number one on that to-do list.

Lea motioned over an assistant whose arms were piled high with files and a silver laptop. The assistant thrust it all at Nikka, who juggled the bundle for a harrowing second before pulling it safely to her chest. Lea took control of the remaining manila envelope from her assistant's outstretched hand. "Call Ace's Town Car Service and tell Mr. We-can't-be-there-for-thirty-minutes he and his company are fired. We're late. Come along."

Nikka hung back, repositioning the papers and the computer into a more comfortable load, until she registered with a jolt that Lea was talking to her and scurried after her to the elevator.

Lea punched the down button as if she owned it. Maybe she did. There had been a rumor on the ninth floor last year that she had actually bought the building.

Once inside and only inches apart, Nikka took stock of her boss. Tall and thin, almost to the point of wiry, Lea radiated power. Nikka had been this close to her once before, when she was hired. Then, there had been a handshake that had crackled with energy, but now that same power hit her in a wave. This was what success looked like, and if she was being honest, what sexy looked like too. Boss or no boss, Lea was hot. Ice-blonde hair fell in a trendy razor cut over high cheekbones and sharp blue eyes, and even the age lines around her mouth gave her an alluring air of experience.

"What floor are you parked on?"

"Oh, C. Level C." Nikka dropped her gaze. This was work, not a date. Although since she could count the number of dates she had been on in the last three years on one hand, she was surprised she could remember the difference.

Nikka shifted the bundle in her arms so she could get the keys out of her purse before the doors opened and not waste a precious second. Even before they were out of the elevator, the beeping from the pristine white Outback greeted them from a nearby parking space.

"Better than I had hoped." Lea peered through the car's tinted back window. "There's a computer plug in the center console, right?" She opened the door before Nikka had a chance to answer. She shoved over a yoga mat, hopped in, and held out her arms for the laptop and files. "Glad to see the ride out there won't be a total waste. Get in, and I'll give you the address."

As Nikka pulled up her navigation device, her heart sank. Lea didn't want an associate to run ideas by; she just wanted a chauffeur. How was she going to find opportunity in being used for a full tank of gas and a GPS? Her father didn't have a saying for that.

When Lea paused to boot up her laptop and slip the charger into the plug between the front seats, Nikka asked, "What city?"

"Steelhead Springs."

Nikka had tapped the S and the T into the console when her heart flipped over in her chest. Steelhead Springs? No way! Wasn't that the official name for the Springs, a tiny town on the Tall Tree River about two hours north of the City? Maybe this day wouldn't be a complete waste after all. The Springs was the home of Truman and Steinbrecker's celebrated client—famous lesbian author and recluse Beth Walker.

Holy shit.

Gigantic, huge opportunity.

Maggie Chalon slipped her paring knife into the radish, carving the last delicate petal of the intricate flower design. She dropped the edible rose into ice water to keep while she cut the tomato for the sandwich. She didn't know why she bothered. Her little works of art were never appreciated. Hell, a good day lately was when the sandwich came back with two bites out of it.

"Is lunch ready? I need to take it up." Vivienne stuck her head into the kitchen. As usual, a nametag reading *Vivienne Tenney, Physician Assistant* rode above the left breast pocket of her polyester scrub top.

Why the hell didn't she take that relic from another job off? It wasn't as if they were working with dozens of new patients or staff members who didn't know her name.

"Yep. Almost ready." Maggie placed the rose radish next to two elaborate pineapple happy faces. "How is she feeling today?"

"Anxious. Irritable. It's not a good day, the poor girl," Vivienne said, but there was no kindness in her voice. She pulled two twenties out of one oversized pocket and slid them over the counter with a wrinkled finger. "Beth asked for broccoli soup tonight for supper. Be a dear. Zip over to the farmers' market and get the ingredients, will you?"

"We have what we need here." Maggie waved to the huge subzero fridge behind her. It sat like a monster from the future in the retro kitchen.

Vivienne pursed her lips, adding even more wrinkles to her face. "Beth especially asked for fresh broccoli."

"Really?" Never once in the six months that Maggie had been Beth's personal chef had she made a request.

"Yes. That's a good sign."

"I guess." How would she know? Maggie hadn't seen Beth Walker in those six months either.

Although she shouldn't be surprised. That tall lawyer, Lea, had been completely upfront when she had hired her. "Vivienne will be your only contact in the house while you're there. Are you okay with that?"

"Sure, sure," Maggie had said even though Lea leaning in to make her point made her skin crawl a little. Frankly, she would've said anything at that point to land the job.

Lea had scanned her face. "Other people I interviewed asked why."

"Okay, why?"

"My client has a long history of being very, very private, and sadly now on top of that, she is tottering toward dementia. Strangers confuse her, and her routines must be set and predictable."

"Okay."

Another long look. "We'll run a background check. We'll find out if you're in trouble."

"I'm not sure you can call it trouble exactly." Maggie had jostled her head around, trying to look cute. She got a lot of first dates with that look, why not a job? "I work for my ex, and it's great and all. But I'm not sure it's the best situation for either of us."

Lea had glanced at her phone rather than answer, so Maggie had changed tactics.

"No worries. Lauren will give me a great recommendation. Does Beth like sweets? I make these little cake pops that..."

"Lauren?"

"I thought with this being Beth Walker and all, *that* wouldn't be a problem."

"It's not." Lea had nodded and leaned back. "Girl trouble. I totally get it. You got the job."

The firm had run the background check anyway.

"It's a beautiful day." Vivienne brought her back to the present as she grabbed the tray with the sandwich. She plucked the rose radish off the plate and tossed it into the sink. "Take your bike to the market. Make a workout of it, as you like to do."

Dark thoughts, and not for the first time in the last few weeks, circled in her mind. Vivienne would rather complain about her wasting time biking to town than breathe. Suddenly, she was pushing an outing?

"Thanks, I will." Maggie tried to infuse lightness into her voice.

Vivienne didn't fool her. She wanted Maggie out of the house. The job, which had never been standard, had just spun from following weird rules to ignoring something that smelled rotten. It looked as if now was the time to start asking why.

Nikka eased her foot off the gas just as they passed the Steelhead Springs sign—Population 14,534—at the edge of town. She had floored the gas pedal most of the way, even though the salesman had told her to break the engine in gently.

Tall coastal redwoods grew on either side of the two-lane highway, and a picturesque river cut into the woods on the left. Signs advertising homey bed-and-breakfasts and womyn retreats popped up along its bank.

"Oh good. We're finally here." Lea snapped her computer shut in the backseat. She hadn't said a word since they had crossed the Golden Gate Bridge over an hour and a half ago. The trip for her had been a steady stream of work as she jumped from cell phone to computer to tablet with rapid-fire precision.

Nikka, on the other hand, had spent the same time stealing glances in the rearview mirror and crafting succinct yet thoughtful answers to any work question that might come up. She wouldn't get a second chance to make a first impression. Whatever this case was, she wanted in.

"Have you ever been here before?" Lea asked.

"Yes, once in college. A friend and I came up for a weekend."

"Let me guess. You had just read *Heartwood* in some women's studies class and wanted to check out the scene."

"Something like that." Stupidly, she hadn't prepared for personal questions.

Lea had only gotten part of the truth, though. Nikka had read Walker's seminal book at UC Berkeley. That much was true, but the real reason she had come to the Springs all those years ago had more to do with Alexis than the book. Alexis, the soft butch who had stolen her heart and her virginity that weekend in the Springs. Alexis, whom she had dumped by text message rather than tell her parents she was gay. Alexis, whom she unsuccessfully had tried to find years later when she had finally come out.

"Beth Walker made this town, you know." Lea waved a hand at the colorful storefronts. The author's face and blown-up versions of her book covers stared back at them from the windows as they drove. Rainbow banners hung down from streetlamps, advertising a dramatization of *Heartwood* at a local coffee house. It seemed as if the town had made Beth Walker.

"You wouldn't recognize this place before Walker," Lea said. "In 1960, Steelhead Springs was just another quiet retirement community up the coast. The only thing they had going for them was the steelhead trout that ran the river from October to April. Then Walker became famous. Not for *Heartwood*, of course. It was for that kids' series…about a magic composition book that grants wishes. I've never read them."

"*Don't Waste Your Wishes*. They're fantastic."

"Right," Lea said, but *right* sounded more like *whatever*. "Then someone, probably from *Heartwood's* publishing house, let it slip that Walker was the author of both. I mean, that's what I would do. The lesbians started turning up in the Springs, looking for her. By then, it was the late eighties; enterprising women jumped at the chance to make a buck, so they turned the town into a destination for women." She pointed to a bustling town center. "Damn. I wish I had thought of it."

Nikka nodded, but she didn't need the lecture. Anyone who had read the book and knew even a little bit of queer history recognized that Beth Walker had captured exactly what it was like to be a dyke in the sixties. From the male oppression and sexism to the hidden life style to wild sex on the banks of the Tall Tree River. More importantly, what it would be like to live free of all that persecution here in an idealized version of Steelhead Springs.

"*Heartwood* is a seminal book in so many ways," Nikka said.

Lea dove back into her files without comment.

Nikka bit her lip. Were there third chances for a first impression? Because at this point she had blown chances one and two.

They were smack in the middle of the town when the navigation device said, "Turn right in five hundred feet."

Nikka signaled and eased carefully into the crosswalk.

Whoosh! A woman on an old mountain bike cut right in front of her, missing her front bumper only by inches.

"Oh my God!" Nikka slammed on her brakes. The car skidded to a sharp stop, and the smell of burning rubber filled the air.

"What the fuck?" Lea cried as her files and computer flew in different directions in the backseat. A packet of legal papers appeared under the front passenger seat.

"She...she came out of nowhere." Nikka pointed to the woman zooming away, her long athletic legs pumping furiously. The biker hadn't even seen them or, at least, hadn't turned around to acknowledge the chaos she created.

Lea stared at the retreating woman until she rounded a bend and peddled out of sight. "Let's continue. Carefully. Can you get us the rest of the way without killing anyone... especially me?"

"Yes, Lea." Nikka fought the urge to switch back to Ms. Truman.

For the rest of the journey, only the cold voice of the navigation device broke the heavy silence as Nikka made a series of lefts and rights. They traveled away from the river and into a beautiful grove of old-growth redwoods.

"Your destination is on your right."

Nikka pulled up to a black security gate rising up out of nowhere in the middle of the trees. She stuck a hand out toward the keypad so she could tap the code in as soon as Lea gave it to her.

Instead, Lea slid out of the backseat and strategically positioned herself in between Nikka and the keypad. Several quick pats and the gate swung open to reveal a long asphalt drive and a soaring estate of wood and glass.

Nikka rolled her car slowly up the driveway, excitement growing in her belly. She was about to meet the Beth Walker. *I'm a big fan.* No, that was way too generic. *Ms. Walker, you taught me who I was.* Better, but a little embarrassing in front of her boss. No matter. She still had time to get it just right.

She killed the engine right by the front door and hurried around the car to open the door for Lea, who was hunting through the jumble of files and papers scattered all over the backseat.

"For God's sake." Lea slid her hand around searching and creating even more mess. Finally, with a huff, she pulled the thin manila envelope that her assistant had given her from the opened armrest. "Could you clean this up while I'm inside? There's nothing private in the files. Just depositions, so just put them back together as best you can."

What? She was staying outside?

Lea cocked her head as if she had heard her thoughts and smiled thinly. "Walker doesn't see anyone she doesn't know and trust. She's only gotten worse since her brother died. You didn't think…"

"No. Of course not."

But they both knew that she had.

"I shouldn't be long."

Nikka stood back by the car, watching the front door open just enough for an older, horse-faced woman to peer around it. As soon as she saw Lea, a wide smile hit the woman's lips but died just as quickly when she noticed Nikka.

"My ride." Lea shrugged and slipped in through the opening.

Nikka's stomach constricted. She had driven two hours and put unnecessary miles on her brand-new car to become *the ride*? She was going places in this job. She would bet her bottom dollar on it, but apparently not just yet.

Nikka soon crouched in the backseat, her behind up in the air as she rummaged around her car, looking for the runaway files. First, she rescued the one from under the car mat and then another from the back cargo area. How on earth had it gotten there? That girl on the bike should really pay more attention or at the very least have thrown up a wave of apology.

She pulled all the files together and stacked them in a neat pile by the computer. That was all Lea had asked her to do, but curiosity got the better of her, and she pulled the depositions to her. Lea had a new case. Different people's voices jumped off the pages, telling their stories. An aging pop singer was suing a soft drink company for using an imitation of her voice in a commercial. The question was always the same. Imitation or inspiration?

Nikka bit her thumbnail. Previous cases on voice imitation claims had supported the celebrities, but one of them was up for appeal. If it was overturned, it would be a game changer. Nikka grabbed her to-do list out of her purse and penciled in *check on BMW appeal* under *get cat food* and *cancel dentist apt*. She tapped on the paper with her pencil point. Lea hadn't asked her to join the case...not yet, at least.

Maggie pedaled up the driveway so furiously that the broccoli, bouncing around in the basket at the back of the bike, almost tumbled out. If she hurried, maybe she could find out why Vivienne wanted her out of the house.

A white Subaru blocked the drive. They almost never had visitors. She'd called it! Something was most definitely up.

She jumped off the bike to walk the last few feet to the car. There was someone in the backseat, messing with papers. Someone not important enough to go inside. Someone like her. Maggie rapped on the window with her knuckles.

The woman inside jumped and dropped whatever was in her hands. She took one look at Maggie and swung the door open, almost hitting her and the bike.

"Hey! Watch it." Maggie stepped back.

"Seriously?" The woman slid out of the car. "You almost kill me and my boss back in town, and you're telling *me* to watch it?"

Maggie glared at her. Who was this lunatic?

That short black skirt and maroon silk blouse screamed corporate office, probably from the City. But she was way too pretty to waste her life away in a cubicle. Dark hair tumbled in thick waves to her shoulders, and her eyes were almost the same color. On second glance, all sorts of different colors gleamed in her irises.

"Sorry? I'm not following you."

"On the main road back in town. You cut us off. Ring a bell?"

Maggie shook her head. A girl could get lost in those eyes.

"Really? I screeched to a halt. You pedaled away like nothing had happened. I—"

The front door opened with a whoosh, and Lea Truman, wearing a cat-that-ate-the-canary grin, darted outside.

Following Lea onto the doorstep, Vivienne stood almost on top of her.

The pretty woman fell quiet as everyone stared at each other.

Maggie broke the silence first. "Lea, I didn't know you were coming."

Vivienne whispered something to Lea that didn't drift down to the driveway.

"That's okay. Go inside. I'll take care of this." She patted Vivienne on the arm.

Vivienne caressed the place where Lea had touched her and slipped back through the door.

"I see you got the broccoli." Lea pointed at the basket on Maggie's bike.

"I did, and I'm glad you're here. I want to talk to you about Beth."

Lea glanced at the driver. Maggie did too. Of course Lea would hire a smoking hot assistant. Or had she brought the woman out as a diversionary tactic? She was totally Maggie's type. Hell, she would be anyone's type.

"She's not—" Maggie began.

"Nikka." Lea came down the steps. "Could you go inside and give this to Vivienne, the woman who just stepped back inside?" She pulled a scrap of paper from her pocket and folded it twice. "Just go into the foyer and call for her."

"Okay." A wrinkle formed between Nikka's brows, then immediately smoothed out. She gingerly grabbed the paper and headed for the door.

Lea waited until the door clicked shut before stepping closer to Maggie. She was a good four inches taller with her overpriced high heels, and she glared down at Maggie. "What's this about Walker?"

Maggie rose up on her toes to split the difference between them. "She's not eating lately."

"Vivienne hasn't said anything." Lea smiled, but it didn't reach her eyes.

"For weeks now, my meals come back barely touched. Whether Vivienne has mentioned anything or not, something has changed up there. I'm worried. And you should be too."

Lea crossed her arms against her chest as her face took on a pinched expression.

Maggie cringed. Dammit. Too assertive. If she wanted to keep her job, she was going to have to tone it down.

"Beth's an old woman. You know how it is. We'll get her Boost or Ensure or whatever that nutritional drink is called." Lea turned away from her. "If you'll excuse me, I have to get—"

Let her go. There are other ways. But almost without conscious thought, Maggie's hand shot out to stop Lea's retreat. "Look. I'm not a nutritionist, I know, but Beth's not eating enough. And seventy-seven's not that old."

"Thank you for caring enough to tell me, but you're right, you should leave the medical evaluations to Vivienne. The professional." Lea glared at the hand on her arm.

Suddenly, it wasn't just about the poor woman tucked away in the depths of the house. It was also about the woman right in front of her. Maggie had never liked a bully. "Is everything on the up and up here?"

Lea raised her eyebrows. "Of course it is."

Maggie fought back the urge to shake a finger in Lea's face and demand real answers.

"When I hired you, I thought I expressly stated that you shouldn't ask why. Are you asking why now?"

Lea was giving her a way out. She absolutely should take it. It would be so much easier to walk away…to not do the right thing. But Maggie had never been one to take the easy path. Why start now?

"Damn right I'm asking why. There's definitely something going on up there."

"Well, then…" Lea shrugged. "You're fired."

Nikka took in the foyer with one glance. Natural wood and stone ran together, creating an air of permanence and calm. Irises stood tall in a glass vase under a skylight, and a stairway to the second floor opened up on the left.

"Vivienne?" Nikka called softly.

No answer.

Nikka wasn't an idiot. She knew the folded paper in her hand was probably blank. Lea had sent her away because she wanted to have a private conversation with that lunatic on the bike. There was so much energy surrounding that girl, she could almost feel it in here.

She had to deliver the paper even if it were a grocery list. But where was Vivienne?

A muffled noise drifted down the stairs. In any other house she wouldn't trot upstairs uninvited, but this situation left ordinary in the dust. Nikka swallowed hard and headed up, her heels making soft taps on the wooden rungs. "Vivienne?"

Another sound, a cross between a moan and a groan, came from the room at the end of the hall. It was definitely a woman's voice. Her heart jumped in her chest as she came closer. What the hell was she supposed to do now? She couldn't barge in.

"Excuse me. Vivienne? Are you in there?" she said for the third time, her hand poised over the door handle.

"Oooh," the woman cried out.

Nikka couldn't let that go. She twisted the handle and swung the door open.

In the middle of the room, slumped in an easy chair, was a small woman with snow-white hair and black rim glasses. Wrinkles sagged around her eyes and mouth. She looked far older and much more tired than all the pictures that Nikka had seen in town. But there was no mistaking it. That was, without a doubt, Beth Walker.

The old woman squirmed in the chair and fixed Nikka with a look that seemed to run right through her. "Please, help me…"

"Are you okay? What's wrong?"

Beth struggled to get up. She favored her right ankle and immediately lost her balance. "Help me!" She teetered—one arm on the chair, the other stretching out to Nikka.

Nikka rushed forward to grab Beth's arm before she crashed. Jesus. The poor woman couldn't have weighed ninety pounds soaking wet. "It's okay. I've got you."

Beth raised her head and met Nikka's gaze. Behind the glasses her eyes were a deep blue and her pupils were dilated. They latched onto Nikka's. Her body shook as she struggled to get her words out. "Help me. I have to get out of—"

Vivienne skidded into the room. Her face and neck turned red all at once. "What's wrong, dear? Are you having trouble getting up? I told you to wait until I came back." Her tone was sickly sweet until she hissed at Nikka. "Get out. You don't belong up here."

"She needed help."

"That's why I'm here." Vivienne drew the words out until they were as sharp as knives. She bent down, wrapped her arms around her patient, and lifted her into a standing position, bumping Nikka away.

"I... I..." Beth opened her mouth, but one quick look from Vivienne made her snap it shut.

"You're making her upset. You need to go."

Nikka backed up a step, but her gaze never left Vivienne. Something about all this didn't feel right. As her father would say, this woman was talking to the right, but looking to the left.

"Ms. Walker? Are you all right?" She tried to find Beth's eyes.

Vivienne shifted her in her arms and conveniently turned Beth away from the door.

Beth didn't struggle.

"See, she's fine. Just the flu."

As an instant dislike for Vivienne rolled over her, Nikka stood her ground. A little stare-down wasn't going to spook her.

But a sharp horn, blaring from outside, made her jump. A summons from Lea was a whole other ball game.

"Shit," Nikka said under her breath. She took another long look at Beth Walker's back before hurrying from the room.

What had just happened up there? Was Beth Walker asking for help getting out of the chair? Did she really have the flu? Or was it more?

It wasn't until she slid into the car that she remembered the paper still in her hand. Oh crap! After a quick check to make sure Lea wasn't watching, she dropped the note to the car's floor. Please let the paper really be an excuse to get rid of her.

"Let's get going." Lea sat calm and cool in the backseat, ready for the trip home. "Traffic's going to be a bitch."

18

Nikka looked around. There was no sign of the woman with the shaggy hair and nice legs. "Right." She pushed the ignition button and tried to shove the last ten minutes out of her mind.

Even before they had hit the end of the drive, Lea tapped her cell phone. "Hi. It's me. I got it." She paused. "Yeah, it's looking really good. A few things we need to clean up, but yes, very good indeed. We can absolutely move forward."

Then Lea ended the call, and they rode in silence.

Unlike the trip up, Nikka wasn't hoping that Lea would engage her in conversation. Lea could have recited the entire US Constitution and its amendments, and Nikka would have only heard the two words that kept circling around in her head.

"Help me."

Chapter 2

February 1960

A SMALL BELL JINGLED AS the front door of the Good Neighbor real estate office swung open.

Beth cringed inwardly at her desk. The bell was a happy sound, but its tingling reminded her that her life was not her own. At this moment it belonged to the Thompsons, a plump dentist and his wife from San Francisco, who were looking for a weekend house in the redwoods. She hurriedly slid loose papers of writing into her desk drawer, revealing a folder from the office. On its cover, *FERN HOUSE* in big, black letters sat over both a photo of a house in a forest and a business card with a golden tooth.

"Yoo-hoo." A man's deep voice filled the room. "We're here!"

The husband and wife standing, no lounging, by the door were most definitely not the dowdy Thompsons. The man—tall, dark and handsome—sported a tie and perfectly tailored pants. He stood next to an elegant blonde with a fresh-scrubbed glow and a crisp, pink seersucker dress.

Wow! Beth almost choked on her own breath. She was a stunner.

The man raised his arm in a wave toward Beth. "We don't have an appointment, but we were hoping that..."

"Oh my goodness." Rachel turned out of the kitchenette and skidded to a halt. "You're James and Dawn Montgomery."

"We are!" James grinned.

"I'm the office secretary." She turned to Beth. "Oh my goodness. You didn't recognize them?"

Beth shook her head. She had been too busy taking in the curve of the woman's neck for their fame to register.

Dawn shrugged, and even that slight movement overflowed with style. "It's always better that way. Not to be recognized. We're just regular people."

"Are you kidding me? You're Hollywood royalty! I'll get Mr. Armstrong, our boss." Rachel giggled and ran into the back office.

A second later, Hank, tucking in his shirt with one hand, darted into the front room, his other hand already outstretched. "I thought Rachel was pulling my leg, but you really are the Montgomerys. What on earth are you doing in Steelhead Springs? Shouldn't you both be in Hollywood, filming a movie or something? I'm Hank Armstrong, by the way. I own this place." He pumped James's hand repeatedly until James finally had to twist away.

Beth suppressed a smile at Hank's exuberance and glanced at Dawn, who was staring straight at her. Their gazes met, and Dawn raised her eyebrows slightly as if to say *See, I told you so. Better not to be recognized.*

Beth gave in to the smile and waited for Dawn to drop her gaze.

She didn't. In fact, she seemed to be staring deeper into her eyes, as if she wanted to root around in all of Beth's secrets.

Beth's heart began to pound. She looked down at the tile floor.

"...driving by and liked the look of the town," James said.

Dang it. She had missed a whole chunk of the conversation. Heat blazed on Beth's cheeks.

"Bless my soul. You want to look at houses here? In Steelhead?" Hank's voice cracked. "But we're in the middle of nowhere."

"That's exactly what we need right now." James wrapped his arm around Dawn and kissed her on the temple. "Do you have any houses we can look at?"

"Well..." Hank wrung his hands. "We're a little low on inventory at the moment. How about a nice one-story on the river? It has a huge deck and..."

"No, something a little more private. In the woods, I think." James glanced around the office and seized on the folder on Beth's desk. He pointed to the picture of the house. "Something like that. No, exactly like that. We want to look at...Fern House."

Hank grabbed the folder, slid Dr. Thompson's business card off the front, and shoved it deep into his pocket. "Just so happens, it's available. Should we go look at it?"

"Yes, siree." James was already out the door.

Hank tripped over himself trying to follow. "Call the Thompsons and reschedule."

"But they'll be here any—"

"Just take care of it." Hank waved off Rachel and shut the office door almost in her face.

"How?" Rachel turned to Beth.

"I don't know." Beth grabbed the keys with the 741 Fern Drive tag from her desk. "I'll be right back. He's going to need these."

Outside, she silently handed the keys to Hank and pushed down the desire to take one last look at Dawn.

"Maybe your girl could tool out with us?" James stood by his convertible Cadillac El Dorado, leaning casually on one of the car's huge, red fins. "The missus and I may want to hit the road once we've seen the house."

Hank couldn't flip his keys fast enough to Beth. "Drive my car out there. Okay?"

"If *your girl's* going," Dawn said, "I'll ride with her. I've had enough wind in my face for one day."

Beth's heart jumped in her chest. Dawn wanted to drive with her? She edged over to Hank's Ford.

James fixed his wife with a look, started to open his mouth, but then seemed to think better of it. "Stay close" was all he said in the end.

Beth slid into the driver's seat with her gaze riveted to the road ahead. Leaving Rachel to deal with the Thompsons on her own was bad, but she couldn't remember the last time adventure had come calling. And in the form of a gorgeous Hollywood movie star? She wasn't about to pass that up.

The two-car procession wound through sleepy streets. Beth tried to see the town from an outsider's perspective—a wood-clapped drugstore, a post office, and a lumberyard filled with roughly hewn logs. *See What We Saw* was painted on a homemade sign in the last window.

Beth's temperature rose even though the cool winter air tumbled in from the vent, and her slick palms slid against the wheel. This place couldn't be farther from Tinseltown.

Dawn had scooted in beside her without saying a word. The silence was comforting at first since Beth hadn't a clue about how to talk to a big-time movie star, but now the quiet was so heavy it almost weighed the car down.

"That's some car. I've never seen one in person." Beth jerked her head at the red Cadillac gliding in front of them. Her voice sounded odd to her own ears, but loads better than the silence. "Does he like it?"

"Probably more than me." Dawn shot Beth a glance. "You're not going to blab that to the tabloids are you?"

The idea was so ridiculous, Beth chuckled. "Definitely not. That's not my style."

"No. I don't think it is." Dawn relaxed against the seat back. "You have me at a disadvantage. You know my name. But I don't know yours."

"It's Beth Walker."

"So, Beth Walker. What's your story?"

Beth chuckled again. "Me? I have no story. I'm a nobody."

"I sincerely doubt that."

Beth glanced over and caught Dawn staring at her again. They locked gazes once more, and this time Beth's lingered so long that when she finally looked back to the road, she was only inches from the Cadillac. She slammed on the brakes with a jolt. What on earth was going on here? What was it about this woman that made Beth lose her way every time she looked at her?

And even when she didn't.

She almost drove right past 741 Fern Drive, skidding into the dirt road at the last minute. She followed the Cadillac, and both cars bumped their way up the drive.

"I can hear Jimmy right now. He's telling your boss that he won't buy the house unless the owners pave over the driveway."

"Hank will do it himself, on his hands and knees if necessary. He'll do anything to sell you this house. He has people believing that he's the celebrity in this town. If you buy the house, he'll milk it for all that it's worth."

"It might happen. Jimmy can be very capricious. He makes decisions with his gut in just seconds and not always with all the right information. The only thing he thinks through thoroughly are his film roles." Dawn smoothed down her hair and brought her hand all the way down her neck to rub it for a second. "My God, sometimes I think I'll grow old and die before he'll sign the contracts. Do you take in many films?"

"No, not really."

"Why not?"

"Steelhead doesn't have a movie theater, for one. But mostly I spend my free time trying to write." The words were out before Beth could bite them back. Why on earth had she said that? Even her own family didn't know she longed to be a writer, and here she was blabbing to a stranger that she had just met.

"I won't tell anyone."

Scary. How did she know what Beth was thinking?

A sudden tingling ran up her arm.

Dawn had dropped her hand on Beth's forearm and gave it a little squeeze. "Seriously. If you keep my secret, I'll keep yours."

Secrets? What was Dawn talking about?

Thankfully for Beth, the house loomed up in front of them, and she didn't have to answer. James had stopped his car right by the front door, leaving Beth just enough room to scoot around to park by the garage. By the time they joined the men, Hank was already into the hard sell.

"Look at those trees." He bowed reverently to the small grove of California redwoods just beyond the house. "They can live over two thousand years and grow to around three hundred and fifty feet. Down by the river is the actual Tall Tree, which is where the river got its name. We can go visit it if you want. That one, they say, is taller than the Empire State Building."

James's eyes widened.

"Your boss is very good," Dawn said so only Beth could hear. She stood so close to her it seemed that this was yet another confidence they were sharing.

"Now, the architect who built this house was a student of Frank Lloyd Wright at Taliesin West in Arizona. You'll see that the house complements the forest and nature outside. He mined the harmony between them to create a grace only seen at Falling Water in Pennsylvania. Shall we go inside?"

"Ooh. There's his first mistake," Dawn whispered.

Sure enough, James slapped his thigh with his hand, and a popping noise echoed through the trees. "I'm not buying a work of art, Hank. I'm buying a pad for me, my wife, and the couple of ankle biters we plan to have. I don't give a flip if nature and the house have a party. I just want a place that we can hide from all the craziness in Hollywood. Can we do that here?"

"Yes. Yes, you can," Hank said. "Come inside. I'll show you."

James tailed after Hank as he unlocked the front door and stepped inside. Fresh air poured out from the stone and wood foyer as an invitation to enter.

Dawn shuffled her feet but didn't make a move to follow.

"Don't you want to see the house too?" Beth asked.

Dawn shook her head. "It doesn't matter what I think. Hank did well. Jimmy's going to buy the house. I was never really part of that equation."

Beth glanced over, but this time Dawn didn't meet her gaze. Apparently, *why* wasn't a secret that they were sharing.

Beth thought about Dawn almost constantly over the thirty-day escrow. She found herself working obscure references about the star into conversations with her family, doodling Dawn's name onto loose pages instead of writing, and even driving all the way to San Francisco one rainy Sunday morning to see her latest release, *Woman About Town*. When Hank announced that the couple was coming up to get the keys to the house personally, Beth's heart flipped over and her knees went weak. She had to grab hold of the back of her desk chair to steady herself.

In her saner moments, she kept telling herself she was being silly. She had spent all of one afternoon with the woman. Their worlds were miles apart. Dawn was a bona fide movie star, and Beth was a real estate assistant in a little town no one had ever heard of. And to top it all off, Dawn was married to hunky James Montgomery, no less. There was no way in hell that America's Sweetheart was even giving her a second thought as she flitted off to parties and premieres in Los Angeles.

When the day finally came, Beth took extra care with her appearance. She grabbed a new shirtwaist dress out of the closet and slid it over her body. The black stripes made her look taller than her five foot two, or so her mother had said, and the tight belt accentuated her best feature, her nice, flat waist. She fluffed up her short brown hair and pulled a few pieces down by her ears, trying to bring a pleasing roundness to her face. A splash of lipstick and she was done. She nodded at her reflection in the mirror. Beth Walker wasn't going to win any beauty contests, but the villagers weren't going to chase her out of town with torches either.

"You look nice." Rachel gave Beth a little wave when she entered the office. She had cleared her desk and was arranging a pitcher of something fruity, glasses, and a plate of cookies on its surface.

"What's going on?" Beth asked.

"Oh, you know Mr. Armstrong. He hired Michael from the *Sentinel* to come over to take a few pictures when he gives the Montgomerys their keys at two o'clock. And then Mrs. Armstrong found out. So now, I think, her bridge club and a couple of Mr. Armstrong's fishing buddies are coming too. Oh, and Sheriff Tom said he might stop by as well."

By two, the office was jammed full of people who just happened to be in the neighborhood. By three, the cookie plate held only crumbs, and by four, only Beth, Rachel, and Hank remained. Everyone else had gone home, grumbling that Hank had pulled one over on them. He didn't know any movie stars, and this was just one of his crazy stunts to get more attention. At four thirty, Rachel gathered the glasses of what had turned out to be strawberry lemonade and brought them into the kitchenette. Beth rolled up her sleeves and began to scrub them clean.

The jingle of the bell broke through the heavy silence. Beth couldn't see who it was, but she knew the deep voice instantly. "Sorry we're late. Anyone still here?"

Hank couldn't scurry out of his office fast enough. He flung a glass of lemonade that reeked of mostly vodka through the kitchenette doorway into Beth's hand.

"You're here. You're here! I thought maybe you had changed your mind."

"Nope." James puffed out his chest. "Once I've signed, I never back down from a deal."

In the kitchenette, Beth took a deep breath. Was Dawn here too? She hadn't heard her voice or any evidence of another person. She almost didn't want to look. If Dawn wasn't there, the disappointment would hit her like a sledgehammer. She rolled down her sleeves, ran a hand through her hair, and stepped into the room.

There she was standing off to the side, quietly rocking back and forth on her heels. Dressed in a tailored red suit, she looked as if she had just stepped off a Hollywood photo shoot. She was scanning the room, and when she lit on Beth, she stilled. A smile crept to her lips, and she raised a hand in greeting.

Had Dawn actually been looking for her? Beth shyly waved back. Relief flooded her chest, making it hard for her to catch a breath—a sledgehammer either way, apparently.

"Do you want some cookies? My wife made them especially..." Hank turned to only crumbs on the plate. "Do we have any more cookies?"

"No, Mr. Armstrong." Rachel's bottom lip trembled.

"What?"

"No matter. We don't eat cookies." James laughed and spun Hank back toward him. He leaned in, focusing all of his attention on Hank. "I'm under contract with my studio to lose weight for my next picture. I'm a warrior in Alexander the Great's army, fighting for glory and money so I can rise up in ranks and marry the woman I love."

"It sounds amazing." Standing only inches from an A-list movie star, he swooned like a teenager. Now his bottom lip was trembling as well.

"The studio and I want to ride the *Ben Hur* wave of success. Actually, it's almost a copy of the film without all the religious stuff. It's a really good role for me. My shirt is off for over sixty percent of the film." He flexed, and his pecs jumped beneath his shirt. "Yes, siree. I'm ready."

Dawn stepped out of James's shadow and strode over toward Beth. "We're both only going to be here for a couple of days, but I was thinking that maybe you'd want to come out to dinner tomorrow."

Beth, dumbfounded, couldn't speak.

"To celebrate and all."

"Yes. I would love to." Beth found her voice and rushed the answer out before the stunning woman in front of her changed her mind.

"Good. Around six? You know the house, of course." Dawn stepped back to James's side. She took his arm as James regaled Hank with more stories about the film. He glanced at his wife and smiled offhandedly.

Beth spent the next twenty-four hours spinning the conversation around in her head. The exchange had only been a couple of sentences, but surely there was more to it than an honest invitation to dinner. What had she missed? Maybe there was some paperwork to bring out. But both Hank and Rachel told her everything was filled out. Maybe it was a housewarming party, and lots of people would be there?

She knocked on the door at 741 Fern Drive exactly at six. One hand held a purple flowering rhododendron plant, the only flowers she could find in February, and the other clutched a bottle of champagne that Hank had given her at Christmas.

James opened the door and craned his head around her. "That yours?" He pointed at the black Chevy truck in the driveway.

"Ah...yeah. I bought it two months ago." The truck gleamed from a wash just that morning—one of the few things that made the job at Hank's worth it.

"Good." He took the champagne and grinned. "Come in. Come in."

Beth shook off the odd question and followed him into the living room. Even though she had been involved in selling this house first to the Thompsons and then to the Montgomerys, she had never been inside. The dynamism of the room hit her immediately. Waxed stone floors drew her gaze to the fireplace at the far side of the room. The stones of the hearth were left plain and when coupled with the highly polished floor, Beth imagined she was flowing down a river to an outcropping of natural rocks. Not to be outdone, the back of the room cantilevered out into the redwood forest behind the house.

Hank might be a brownnoser through and through, but he knew design. This house really was a tour-de-force of organic architecture. No wonder the Thompsons had threatened lawsuits when Hank had withdrawn their offer.

Dawn sat by the fireplace in a striped wing-tip chair, wearing capris and a thin scarf. Her curls fell loose and soft around her face.

Beth had to look away she was so lovely and then gasped. There was no one else in the room!

"It's just the three of us." Dawn's ability to read Beth's mind was unnerving to say the least.

James handed her a flute of the champagne she had brought. "But we'll have lots of fun anyway."

"Don't mind him." Dawn got out of the chair to join them and took the plant with a smile. "I'm glad you came."

"Me too." Beth forced the words out more to be polite, even though up to five minutes ago, spending time with Dawn was one of her greatest desires. But now with that wish playing out as an intimate dinner with the Montgomerys, anxiety rolled in her stomach. What was happening here didn't fit any of the possibilities that had danced in her head all day. Mostly, she had envisioned standing off to one side of a grand party and watching the excitement all around her. She shook her head to clear it only to note that furniture filled every room.

"How did you get the place together so quickly?"

"Oh." James laughed. "We have people for that."

"And they also delivered dinner. Should we eat before it gets cold?"

Beth followed them into a dining room that could've easily been a spread in *House Beautiful*. A long, polished table was set for three at one end—china with domed covers, wineglasses already filled with a rich, red liquid, and simple green salads off to one side.

When she sat down, a delicious smell of puffed pastry greeted her.

James, delighted by the theatrics of it all, ran around, pulling the covers off with loud ta-da's.

One bite and Beth's nerves completely melted away. "This is one of the best things I've ever had. Is this Beef Wellington? I've only seen it in magazines."

"There's this little bistro in the City," James said, his mouth already full. "No one does it better."

"Mmmm." The night was full of mystery. How they had gotten it here and kept it so warm and fresh was beyond her. But another bite told her she really didn't care. These people didn't have to abide by the same rules as everyone else did. And here she was sitting right beside them.

"We don't eat like this every night," Dawn said. In fact, she wasn't really eating at all. She poked at her food with her fork, taking only a small bite of the baby carrots every so often.

Was she sick? She looked positively glowing.

Waving his fork around while he spoke, James launched into tales of his last picture and the crazy director at its helm.

Beth laughed so hard she almost fell off her seat. Maybe it was the wine talking, but somewhere in the middle of a story about the director trying to convince him to wrestle a live lion, his charm spilled over and filled the room. No wonder Dawn was attracted to him.

After dessert—a chocolate cake so moist that it melted in her mouth—James leaned back in his seat and twirled the nearly empty wineglass in his fingers. "This was fun, Beth. But I'm sure you're wondering why we invited you out here."

"I am. A little."

"We need to ask you a favor."

Beth looked to Dawn, who nodded ever so slightly.

"You see, Dawn needs to take a break from Hollywood for a while. Live up here while I shoot *Conqueror of the World*. I'll be overseas for months, and she can't come with me. I need to know that she will be righti-o here, away from it all."

"Okay." Beth waited for James to continue. He didn't. He just sat in his chair nodding slightly. "And how does that involve me?"

"We want you to look after Dawn while I'm gone. You'd have to run errands, do whatever she needs here, and generally make sure the people in town give her privacy. She can't drive. So we need a driver, obviously, and a Girl Friday, but we also thought it would be better if it was someone people in Steelhead already know."

Beth glanced back and forth between the two. Her mind spun in a million directions.

"I would stay, but you see I'm taking a big chance with this film. No salary, just a cut of the profits, so I've got a lot riding here. Otherwise I wouldn't leave Dawn, of course, but I got to think about my future." He looked at his wife. "And my future's our future, right, sweetie pie?"

"Jimmy, she doesn't care about all that." Dawn wrinkled her nose as if the beef had suddenly gone off. "Look. Here's the thing. The hours and the money are great, but the best part is that you wouldn't have to work at the real estate office anymore. You'd have enough time to do something else on the side. Something you wouldn't have to hide in drawers."

Beth flinched. How could Dawn know about that? Her mind leap-frogged over that puzzle and straight into writing almost full-time. Excitement gripped her. She had been wrong before. Becoming a real writer was her deepest desire. Friendship with Dawn was just icing on the cake.

Were they really offering her a way to do both?

"Why do you need someone to take care of you? Are you sick?" That would explain the dinner of only carrots.

"No." James downed the rest of the wine in one gulp. "She's not sick. She's pregnant."

Seriously? She studied Dawn with this new information. She didn't look pregnant. Not that she would know. None of her friends, even the few who were married, had kids.

Dawn met her gaze and nodded. "That's why we wanted a house up here, away from it all. And he's right. I'm going to need help." She tilted her head and gave Beth an Academy Award-winning smile. "So what do you think? Could you take me on?"

Chapter 3

"You have twenty minutes to get your stuff together and leave." Vivienne spat the words at Maggie like bullets. "And don't be taking any equipment that doesn't belong to you. In fact, I have a full inventory upstairs. I'll get it so we can compare notes before you go."

"I bet you do, bitch," Maggie muttered once the kitchen was empty. She banged open a green enamel cabinet and pulled out a black case containing all her *stuff*—as if ergonomic knives, peelers, and zesters costing a small fortune could ever be called *stuff*. Tools maybe, fine instruments definitely, but never just *stuff*. Jaws clenched, she unfolded the case to reveal one empty slip.

The paring knife was missing. She had been using it right before Vivienne rushed her out to get the broccoli. Back when she actually had a job. It still had to be here somewhere.

Maggie rooted around in one drawer and then opened the dishwasher. Where the hell was it? The kitchen was clean except for the plate in the sink. As usual lately, Vivienne had returned Beth Walker's sandwich completely untouched and had dumped it there.

Old woman, my ass. They're hiding something. I just know it.

Picking up the plate, she found the paring knife. It had been hiding under the dish right by the radish that Vivienne had tossed away earlier. She grabbed it, swiped down both sides with a kitchen towel, and slid it back where it belonged. The case was full, and since there was no way in hell she was staying for Vivienne's last power play, she marched out of the room. She had her hand on the front door, ready to jerk it open, when she froze.

She was fired. She couldn't be any more fired. Should she...?

She might as well.

Clutching the case to her side, Maggie started up the stairs. When her boots slapped the wood, she crept up on her tiptoes to kill the sound. At the top, she stiffened. There were closed doors up and down the hallway. Which one? She had to pick a side.

She went left and peeked into the first room. It was empty, so she tiptoed to the next one.

The door was ajar, and scuffling noises drifted toward her, sounding as if someone was flipping through papers.

She held her breath and scooted forward.

Vivienne's broad back hunched over a file cabinet.

Two quick steps and Maggie made it past her.

A dim light came from beneath the door at the end of the hall. That must be the one.

She pushed the door open just an inch and paused. When no poison darts shot out at her, she swung it open the rest of the way.

It took a second for her eyes to adjust to the light.

A small woman lay on a hospital bed at the far end of the room. She wasn't moving. Maybe she was sleeping really deeply, but Maggie couldn't see the rise and fall of her chest. She had to get closer.

Maggie glanced both ways before stepping into the room. Stepping up to the bed, she whispered, "Ms. Walker, are you okay?"

No response.

Maggie drew a finger along Beth's wrist, feeling for a pulse. There it was—regular, if a bit slow. She was alive, but that didn't mean she was okay. Maggie circled the fragile wrist with her whole hand and shook it gently.

"Ms. Walker? Ms. Walker?"

Her eyes fluttered open at her name but, within a beat, closed again.

This wasn't an ordinary nap. She almost looked drugged.

Maggie scanned the bedside table. A pill bottle on its side and a bunch of pills lay scattered on its top. A few had even fallen to the ground. Vivienne didn't strike her as the clumsy type. What if Beth had tried to do something stupid? She reached out.

"Leave her alone!"

Maggie jumped back about a foot as Vivienne spun around the corner.

Beth let out something between a moan and a sigh and rolled over, away from them both.

Maggie fought the urge to rush back to the bed and shake Beth awake. Instead, she thrust her knife case out toward Vivienne and tried to look innocent. "Sorry, I thought I was supposed to come up here to show you what I was taking."

"I was coming down to you!" Vivienne waved the inventory list in the air.

"Oh, sorry." Maggie shrugged and took a small step back to the bed.

"No, you don't. You need to leave!" Vivienne herded her to the door. She waved her hands aggressively; the list in her right hand snapped in the air with the movement. "First I catch that other girl snooping around up here and now you."

The other girl? Maggie filed that tidbit away for later and motioned to Beth. "What's wrong with her?"

"Nothing. She's just sleeping."

"That isn't just sleeping. Do you think I'm an idiot? What are those pills?" Maggie tried to dart back to the bed.

Vivienne lurched and cut her off at the pass. "Everything's fine, and you need to lower your voice or we'll wake her. She always takes a nap this time of day," Vivienne said, but her voice had a pinched quality to it. She directed Maggie to the door and, as soon as they were outside in the hall, shut it tight.

"So you're staying with that. She's napping?"

"I am. And now you need to leave. You no longer work here. If I have to, I will take more stringent measures."

A crazy vision of bonking Vivienne over the head with her knife case and rushing the room rose in Maggie's mind. But then what? Sitting by Beth's side until she woke up? Shaking her violently awake until she gave the woman a stroke? She had to go about this much more systematically. "Okay. Okay. I get it. I'm going. Just promise me you'll get her to eat."

"That's no longer your concern."

"Yeah. I get that too."

Vivienne grunted her response and jabbed Maggie's shoulder with a thick finger to get her moving toward the stairs.

Outside, straddling her bike, Maggie took one last look at the house. It sat serenely in the forest, the afternoon sunshine streaming onto its roof. From this perspective, Maggie could actually believe that everything inside was on the up and up. That the little old woman was napping and that Vivienne, working all on her own out here, was just really rough around the edges. It certainly would be easier to ride down the driveway and leave it all behind if she believed that. No good could come from her digging around anyway. Her gut had gotten her into trouble before. Lots of times, actually; she just couldn't help herself.

No longer my concern? We'll see about that.

Maggie pedaled rapidly through town, cutting around cars and tourists, barely missing some by inches. Finally, she skidded up to the shopping center in the middle of town and clambered off her bike. She wheeled past The Lumberyard, the Springs's trendy gastro-pub. Women of all shapes and sizes spilled out onto the terrace with pint glasses of craft beers and sunburns probably from a day on the Tall Tree River. Two shops into the mall, Maggie leaned her bike up against the colorful storefront of Made From Scratch and popped inside the bakery.

Lauren, her ex, handed a red velvet cupcake to a giggling couple whose arms were wrapped so tightly around each other they might as well have been one organism. One of the women reached into her pocket for money while the other took the cupcake. Cooing, the second woman fed little bites to her partner as they walked out.

"Were we ever like that?" Lauren stared after the departing couple.

"God, I hope not. They're way too into each other." Maggie watched as one woman slid a hand into her partner's back pocket. "But that might have been the problem."

"Yeah, that and a few other things." Lauren laughed and threw her an air kiss. The laugh turned into a true smile. "What do you need, Mags?"

"Do you have any Lemon Lovers left?" Maggie scanned the case below the counter. "I don't see any."

"There's a few in the back. How many do you need?"

"Just one."

"Going to see George?"

"Yeah. It always gets me in the door."

"Do I even want to know why this time?"

"No."

When Lauren headed toward the back of the store, Maggie watched her. Her graceful walk was by far her best trait. Even now Maggie found it mesmerizing. They had been good for a while, but never great. And when they both realized that truth, the parting had been remarkably easy.

Lauren returned with a small blue bag and handed it to Maggie.

"Thanks."

"No problem. Hey, you teaching out at the gym tonight? Chris still hurt?" Lauren asked.

"Yeah. You coming?"

"Probably. I'll see you there if I do."

Maggie was halfway out the door when she eyed the empty space in the case where the Lemon Lovers should have been. She spun around as an idea jumped in her mind. "Lauren? Can I have my old job back?" She hurried the words out, but not as fast as the heat flooded into her cheeks.

"Oh, Mags, what happened with Beth Walker?"

Maggie shrugged. "It didn't work out."

Lauren raised an eyebrow.

Maggie shuffled her feet in response. Lauren always made her feel a little too much like a kid with her hand caught in the cookie jar. Usually, Lauren was right. That had also been part of the problem.

"I don't know," Maggie said. "The bitchy physician's assistant or whatever the hell she is, we didn't really get along. And today I might have let fly a few things to the boss lady from the City that I shouldn't have."

"Well, there's a shocker."

Rolling her eyes, Maggie opened her mouth to tell Lauren what she had seen upstairs, but then she changed her mind at the last minute. "So what do you think? Is there a place for me here?" She slapped the blue bag against her leg nervously.

"You know you're going to have to get up early again?"

"I do."

"So will you? I mean repeatedly, not just once."

"I will." She cringed at the harsh edge to her voice and tried to beat down the embarrassment over her situation. Several deep breaths later she said, "Five o'clock sharp. I'll be the model employee." When that didn't get her anywhere, she added, "Lauren, I'm in a bit of a tight spot here. What do you say?"

Lauren bit her lip while her gaze darted around the store. "We're good friends now, and I'm not sure that our working together is the best idea."

Maggie nodded. She understood. She had left Lauren a little bit in the lurch when she quit last time.

"You know you change your mind at the drop of a hat. Have you really thought this out? This is what you want?"

Maggie nodded a little too quickly.

"I'd be crazy to say yes. But I'd be a fool to say no too. You're the best pastry chef I've ever met, and I shouldn't tell you this, but my sales fell by twenty percent when you left. Besides, Pick of the Litter has just ordered a hundred of those doggie cake pops. No one decorates them as well as you do. So what do you say? You want to start right away?"

"Absolutely!" She grinned. "But I got something to do first. I'll be right back." She opened the front door again. "Thanks, Lauren. I owe you."

"Okay. I'll be here…waiting… As always." Lauren pursed her lips.

She was right. Maggie couldn't blow this. There wouldn't be another chance. Maggie rushed up to Lauren and threw her arms around her. Lauren felt big and solid, like the rock of Gibraltar, in her arms.

"I really mean it. I won't let you down this time. Thank you."

Lauren squeezed tight and then pushed her away, laughing "Okay. You goof. I'll see you later. Just don't leave me hanging."

Leading with the blue bag, Maggie marched down the hallway at the Steelhead Springs sheriff's station. She stuck only her hand into an open door and waggled the bag back and forth.

"That better be a Lemon Lover, and it better come with no strings attached." Her brother's strong voice flowed into the hall.

"You got it half right." Maggie grinned and scooted into the small office.

Her brother sat behind a big desk with a Deputy George Chalon nameplate on the edge. Paperwork was spread so thick on its surface, no wood showed at all. George let out an exaggerated groan as his hand jutted out for the bag. "Yes, please." Sinking his teeth into the cupcake, he groaned again. This time with happiness. "Oh, I've really missed these." His mouth was full to overflowing. "I think I was sadder than either you or Lauren when you two broke up."

"Yeah. I think so too." Maggie slid out the extra desk chair and sat down. She watched her brother tear into the cupcake with a smile. Like all chefs, she enjoyed watching people eat with gusto, especially when the recipe was hers. For a few minutes the only sound in the room was contented chewing.

George licked his fingers and stuffed the cupcake wrapper back into the bag. "Why do I feel as if I've just made a deal with the devil?"

"All you have to do is listen." Maggie scooted the chair closer to his desk. She told him the whole story right from the beginning when Lea had told her never to ask why to that afternoon.

"But she was alive, right?" George asked when she had finally stopped talking.

"She was. But not really responsive."

"Because she was sleeping."

"Well, yeah, I guess. But what about those pills? Why would they be spilled all over the table?"

"Did you see a medical chart?" Her brother avoided the question.

"No, of course not."

"So you don't know what they were. They could have been prescribed or vitamins. Did you see any sign of distress other than her sleeping deeply?"

"George—"

"This may come as a shock to you, Maggie, but you're not a doctor."

She rolled her eyes. "You got to believe me. There's something not right out there. I know it."

Her brother just pursed his lips and shook his head.

"George, seriously, I'm not making this up."

"Cuz you certainly don't have a history of that type of behavior. You never imagine scenarios that aren't true." When Maggie sent him a questioning look, he threw up his hands. "In third grade you were convinced that Mrs. Marsh was selling secrets to the Chinese, remember? You got suspended for three days when they caught you spying on her in the lunch room."

"Oh, come on. I was just a kid."

"Or what about last month when you decided that that valet guy at Roscoe's was driving the cars while we ate."

"To be fair, he quit before we could make a final determination."

"Maggie, everyone knows that Beth Walker is a recluse. No one has seen her in town for decades. Since she bought Fern House in the eighties I think. Besides, there's never been a hint of trouble out there, and her own brother told us all that she was heading downhill, both physically and mentally, before he died."

Maggie swallowed while she considered how to handle this. George was Beth Walker's best hope. "Make fun of me all you want. But I know that I'm right this time."

"Are you sure this isn't about that physician assistant out there? You know how you get when you're excited or when people get in your face. I've heard you tell Mom more than once that Vivienne's a bitch."

"That's not the word I used. And, yes, I'm sure this isn't about Nurse Ratched. George, can you just this once trust me and look into it?" George was her best friend. When they had been kids, he'd always had her back, and to have him not believe her now stabbed at her heart.

He sighed and rolled his head around in a half-nod. "Okay. I'll poke around in this a little bit. Let's get this clear, though. I'm not going to put my neck on the line, but I'll see what I can dig up."

Maggie pursed her lips.

"It's the best I'm willing to do."

"Okay. It's a start." And it was. If she was being honest, Beth Walker might have only been sleeping. She knew lots of people took sleeping pills or pain pills by their own choice. Maybe she had overreacted.

And George was right too; the bad vibes had really come from Vivienne and Lea, and now that she had no access to the house anymore, this wasn't going to be an easy fix. She could kick herself for not being more aggressive when she had the chance. But life wasn't lived on should'ves and could'ves. Only in the now. She had to be sure for her own sake as much as Beth Walker's.

"You coming out to Mom's for dinner tonight?" George broke into her thoughts.

"No, Chris's hurt, so I'm taking his class over at the gym. You want to come out there and climb some rock walls instead? Get away from Sarah and the girls?"

"I'd love to, but Sarah would kill me."

"Then don't. Despite what you may think, I can only handle one crazy scenario at a time." She held out a closed fist for her brother, who bumped it immediately. "Thanks, bro."

Nikka pulled into the garage of her condo building well after dark, tired but clearheaded. Somewhere on Highway

101, she had mostly convinced herself that she hadn't seen anything out of the ordinary up in Steelhead Springs. Just a woman who needed extra help with her daily routines and was plainly asking for it. Nikka had no room in her plans for a woman in need of real help. Besides, the crumpled-up piece of paper on the car's floor mat started to loom larger and larger in her mind. What if it wasn't just an excuse for Lea to have a private conversation with the crazy bike woman? What if she had really wanted her to deliver it to Vivienne? Nikka liked her days wrapped up in neat packages. The loose end of the note niggled at her.

She wasn't used to spending so much time behind the wheel, and when she pulled herself out of the car, her muscles tensed. She whispered a promise to throw more yoga into her daily routine and squatted down stiffly to pat the driver's side floorboard. Where was that note?

She found it tucked under the mat, just its corner peeking out. A careful unfolding revealed a phone number written out in pencil.

Oh shit. This might have been real. She actually may have wanted me to deliver this.

In the elevator up to her condo, the question of what to do raced around in her brain, bouncing back and forth between possible solutions. She could say nothing, and if it came up, maintain that she had given the paper to Vivienne. The mistake must be on Vivienne's end. Or she could come clean and admit that she had been so flustered by the whole experience that she had dropped the ball.

I'm screwed. Either way she came off like an idiot and certainly not future partner material. Maybe there was another solution. Her fingers itched for her iPad. She needed to get on MindNode as soon as possible to create a brainstorming chart and systematically figure out how to get out of this pickle.

Desi and Lucy greeted her at the door with loud meows, and she immediately grabbed the kibble out of the cupboard in the laundry room. She dug deep into the container and remembered that she had to buy cat food. They purred and wrapped themselves around her feet until the tinkling of kibble dropping into the bowl told them that dinner had arrived.

She hit the blinking play button on her answering machine as she dumped her briefcase onto the dining room table. Neat stacks of mail, files, and legal pads spoke to office work more than fine dining. She slid into an ergonomic office chair at the head of the table and grabbed her iPad out of her briefcase.

"Nikka." A thick Russian accent poured out from the machine. "It's your father. I want to know how first day went. Call back."

"Nikka, this is Dr. Robin's office just confirming your dental appointment on Thursday. Your mouth guard is ready. Hope to see you then."

"Nikkkkaaaa! We're at the bar. Come on down. There's a hottie here we all think you should meet. No excuses this time. We'll be here until ten." Her old college roommate yelled over chatter in the background.

"End of final message," the mechanical voice said.

There it was, the state of her life outside of work in three messages—a father who was a little too involved, a propensity to clench her teeth, and absolutely no love life. It wasn't pretty.

Despite herself, she wondered what the girl at the bar might look like. Tara knew her type almost better than she did. Athletic, legs that didn't quit, a shaggy bob with soft, sweeping bangs, maybe brown eyes a shade or two lighter than her hair...

Wait a sec... That was the crazy bike lady from the Springs. What on earth?

All thoughts of heading out to the bar died instantly. Besides, even if Tara's choice was that sexy, she'd also probably be a sports fanatic. She knew she was stereotyping in the worst kind of way, but the girls who turned her on in bed usually turned her off once they threw off the covers and started talking about football or baseball or whatever sport was in season.

For now at least, she had sworn off love. There would be plenty of time for that when she made junior partner. Besides, a drawer full of anatomically correct toys thankfully had no opinions on penalties against a defenseless receiver on the football field.

She typed a new title, *Phone Number Fiasco,* into MindNode and started plotting any idea that might help. A half hour later she was no closer to a solution than she had been in the elevator, but just creating the mind map with its different colors and spiraling nodes had calmed her down. Besides, the two yoga poses of Downward Dog and Happy Baby were calling her name.

The next morning, she walked into the tenth floor at Truman and Steinbrecker, nursing an upset stomach and no clear plan of action regarding the note. As soon as she rounded into her cubicle, the man with the red beard popped up.

Nikka stretched out her hand to play nice. "Hi, I'm Nikka."

"I have a full tank today." He eyed her like the competition.

"So do I." Nikka glared right back. "And the inside track from yesterday." She might have a nervous stomach, but only she had to know that.

She pulled her chair up to the desk and looked for the red blinking light on her phone. It wasn't lit. That was one hurdle behind her. At least she wasn't going to be called on the carpet before her day even started. She still hadn't decided what to do about the phone number and instead dove into the case files on her desk.

At lunch, she stayed put to look up that appeal on the BMW case. It hadn't come down yet, so she called the dentist to cancel. Two things to cross out on her to-do list. Already she could feel the spike in endorphins even before she slid her lucky metallic pen across the entries. It was why she went old school and hand-wrote her to-do list. No Todoist or Wunderlist for her.

She hunted around in her purse for the paper but couldn't find it. In the end she had to make a new list, and true to the rules of the to-do list manifesto, she couldn't put down something she had already done. Damn.

Around two, the phone rang shrilly, startling her. She was thigh-deep in work, drawing up a trademark contract for a lead attorney, and wasn't ready for the voice on the other end.

"Hi, this is Alison, Lea's assistant. She would like to see you. Can you come to her office?"

"S...sure. I'll be right there." Nikka put down the phone with a shaking hand. When she stood up, thin ribbons of pain ran through her stomach again. Here it was. The moment of truth. To tell or not to tell.

She stepped into Lea's office focused on exactly what she was going to do and stood in the middle of the room while Lea finished up a phone call.

"That's unfortunate, but all you have to do is keep it together up there for a few more days. Don't worry. I'll take care of her."

Nikka almost felt sorry for the "her," poor person, and straightened the hem on her skirt for the third time since she'd entered the office.

"Yes, and then we'll go out and celebrate... Sure, that place with the craft beers... Yes, I promise."

As soon as Lea dropped the phone back into the cradle, Nikka made her move. "Look, Lea. I need to tell you what happened yesterday when you sent me into Beth Walker's house with that note."

Lea raised an eyebrow. "All right."

"I meant to give that note to Vivienne, but I stupidly stumbled into Ms. Walker's room. Vivienne was nowhere to be found when I went in, and I heard noises. And I just assumed... You were absolutely right. Ms. Walker isn't at all well, and I think I startled her. When Vivienne came in, she went straight to Ms. Walker to help her, and in the commotion I forgot to give her the paper."

Lea leaned back in her desk chair and folded her arms across her chest.

She thought she would feel better after the confession, but pain jabbed her in her gut again. Lea was wrong. This was exactly like being in a headmistress's office. Or so she imagined. Her parents had never had the money for a ritzy private education.

"Why didn't you tell me that when you got in the car?" Lea asked.

"There's no excuse for that except I wanted to make a good impression. I've worked here three years, and all I've said to you in all that time is 'thank you for this opportunity' when you hired me. I didn't want the next statement to be something like I can't even deliver a piece of paper. It's silly, I know, but there it is."

Lea just stared at her, her hard gaze traveling up and down for a long, long moment. So long that Nikka had enough time to mentally pack up her things at her new desk and start composing her phone call to her father to explain how she had lost her new position in just over twenty-four hours.

"Well, the silly thing is you did."

"Sorry?" And when Lea didn't answer, she asked, "Did what?"

"Make a good impression."

"How?" Nikka looked around. Was she being punked?

"I think I have something of yours." Lea handed her a piece of paper with *TO-DO* written in bold letters at the top.

Nikka felt the heat on her face as she plucked it out of Lea's outstretched hand. No wonder she couldn't find it. When that crazy bike woman startled her, she must have dropped it into the depositions, but how on earth was this particular OCD compulsion impressive?

"Despite what you may have thought, I didn't call you in here to grill you about the note. Actually, I called you in here to ask you about something on that list. The BMW appeal. Did you look it up?"

"I did. It's still pending, but if it—"

"Yes, I know. I'm tracking it too." Lea tapped the files on her desk. "This whole case hinges on the result, and I have to say, I'm impressed that from just cleaning up your car, you recognized that as well."

Nikka stood up a little straighter. "Thank you...Lea."

"So I checked around a little this morning. Word in the office is that you have a first-rate legal mind, a flair for innovation, and a knack for tying up loose ends."

Nikka nodded, trying to mentally jump ahead of the compliment. Where was she going with this talk?

"You've seen for yourself what kind of shape Beth Walker's in. There was an accident in her past that has always made her physically fragile. And I'm afraid that she's tottering in and out of dementia. What a shame that such a great author would end up like this. And so we need to rally around her. If times get any tougher for her, I want to make sure that her revenue stream is in place."

In her mind's eye, Nikka put all her belongings back on her desk. "What do you need me to do?"

Lea got up and walked around her desk to lean on it, bringing herself down to Nikka's level. "It involves some time out of town. Can you get someone to look after your cat for a while? I assume that's who the cat food was for."

"Yes, I can." The heat in her cheeks rose again.

"Good. I need you to go back up to Steelhead Springs and be my ears and eyes on the ground. Walker's brother was a horrible businessman. He never negotiated any real licensing deals. Just Mickey Mouse contracts that practically invited the town to take advantage of Walker."

"Got it."

"We need to tighten up the commerce in that town and make sure that poor Beth gets the money she deserves from all those trinkets that are being sold up there. You'll have to be a bit of a hard-ass with the mom-and-pop stores up there. Will that be a problem?"

"No. The law speaks for itself."

"It certainly does." Lea nodded once. "Glad you're on board." She got up and walked to the glass door, calling to her assistant, "Alison? Is the paperwork for Steelhead Springs ready?"

Nikka watched in wonder as Lea crossed the room. Everything around her boss had suddenly come into focus. The custom-built modern furniture, the breathtaking view of the bay, the sheer size of the office—she hadn't seen any of it before. When she crept in, she had been so nervous. Now, her possible future materialized right before her eyes.

On board? She couldn't get any more on board if Lea had hung down a ladder and pulled her up herself.

Alison jumped up from her desk and handed Lea a file. She checked it and then passed over a long, numbered list of all that Nikka would have to accomplish up in the Springs.

"Just put a to-do at the top here, and you should be right at home."

Nikka searched Lea's face. Was she being snide?

A smile flashed for an instant at the edge of her boss's mouth. Nikka's stomach flipped over one last time and was silent.

Look at her. Joking with the boss.

Lea slid one hand down the file. The other, she placed lightly on Nikka's arm. Her touch made Nikka's whole arm tingle. "And here's my private number. Call me if anything comes up."

Nikka let her gaze fall to the bottom of the page. Wait a sec...

That was odd. The exact same number on the note. Why would Lea ask her to give Vivienne her private line? Wouldn't Vivienne already have it? She immediately dropped the thought like a hot potato. She was in the inner circle. It was nice and warm in here, and she'd be crazy to open that door and let the cold air in.

File in hand, Nikka strode down the hallway back to the cubicle farm as if she owned the place, a much different walk than the one a few minutes ago.

The red-bearded man threw her a questioning look as she passed.

She gave him a shit-eating grin and a knowing wink as she grabbed her purse and her keys.

Let him sit there and wonder.

Chapter 4

March 1960

THE OBVIOUS ANSWER TO—HOW HAD Dawn put it?—
could you take me on had to be a determined *no*.

"I don't have any experience with babies," Beth said. "I
haven't even held one. You should get someone like a nanny
or a midwife or, I don't know, someone who could actually
accomplish something in an emergency."

"That's not what we're looking for," James said. "Dawn's
as healthy as a horse. We need someone who can drive her
around on a daily basis. Dawn can't drive."

"I can, but not well," Dawn said.

"It's the same thing. Besides we need someone just to
make this house feel a little less lonely. Someone who won't
bug out being with a movie star. Someone who's cool with
the whole situation and will treat her like a normal person."

"And you think that's me?" Beth's palms sweated every
time she just glanced at Dawn.

"It will be, once you realize that I'm just like you." Dawn
cocked her head and gave a slight shrug.

Beth shook her head. There was no universe where Dawn
and she were the same, but it was a nice idea.

James topped off her wineglass. "We'll make it worth
your while."

"It's not that."

"What is it, then? We need to get this resolved quickly before I leave."

"I don't know." Beth let her gaze shift to Dawn's face. "I've never been asked to do anything like this before."

Dawn caught her glance. "We can drop it. We don't mean to make you uncomfortable."

Too late. They had zoomed past uncomfortable the moment she walked in the door and found there was no party. She had no idea what this feeling was—the one that made her nerve endings tingle. Truth be told, the proposition scared her down to her toes, but the thought of dropping it scared her even more. Dawn had even implied that she might be able to write when she was out here. She wouldn't get another chance like this.

Dawn and James waited for her answer, their stares boring into her.

She squirmed in her seat. "Okay, if you're sure you want me... But my father will have to agree first."

"Done!" James slapped the table so hard that the wine sloshed around in his glass.

Had he ever heard no?

The check written out by James's own hand, matching her whole salary for a year, arrived at her parents' house the next day. Her father did a double take and pointed to the four zeros all neatly in a row.

"What exactly are you going to do out there?" he asked.

"Drive her around, run errands, help around the house."

"Seems like an awful lot of money for a Girl Friday."

"Mr. Montgomery needs to have this settled before he leaves for Italy." Beth took the check back. Her father was right. It was a ton of money. She was playing in a whole new league with the Montgomerys. Maybe that's how movie stars did things.

"You're going to have to tell Hank." Her father reached for the drink on the coffee table.

"I know." Beth grinned.

Beth chose a time when the office was empty and Hank had his flask out openly on his desk.

"Hank, do you have a minute?"

He grunted.

Beth wasn't sure what that meant exactly, but she sat down across from him anyway. "I found another job. Starting tomorrow, I am working for Dawn Montgomery."

"Are you serious? You'll see Dawn Montgomery every day?" His eyes doubled in size, and his mouth stayed open with the question.

"Absolutely. They invited me out to dinner yesterday and asked me." She felt a little like a celebrity herself.

He flounced back against his office chair, eyeing Beth up and down as if he were looking at her for the first time. "Well, go figure. Who would have thought it?" He licked his lips greedily. "And when their friends come up and see what a great town Steelhead is, you'll invite me over, right?"

Beth laughed.

"No, seriously."

"I think Mrs. Mont…Dawn's buying a little bit of privacy with this house, Hank. Maybe that's the point." *Dawn* rolled off her tongue easily, and Hank was eyeing her as if she mattered. Yep, she could get used to this.

"I'm not an idiot. I get it. I'm not inviting myself over for tea and a game of bridge, just a meet-and-greet with some people who have ready cash to plunk down on vacation homes. It's a whole new market, this Hollywood crowd. I'd be foolish not to tap into it. And you could help me, you know. I'd even throw a small commission your way if we could pull this off." He reached across the desk and grabbed her arm for emphasis.

Beth cringed the moment his fingers dropped on her skin, but she couldn't shake the knowledge that she might need Hank again if her new dream job went south. "They'll have to bring it up."

He moved his head up and down so rapidly his stringy hair flapped against his forehead.

"And we'll come to you, if they do."

"Of course. Of course." He released her.

She rubbed her arm with her other hand and quickly spun out of his office without waiting for his dismissal.

"Keep in touch, Beth."

Beth didn't reply. She just walked out the door. With a little luck, for the very last time.

As Beth was standing on Dawn's stoop, all of her little victories behind her, her initial fears returned in a rush. What was this job really? Would she be more of a friend or a maid or something in between that had no clear label?

I can't do this. She fought down the urge to race back to her truck and drive away like a bat out of hell. As it was, she swallowed hard as she worked up the courage to knock.

Just as she lifted her hand, the door swung open.

Dawn, lovely as always, stood just inside, a smile playing at her lips. "You do know that the job's inside the house, right?"

Heat rushed across her cheeks, and Dawn bit her lip to kill the smile.

"I'm sorry. I forget I'm not in Hollywood anymore. Everything doesn't have to be a quip or a sound bite for the press." She cupped Beth's elbow and guided her inside. "You don't have to be nervous. I don't bite. And the sooner you come in, the sooner we can get comfortable around each other."

Beth's arm tingled, and her heart started pounding a mile a minute at Dawn's light touch. She silently counted to ten, trying to calm her nerves as she let herself be pulled into the foyer. It didn't matter what Dawn said; just her presence was enough to send Beth into paroxysms.

At the number ten, her heart stopped slamming against her chest, and she was able to look around. Once again, the architectural beauty of the house grabbed her. The early morning sun flooded in through a skylight right above them and gave the small room a golden glow. The Montgomerys had been unbelievably lucky to get such a house.

"I know. Can you believe how pretty it is in here in the morning? We were really lucky."

It was uncanny. How did she always know exactly what Beth was thinking?

"Can you read minds?" The words popped out before she had really considered the question. She looked down; she couldn't meet Dawn's gaze.

"No, of course not." Dawn chuckled. "But I can read people."

The laugh was so gentle that Beth raised her head back up.

"That's different? How?"

"There's nothing mystical about what I can do. People's expressions, how they hold their heads, the way they stand and move. It's like they're speaking out loud to me."

Beth raised her eyebrows, and Dawn shrugged, an elegant little flip of her shoulders, perfected on a thousand movie screens. "I've always been really, really good at it. I had to be, and you'd be surprised what people give away without even knowing."

"They do?"

She met Beth's gaze and held it. "Do you want to know what you're telling me right now?"

Beth's heart flipped in her chest and started pounding all over again. She couldn't find a spoken answer; the question, the look—she wasn't used to having all the focus in the room turned on her. It was unexpected and very intimate. All Beth could do was nod.

"Okay. You're telling me that you'd be more comfortable in the kitchen with a cup of coffee in your hands, making a list of what this job might entail. Am I right?"

"Yes." Beth's response was little more than a breath.

"Don't look at me like that. I told you it wasn't magic."

"I'm not buying it, because honestly, that's exactly what I was thinking." Beth found her voice.

"Your feet are pointed in the direction of the kitchen. People always aim their feet where they want to really be and give their true feelings away. In fact, your whole body is leaning that way as well, so I guessed you're a little anxious."

"I am. Sorry."

"I'll share a little secret with you. Me too. Don't forget, this is new for both of us." She smiled. "Should I go on?"

Beth nodded.

"It's early in the morning, and so I guessed maybe you didn't have coffee yet or you could use another cup. I've already made a pot, so really I took a shot in the dark on that one. And finally, it would only be human nature to wonder what the hell you had gotten yourself into by accepting this job." Dawn raised a hand toward the kitchen. "After you."

Beth's shoulders dropped as she led the way. The first exchange had gone well; maybe there was hope for her yet.

The kitchen was a showroom of modern luxuries. Green cabinets of enameled steel gave way to stainless steel counter tops and blended in beautifully with the wood on the floor and around the windows. The white refrigerator with separate freezer doors—Beth had never seen such a thing—looked as if it had been bought yesterday. A shiny copper smoke hood soared over an indoor barbecue, and a large cooking top with a grill added the architectural flair seen so clearly in the rest of the house.

"Wow," Beth said as soon as she rounded the corner.

"I know. Best room in the house. I didn't read your mind on that one either. It's just the truth." Dawn scooted around Beth and picked up a cup next to a pot of coffee on the cooker. "Coffee?"

"Yes, please."

Ten minutes later, they sat at the small breakfast table in the kitchen, and Beth began to understand a few things about Dawn. She liked things sweet and easy. She dropped three cubes of white sugar into her coffee, and when she started to talk about the job, she relaxed completely into her chair.

"Look, I don't know what this is either. I hope you'll feel comfortable keeping the house stocked with groceries and supplies. I've even started a list of some of the things I would like." She gestured to a paper on the counter. "But we've hired a cleaning service who will come out when needed, and Jimmy insisted on having dinner delivered, so no real cooking either."

"Okay." Beth let out a breath she hadn't even known she was holding. She had jumped the first hurdle—she wasn't a maid.

"I think your main task, if you're okay with it, will be just what Jimmy said. To be around so the house isn't so empty. I think they used to call it a companion in the olden days. Oh, and drive me around. I can drive, but I'm terrible at it. Seriously, a car crash just waiting to happen."

Dawn chuckled at herself first, and Beth, sensing it was okay, joined in.

"So, the weekdays for sure, but maybe the weekends too? At first I thought I would like the quiet. There's always a ton of people around you in Hollywood, telling you what to do and how to think and act, but here the quiet is just so…still. So can we play Saturday and Sunday by ear?"

"Yes, of course." A thrill ran through Beth. This wasn't at all like when Hank asked her to work the weekends. "I would imagine the pace in Steelhead takes some getting used to. The change must be huge."

"Will you help me?"

Dawn's lingering gaze cut her to the core. Beth wished she were the one who could read minds or at the very least read her own. It was a jumble in there. Emotions, feelings, and possibilities all turning in on themselves. She had never felt like this with anyone and was beginning to think it wasn't a simple case of being starstruck. She pushed that last thought away as quickly as she could.

"Of course, I will." Her voice was thin and unsure, like a child's.

"Great." Dawn looked away and broke the contact.

The tension mounting in Beth rode back like a wave.

Dawn bounced up from her seat. "Come see the rest of the house. You didn't get to see it all last time you were here."

The tour took them all over—the den at the back, a huge wooden porch that ran all the way around the kitchen. Dawn headed upstairs, taking them two at a time, and then bounced on her feet as she waited for Beth to reach the landing. She showed her two extra bedrooms and the huge master in the back before pausing outside a closed door near the stairs. "I saved the best for last. Look!" She swung the door open.

Beth poked her head inside: a guest room with a daybed along one wall and a desk with a typewriter and stacks of brand-new composition notebooks along the other.

"Nice office. What work will you do here?"

"No, it's not for me. It's for you."

"Me?" She took a step back. Surely she had misunderstood.

"Yes, you. It's your writing room. I know lots of screenwriters in Hollywood, and they all say that they have to have a place to write that's safe and protected from the outside world and a set of books to keep everything organized. You can't keep writing on pages that can get lost at the drop of a hat. You want to be a serious writer. Right?"

Beth opened her mouth but couldn't speak. This was beyond crazy. It was by far the nicest thing anyone had ever done for her. But Dawn didn't even know her. Why would she do such a thing? Beth stepped up to the desk to buy herself a minute and ran a finger along the black-and-white covers of the composition notebooks. Pencils sat neatly by their side, sharpened and ready for use.

"You did all this for me?"

"Of course." She tossed Beth's question casually aside. "Who else would I do it for?"

"How do you know I can even write?"

"I think we've already established that I know things. Look at your feet and your hands. They're trembling. You can't wait to get into that seat and get started."

Beth pulled her hand away from the desk as if it had burned her. It was true, though. Visions of working here already danced in her head. She would have to be more careful around Dawn if she wanted to keep anything to herself.

"Why would you do all this for me? We just met."

"Yes, I know. It's extreme. Jimmy is always going on about that too. You see I can't do things by halves. But I also know this, whatever it is..." She waved her hand back and forth between them. "...has to work for both of us. Doesn't it?"

"Yes, but..."

"You need to take *but* out of your vocabulary. They're no buts anymore in your writing career. Besides, I plan to take a lot of naps, and since I'm sleeping for two, I thought you should have an activity too."

The room and the fact that Dawn had even thought of it were unbelievable. Almost too good to be true. Had she walked into a living fairy tale when Dawn opened the front door?

"Thank you," was all she could muster.

"Isn't this what friendship's all about?"

There it was. Dawn had finally defined the job with one simple word. *Friendship.*

How about that?

After lunch, Beth and Dawn strode deep into the redwoods behind the house. Tall trees towered over them, their branches creating a protective canopy over the green moss and ferns and a little path that disappeared deep into the grove. Afternoon sunlight filtered down among the leaves and dappled their shoulders and heads with an almost magical glow.

Dawn stretched out her arms and whirled around, spinning in the light. "This is like a fairyland. I can hear the music. The trees are singing."

"So you can read plants as well as people?" Beth cringed. Had she gone too far?

Dawn laughed and patted the nearest tree, a grand giant disappearing into the blue sky. "You don't need any special skills to know how happy they are here. You probably just have stopped noticing. You've lived here all your life, right?"

"Is it that obvious?"

"Yeah, it is. Look at you. You walk as if you belong here. Nothing timid about the way you move in the forest. You should move through life like that. You're more timid in other places, like the real estate office."

Was Dawn always watching her? Goose bumps rose all over her body, even on her stomach. Being the center of someone's focus was crazy and brand-new, but so exciting. She was used to fading into the background, first at home, playing second fiddle to her rowdy brother, and then at the real estate office with Hank. Men tended not to notice her, at least not in the way they looked at other women. That had been okay with her. She had never wanted all the extra attention…until now.

"How old are you, Beth?" Dawn whirled so close, Beth could see the light sprinkle of freckles across her nose.

"Twenty-two." She tipped her head with pride at the number. She felt so mature and experienced walking along a forest path with a gorgeous movie star.

"Oh, that's a wonderful age. I wish I were twenty-two again. Young enough to believe that anything is possible."

Beth studied this gorgeous creature beside her. Dark Wayfarer sunglasses hid her eyes, but there wasn't a line or wrinkle on her face. Her complexion was clear and flawless all the way down to the thin strand of pearls that circled her neck. Beth's gaze lingered where the pearls ran over her clavicle, and she fought down the urge to run a finger down its soft curve.

"How old are you?" She pulled the hand into a fist at her side.

"Old enough to mind the question."

"Sorry." The heat ran all the way down her neck and spread along her chest.

"Don't be. Age is a deep, dark secret in Hollywood for women." Dawn linked her arm with Beth's.

Her embarrassment eased, but still her tongue was tied.

Dawn pulled her close. "Do you want to know an even better secret?"

Beth leaned in to her, basking in her forgiveness, and nodded.

"Jimmy tells everyone that he was just strolling by that coffee shop in Hollywood after high school one day when a casting director from Warner's rushed out and begged him to sign with them."

"I've heard that story. Everyone has."

"But here's the thing. It didn't happen like that at all."

"No?"

"God, no. Jimmy cut morning classes and took two busses for a month straight to get to that shop by lunch. He knew the casting directors ate there, and he begged them every day to give him a screen test. The restaurant even posted a waiter at the door to fend him off, but he always found a way in. He even climbed in through the trash chute once. Finally, Paul Hanley said he'd bring him into the studio just to get Jimmy off his back. None of them thought he had much talent, but you know Jimmy. He doesn't let an opportunity pass him by. He got in front of that camera during the screen test at the studio, ripped his shirt off, and the rest is history. With someone that handsome, no one really cared if he could act. They still don't."

"His movies are really popular." Beth took a chance and squeezed the arm wound with hers. When Dawn didn't pull away, happiness flooded through her; she felt as if she were a popular schoolgirl gossiping about the football quarterback.

"Oh, Jimmy breathes charisma. I'll give him that. Once he got his foot in the door, he charmed everyone under the sun, even me." A hint of harshness had crept into Dawn's tone, and her mouth, just for a second, turned downward. She dropped Beth's arm and danced up the path.

Beth raced to catch up. "Is it true, then, that you two met at that screen test for *Drop in the Bucket*? Did you really take one look at him there and know he was the one?"

"Oh no. The studio set us up long before that. The real story is that we just happened to be filling out paperwork in the same office one day. An executive from publicity happened to be walking by. Clean-cut boy standing by the girl next door. He thought we looked really good together, and when we tested well, they fabricated a relationship."

"But you fell in love, right?"

"Of course. He's so handsome; who wouldn't love him? But there was more to it."

"In what way?"

"In the way that was good for our careers. Alone, we couldn't catch a break. Jimmy had those Coca-Cola commercials and some bit parts. And me? The studio was on the verge of releasing me." She licked her lips as if to get rid of the bitterness of that statement. "Together, as a couple, it was a completely different story. Suddenly, we were America's sweethearts. We got the leads in *Drop in the Bucket*. I nailed the death scene, and Jimmy just managed to not overact being heartbroken. It did well, and we never looked back."

Beth stopped in the middle of the path. "But that's not what they say in the magazines."

"Oh please tell me you don't read those rags."

Beth visualized the stack of tabloids sitting at that very moment on her bedside table. She had pored through them, looking for any tidbit about Dawn, while she waited for the escrow to close. "Sometimes—"

"Well, don't. They're all lies." The bitterness was back, and for some reason now it was directed at Beth.

"I... I..."

Dawn closed the space between them with two steps. She reached up to cup Beth's cheek.

Her fingers felt light and cool, and Beth couldn't help herself; she leaned her head into the hollow of Dawn's palm.

"You don't have to read them anymore." She slid off her sunglasses and met Beth's gaze. "Look at me. You've the real thing right in front of you. Okay?"

Intensity swirled in the irises of Dawn's eyes. They played much greener in person than they did in the movies. Standing this close made Beth's throat close up, and she had to swallow twice before she could get even one word out. "Okay." Even so, it registered more as a squeak than a sound.

"That's my girl." Dawn patted her cheek with a smile and spun away. They continued the walk as if the moment had never happened.

As soon as Beth got home, she gathered up all the magazines in her bedroom and dumped them straight into the trash out back.

Her brother, Sammy, still wearing his football uniform, materialized on the doorstep. "If you're getting rid of those, I'll take a few."

"No, I'm throwing them away. They're all full of lies."

"You spend one day with a movie star and suddenly you're a know-it-all?"

Beth elbowed him aside as she attempted to get back into the house. "What if I am?"

He grabbed her arm and pulled her back. "Come on, sis. Spill. What's she really like?"

"She's wonderful." She threw the statement at him like a weapon. It felt good to have the upper hand with him for once.

"No fair." He drew the words out in a long whine. "Let me meet her. Please. Just let me drive you out there one day. I don't have to stay, but I could say hello."

"My answer hasn't changed from the last time you asked. It's still no." The last thing she wanted to do was share Dawn with anyone. She wrenched her arm out of his grasp and shook him off.

"What if I run interference with Pop? Get him on your side."

She spun around to look at her brother. His face had none of that snarky quality that usually took up permanent residence there. "You would do that?"

"Yeah, tonight at dinner. If I get Pop to really sign off on your new job and not just the money, can I meet her then?"

Beth shifted from one foot to the other. Letting Sammy in was chancy. He had a way of making everything about him, but her father was way more dangerous. He could pull the carpet out from under her at any moment by demanding that she return to the real estate office or, worse, go back to not working at all. What had he said? "People will think you have to work and that I can't take care of my family. Working for Hank looks like a favor to a friend, but this is just plain crazy. Why can't you just find a husband and settle down?"

That was the million-dollar question she had been avoiding for a while. From her father and, if she was being honest, from herself as well. Sammy might just be what the doctor ordered. If she could control Sammy—and that was a big, big *if*—she might be able to get ahead of her father and this whole situation.

"You get Pop to say it's okay tonight and every other time he brings it up, because we both know he will. You do that, and we have a deal."

"What? That's way too much."

"Take it or leave it." Beth bit the side of her lip. Sammy might not jump.

"All right." He thrust his hand out for the shake. "Deal."

She dropped her hand into his. "Deal."

Sammy was better than his word. At dinner, between the fried chicken and the Jell-O ambrosia, he went to town, playing their father like a fiddle.

"Someone is always going to have to take care of Beth." He ended with a crescendo. "Make sure she's making the right choices."

Carl dropped his spoon into his empty Jell-O bowl with a clatter. "You know, Sammy's right."

Her brother grinned broadly as his face puffed up in victory. Even as a little boy, he had never worn his success well.

Beth's heart sank. Could she have been any dumber? She should have asked him how exactly he was going to swing their father her way.

"I will feel better about your working for Mrs. Montgomery if I know her. See that she's... what did you call her, Sammy?"

"Bona fide, you know, Pop, totally legit."

Carl nodded first to Beth and then to the rest of the table. "He's right. We need to make sure that her heart is in the right place where you're concerned."

The writing sanctuary and all its luxuries rose before her. "Trust me, Pop. It is, but—"

"No, no." He held up his palm to stop her. "My mind's made up. In fact, ask her over for dinner next weekend. Your mother will make a pot roast, and we can really get to know each other. Then sending you off to her house each day won't seem so strange."

Beth fumed. Her father was treating her as if she were four and her job with Dawn as if it were an elaborate play date.

Sammy, at least, had the decency to avoid her glare and began to pick at the napkin in his lap.

"Pop, she came out here for some peace and quiet," Beth said. "That doesn't include dinner at our house."

"It would be nice to see what she's all about." Her mother fingered the cross at her neck.

What was that about? Beth by no means had Dawn's skills, but her mother was an open book. When she was nervous about something, her hands were all over that cross. She glanced back and forth between her parents. The hard stubbornness in their stares told her she was beaten.

"Okay. I'll ask her. But I can't make her come."

The invitation lodged in Beth's throat every time she opened her mouth. They were just getting into a rhythm out at the house, and she didn't want to throw a wrench into the easy companionship that was quickly developing.

Beth would stop in town on her way out and pick up groceries and anything else Dawn might need. Then they would sit in the kitchen with steaming cups of coffee and ramble on about their lives, hopes, and dreams. Dawn asked as many questions as she answered, and Beth found talking to her was remarkably easy. When their mugs were empty, they would move outside to "take the air" as Dawn called it. So far that involved planting flowers in big pots by the door or Dawn drawing something "straight from nature" in her sketchpad. Not one of the gossip magazines had said anything about Dawn being such a great artist, and Beth carried the secret around with her like a hidden treasure. After lunch, Dawn would take a nap in her bedroom while Beth stole away to the writing room down the hall.

Soon her notebooks were heavy with words and stories. The pencil sped across the paper as if it had a mind of its own.

"Are they possessed? Have I sold my soul to the devil?" She waved one at Dawn after a particularly fruitful session. "Or are they just magic?"

Dawn laughed. "No. They came out of a regular box just like ordinary pencils."

Beth wasn't convinced; her stories breathed with a grace and excitement that was brand-new to her. Okay, not the pencils; maybe it was the notebooks—ordinary on the outside, full of inspiration on the inside. Whatever it was, she always walked out of the room at the end of her sessions with a bounce in her step.

One afternoon, Beth wrote *THE END* at the bottom of the page and put down her pencil with a contented sigh. Yes, she had completed her very first story. She gathered the notebook up with shaking hands and made her way downstairs.

Dawn sat in the same wing-tip chair in the living room as she had on Beth's first night in the house. Although this time, she had angled it out toward the wall of windows to take in the view, and Beth could only see blonde curls spilling over the back of the chair. The head underneath was as still as stone, and her sketchpad lay discarded on the floor.

"Dawn, are you okay?" Beth stepped deeper into the room.

Dawn craned her head around the side of the chair and met Beth's gaze. Her face and expression were strangely blank as if she had wiped her emotions away with an eraser as she pivoted. "Yes, I was just thinking."

"About what?" Beth shivered, although the room was warm enough.

"About life and how it turns out. I'm just feeling a little blue, I guess. When you're in my condition, I hear that happens sometimes." She waved her hand toward the couch. "Sit. I can see you've something to tell me."

"I do. But if you're not up for it, I can wait."

"No, please. I need something to take me out of this mood."

Beth sat on the very edge of the couch and clutched the notebook protectively to her chest. "I finished a story."

"That's fantastic. Read it to me." The warmth seeped back into Dawn's eyes, and she let her head drop against the side of the chair.

Excitement swirled up in Beth. An audience, well Dawn's approval really, was what had drawn her downstairs with the notebook in the first place. But now the idea of reading it out loud sent a jolt racing through her.

"Don't be scared," Dawn said in that prescient way of hers. "Don't get me wrong. I'm going to tell you the truth, of course. All artists should only hear the truth about their talent. Believe me, I've seen actresses completely ruined when the studio coddles them after a bad performance."

Beth gripped the notebook more tightly.

"But I already know I'm going to love it."

"You can't possibly know that."

"Try me."

Dawn had expertly backed her into a corner. Reading out loud was now both an invitation and a challenge. Beth marveled how easily Dawn had manipulated her into the one act that scared the bejeezus out of her. But still, she had to know. If she couldn't get Dawn on her side, she might as well snap the magic pencils in half and throw the enchanted notebooks into the trash.

With a voice that shook both with eagerness and anxiety, Beth began to read. "On her twenty-second birthday, Karen woke up to find that she couldn't recall even one mildly interesting incident about her life."

As the narrative unfolded, Karen bought herself a ticket to the traveling circus that had taken up residence in the next town over and found herself at the end of the night in the fortune-teller's tent. The tarot card reading didn't go well. The woman with the luminous green eyes turned over one blank card after another until the state of Karen's life was patently clear. Finally, she told Karen that there was nothing for her here and that she might as well do something completely crazy. As Karen spun the possibilities around in her mind, the blank cards on the rickety table magically shone with colors and events so improbable that Karen gasped out loud. Her future, full of enchantment and adventure, was laid out before her, and all she had to do was grab it and never let go. When the circus left the next morning, Karen did too. She stood on the train next to the green-eyed woman and never looked back. Her parents woke up to an odd feeling that the house was strangely empty, but they immediately chalked it up to their missing dog that they thought had run away during the night. No one, as it turned out, remembered Karen at all.

As she read, Beth stole glances at Dawn, who had sunk deeper into the chair with the first words. From then on, she gave nothing away. By the time Karen pulled back the thick curtain of the fortune-teller's tent, Dawn's eyes had fluttered closed. And she was so still after the last lines that Beth was sure she had fallen asleep.

She closed the notebook with a soft rustle and started the criticism in her own head. *Too derivative, too immature, too personal, too—*

"Sure, you can tell you're young, maybe haven't written a lot, but, Beth, as you read it, the story came alive. Just like a movie. No, better. I felt like I was there with Karen and Madame Valentini, standing in that tent."

Beth's heart skipped a beat. "Really?"

"Yes. And that's something you can't learn." She clapped her hands.

"You really liked it?" Beth needed to hear the compliment again.

Dawn nodded. "Tomorrow we should start talking about another story, maybe something longer, bigger in scope."

"That would be amazing." Beth sank back onto the sofa, grinning from ear to ear. Dawn was the real magic. She couldn't lose this job. "Oh. Tomorrow. I forgot. My parents want me to ask you for dinner. I know it's last minute and all. You don't have to say yes, but I told them I would ask."

"That's a lovely idea. I'd love to come."

Her heart dropped. She had been hoping that Dawn would say no, and all this would stay private.

"Don't fret. It was bound to happen sooner or later. Your parents just want to see what type of mysterious woman you've taken up with."

"No, it's not that. They just can't believe that this is a real job."

"Oh, sweetheart. I'm pretty sure I'm right."

Like a cat, Dawn uncurled herself from the chair and was suddenly by Beth's side. She took her chin between her thumb and forefinger and held it steady while she bent down and pressed her lips gently to Beth's. They were firm and comforting as the shock rolled through Beth.

When the surprise subsided, her lips softened and the kiss deepened. Dawn's hold on her cheek grew into a caress. Beth leaned in to her hand as a warmth fluttered below her stomach and threatened to take her over completely.

Then, just as quickly as the kiss had started, it was over. Dawn drew back, smiling gently.

"What...? I...What was that?" Beth's breath puffed out in little gasps.

"What else? I colored your tarot cards. Isn't that what you wanted? What you asked for with the story?"

Dawn dropped her chin, and Beth felt the loss of her touch down to her toes.

"But mostly teaching you that there are far worse things than kissing a girl."

Beth froze, not able to process even a little bit of what had just happened.

So Dawn helped her out. She tenderly drew the notebook out of her hands and dropped it to the coffee table. Then she pulled Beth off the couch and led her to the front door.

"Can you pick me up at four tomorrow? There are a few things I need in town before we have dinner with your family."

The door opened and closed, and Beth stood all alone in the cool afternoon air. She ran her fingers over her still tingling lips. Was Dawn right? Did she want the kiss? Was that what the story had always been about?

The answer struck her hard, and her entire world opened up right there on the front porch of 741 Fern Drive. Suddenly, she knew things about herself that she hadn't known ten minutes before. A bunch of things that she would have to unravel later, but the main one was that Dawn was right. There *were* far worse things than kissing a girl.

The worst being that she had liked it.

A lot.

Chapter 5

DIMITRI'S GRAVELLY VOICE ECHOED THROUGH the Outback's speakers. "When opportunity knocks, you open door."

"I know, Papa."

Her father had a saying for everything. Not one was original, but Nikka thought it endearing how he said them as if they were and he had just come up with them out of the blue. The cheesy sayings aside, she had inherited her drive from her father, and for that, she was eternally grateful.

"This is why we come to America. I opened door, and now my daughter will be partner in law firm."

"Slow down there, Papa. That's a long way off, if ever." But her voice also sang with the brightness of that distinct possibility. "Let's not get ahead of ourselves. This is just one case, and I have to shine."

"You will."

"Part of what I have to do here is grunt work, and I'm not going to be popular." She made the turn off the main highway and eased onto the road to Steelhead Springs. "A lot of people will look at me like I'm the bad guy when I give them this new information."

"Are you? Bad guy?"

"No. The law is very clear in this case. Ms. Walker's books aren't in the public domain, so all the stores in Steelhead

Springs are violating copyright. More importantly, I'll be helping someone who can't help herself. Not many people will see it that way, though."

"Then you make them see it. You have good plan?"

"I think so. I hope so."

"You need good plan. Good plan is like Google road map. It puts flag at final destination in mind and big blue line to get there."

"Yes, Papa." That was one of his favorites.

"That's my good girl." Dimitri's voice faded as he pulled the phone away to hang up.

"Oh, Papa?" Nikka yelled into her car. She wasn't used to the Bluetooth yet.

"Yes?"

"Can you make sure Sasha feeds Desi and Lucy?" Darker visions of her brother with his head in her liquor cabinet as the cats pawed empty bowls pushed the other shiny ones away.

"He is big boy."

"Yes, but he doesn't always act like it."

"I make sure."

"Thanks. I love you."

Dimitri grunted his love and hung up.

Nikka tapped her iPhone sitting in the cup holder, and another voice, this one calm and female, carried Nikka into the latest Booker Prize winner.

Forty-five minutes and several chapters later, Nikka pulled into the Riverside Inn & Resort parking lot. As generic as the name of the hotel was, the actual property was breathtaking. A wooden slat building painted sunshine-yellow sat among pine trees right on the bank of the Tall Tree River. A huge, grassy lawn ran down to the water's edge, and big decks soared off both the top and bottom stories, giving every room a gorgeous water view. Nikka smiled as she got out of the car. There were certainly worse places to work.

"Welcome to the Riverside." A butch woman with ink-black hair and several piercings popped up from behind the front desk. Her grin was so wide it worked against her tough image.

"Thanks. This is beautiful." Nikka took in the cozy fireplace and sitting room littered with paperbacks and magazines. "I'm Nikka Vaskin. I think I have a reservation."

"Yes, you do." She hit keys on a desk computer. "Oh, the River Suite. One of our nicest rooms. For a week?"

"Yes."

"You alone?" The butch craned her neck to see if anyone else was coming in from the parking lot.

"Yes."

"You here for business or pleasure?" She gave Nikka a long, appraising gaze.

Was she flirting with her? She would have to put a stop to that immediately. She had no room for distractions of any kind, even if they had such a great smile.

"Work. Nothing but work."

"The Springs has a way of changing that." She winked at Nikka. "Mark my words."

"Not me. I got my priorities straight."

When she entered the hotel room, she slid the balcony door open to take a quick look at the idyllic view below. The green lawn was littered with deck chairs and umbrellas, and a pile of rubber inner tubes was tied to a post at the water. Beyond them, the Tall Tree River tumbled by with a cadence that could have been the model for a high-end sleep and sound machine. It was peaceful, restorative, and absolutely not for her. She slid the door closed and ran the black-out curtain across the view.

Ten minutes later, she had transformed the holiday suite into a miniature office. Legal software CaseManager sat open on her iPad, and her computer hummed with the Riverside Inn's spotty Internet. Her stomach rumbled, reminding her that she had only snacked at her desk while working through lunch. Nikka toyed with the idea of going into town to get supper but then settled on the much more efficient option of room service and another working meal while she memorized details about the businesses that she would have to deal with first thing in the morning.

Yep, nothing but work.

The next morning the day started out fine...good even. The cute butch whose name was Germaine and who lived on the premises brought her a delicious breakfast of homemade granola with organic plain yogurt and fresh berries in the dining room. The coffee, rich and complex, rivaled her favorite place in the City.

"Excellent coffee," she said when Germaine refilled her mug.

"Roasted at a little place right in the center of town. Can't miss it. They've excellent cinnamon rolls too, if you eat sweets for breakfast."

"I try to stay healthful...at least for the first meal of the day."

"No, I get it." Germaine grinned. "Sweet enough already, huh?"

"Hardly." But despite herself, she smiled back.

She watched Germaine move on to another table and flirt with two older women in big sun hats. They ate it up, giggling and hanging on her every world. Apparently, a little sweet talk came with each breakfast served at the Riverside Inn & Resort.

Thank goodness. Nikka wasn't interested anyway; there was no room in her life for anything more than a little harmless banter. And even that had taken up precious time.

The cease-and-desist letters sat neatly tucked into the briefcase at her feet. She had a long day ahead of her. Lea had been insistent on Nikka serving the restraining order to a Margaret Chalon on Walker's behalf—whoever the hell that was. She pitied the woman. Personally, she would do whatever it took to stay on Lea's good side. No one in her right mind would want Lea as an enemy.

She took a last sip of the smooth coffee. Time to get to work.

The first stop on the list was Home at Heartwood, a bookstore in the town's center. A huge black-and-white school composition book hung in the storefront. The marbled notebook was covered with characters from Walker's *Don't Waste Your Wishes* series and screamed copyright infringement. No wonder Lea wanted to get this town under control.

Inside, Beth Walker's books were on full display, like a shrine to the town's deity. One table held her *Heartwood* book in a spiraling column with a poster of the author like a crown at the very top. The rest of the store was dedicated to the far more lucrative *Don't Waste Your Wishes* series.

On a nearby podium, an electronic notebook, crafted to resemble the one from Walker's series, was connected to a large screen above. A boy and girl stood by the display, scribbling into the notebook with the stylus. As they wrote, their wishes popped onto the screen underneath the words: WRITE A WISH, WIN A PRIZE.

Spread throughout the rest of the store were stuffed toys and action figures of the magical creatures that lived in these books. Nikka picked up a plush version of her favorite character, Citrine, the griffin who stood tall and alone in a clan of dragons. She turned the creature over in her hands. The details were perfect: the eagle's feathers and the lion's fur were so soft and Citrine's eyes so knowing. Suddenly, she was her ten-year-old self, lying in bed at night with a flashlight under the covers, reading and rereading volume seven that had introduced Citrine. How many times had she rooted for Ameliah to save Citrine from the dragons who hated her because she was different?

Still holding Citrine, she cast her scrutiny on key chains, magnets, T-shirts, aprons, children's onesies, and all sorts of other souvenirs from the books. The gall of some people. The owner of Home at Heartwood—a Serina King according to Nikka's study session the night before—exploiting Walker like this. Stealing her name and characters, without offering a lick of compensation back to the author.

Seeing the evidence in front of her and not just on a piece of paper, she had to remind herself to unclench her teeth. Rules were in place for a reason: to protect people like Beth Walker who couldn't defend themselves and to punish people like Serina King who exploited the prestige of a famous person for her own gain. This wasn't going to be an easy week for her here in the Springs, but, law or no law, it was the right thing to do. Walker was old and feeble and needed someone to look out for her interests. She dropped Citrine back into the pile of griffins.

Right. She glanced around. Where was the owner?

A middle-aged woman in a sleeveless striped dress decades too young for her bounced up to Nikka. "You know it's, like, totally okay for you to buy Citrine." Her voice dropped to a stage whisper. "I have the whole collection at home. I tell myself they're for my niece when she comes over, but, I don't know, I just like having them around." She pointed to another large pile featuring Frost, the white snow fox from volume ten. "There's other characters in the back."

Nikka took in the dress, the two blonde braids, and the immature surety that she had already sold the entire stuffed animal collection to another customer. The come-on was way too obvious. Probably not the owner. "I'm looking for Serina."

"This is Serina's day off. When she's not here, I'm the manager."

"Okay. My name is Nikka Vaskin, and I work for Truman and Steinbrecker, a law firm in San Francisco." She pulled a white envelope from her briefcase. "Would you please give this letter to Serina?"

"What is it?"

"Just some legal stuff that she needs to take care of."

The clerk snatched back her hand as if the letter was dripping with disease. "Oh. No. No. I just work here." She spun away from Nikka, bumping into the table and sending a dozen Citrines tumbling to the floor.

Nikka reached out to the woman and touched her briefly on the arm. The problem was that cease-and-desist letters packed no true legal punch. They were basically a warning to knock it off or all sorts of bad things would come down on Serina King and the bookstore. A necessary first step, though, and the woman had to cooperate.

The woman turned back and met her gaze.

Nikka visibly let her own shoulders drop and smiled her best smile.

"Just give the letter to Serina. That's all you need to do." She flapped the letter in front of the woman until she took it. "All Serina has to do is get rid of these knickknacks. Stop profiting from the unauthorized use of the protected name and trademarks of Beth Walker and her books. If she does that, everything will be fine. No harm, no foul."

"We...she doesn't do that."

"Look, why don't you let Serina worry about that? In the meantime, please just give her the letter." She handed the woman a business card. "Here's the card from the lawyer in my office who's handling all questions. Tell Serina to call if she has any. He'll be happy to talk to her and explain it all."

"Okay," the woman said.

"No, seriously. You'll be absolutely fine." Nikka smiled again and nodded. "Hey, where did you get that dress? I really love it."

The woman gripped the letter a little less tightly as she dropped her own gaze to her flowered dress.

Nikka stayed only until she knew she had talked the woman off the ledge. Her next stop was the coffee house, All Jacked Up.

Even though it was mid-morning, the line snaked out the door and down the street. The smell of cinnamon and buttery pastry drifted down to her, and a mostly empty tray of huge cinnamon rolls sat in the front window. This was the place Germaine had been talking about at breakfast. Too bad. After today, she wouldn't be able to come back for a caffeine fix.

She squeezed by a trio of women to get inside.

They glared at her for jumping the queue.

"Sorry. Excuse me. I'm not getting coffee."

All Jacked Up was even busier than the bookstore. Women and a few men perched at the high tables. Some tapped away on computers and tablets; more, however, sat with relaxed poses. Nikka wondered if they were on vacation on this gorgeous summer day in this resort town. Must be nice.

Each customer had a freshly baked pastry on a plate. The smell was even better inside, and Nikka's mouth started to water, protesting her way-too-healthy breakfast.

At the back of the large, industrial room was a small stage. Dark for the moment, but large flags advertising *Heartwood — A Dramatization* hung on either side and promised excitement every night at eight.

Nikka swung to a busboy who was cleaning up a nearby table. "Hi. Is Justine Cammelle here?"

"Yeah," the boy said, "she's in back. Do you want me to get her?"

"If you don't mind. Thank you."

A few seconds later, Justine Cammelle strode out. Her steps ate up the ground, telling Nikka that a compliment on her clothes and a gentle touch weren't going to work here.

She met Justine with her hand outstretched and took her fingers in a strong grip. "Nikka Vaskin. Attorney at Truman and Steinbrecker. We represent Beth Walker. Please accept this cease-and-desist letter. Here is the card of a lawyer at my office who will answer any further questions." She turned, attempting a quick getaway.

"Hold on a minute."

When Nikka turned back, Justine's face was already blotchy.

"Cease and desist what?"

"The performances for starters." Nikka waved a hand at the stage. "And selling those cookbooks as well."

A large stack of *Coffee Breaks — Creative Coffees with the Characters of Heartwood* stood prominently on the counter.

"What are you talking about? Those are my mother's recipes!"

"Put in the mouth of characters from Beth Walker's lawful property. All you have to do is pull the play and the books."

Justine rolled her eyes like a teenager. "Give me a break. Sammy never had a problem with it."

Nikka's dislike rose from her gut. "You had a break for the last ten years as you willfully capitalized on the fame of *Heartland* without the author's permission. Break time is over, I'm afraid."

"You can't do this." Justine raised her voice. The people in line and behind the counter all looked over. "You cut me off, and I'll have to fire people. Besides, Beth Walker needs us. Everyone would forget about her and her stupid books if it weren't for businesses like mine." The blotches had connected, leaving her whole face bright red.

"My advice for you is to call a lawyer of your own, Ms. Cammelle. Emotion can often cloud an understanding of the law." Nikka nodded her dismissal. "Thank you for your time."

"You bitch. You can't just come in here and tell me..."

Nikka stopped listening. Yep. It was going to be a long, hard day at this rate. She pushed past the same three women to leave the store. This time instead of stepping out of her way, they jostled her as she made her way through the door.

"Bitch is right." The heavier one put her hands on her hips to give Nikka even less room.

As Nikka walked away, Justine whipped out her cell phone and punched numbers into its keypad. Maybe there was hope yet. She was taking her advice. Calling a lawyer.

It wasn't until she reached Pick of the Litter, where the collars with the talking dogs and cats from volume three were, that she realized Justine had called someone else.

The owner came at her even before she walked into the shop, eyes flashing and waving some sort of doggie pop treat like a weapon.

"Don't you dare! I know what you're all about. Get off my private property."

Nikka dropped Pick of Litter's letter on the table right by the collars in question and darted out. Back in the safety of her car, she glanced at her watch. Even with the quick delivery at the pet store and the efficient route she had mapped, the letters in her case were still too many for one person, especially if she got another Justine or scared bookstore girl. She had wanted to serve them all herself. Prove to Lea that her trust wasn't misguided.

"Get help if you need it. I want them all delivered before I get there," Lea had said before she left the City.

Damnit. She picked up her phone.

A deep male voice answered.

"Harlan Potter? Nikka Vaskin here," she said through teeth she had to consciously unclench. "I'm going to have to add several more deliveries to your afternoon schedule, if you don't mind."

"No, I don't mind. If you don't mind me adding at least two more zeros to your invoice." He laughed at his own joke.

Nikka sighed. Everyone was a comedian. "You need to call Alison about that." Nikka was happy to pass the buck, literally, back to Lea's assistant who had connected her with Potter in the first place. "My plan is to swing by the courthouse and pick up the restraining order. Can you meet me at Made From Scratch in…let's say," she glanced at her watch, "in an hour?"

"Yes, siree. I can." Potter's pitch was so low, he sounded as if he were auditioning for an animated cartoon villain.

"Great. See you then."

Nikka got to the bakery with time to spare, so she walked around the shopping center. In the middle was a kiosk that housed an old hand-painted sign—See What We Saw—and faded color photos of what the mall had once looked like as a lumberyard in the 1960s. Now, instead of logs, trendy stores filled every corner.

When Lea had said that Beth Walker was a cottage industry for the whole town, she hadn't been kidding. Even the cold-pressed juice shop offered a "Walker" that promised to "give you the zing to find your true love in the Springs." It was crazy. Did Lea really intend to negotiate contracts with the entire town? When Lea arrived after bad cop Nikka had done all the legwork, she would find out. Lea would roll in as the good cop, happy to restore revenue to all these stores as long as they played by the new rules. And with a little luck, Nikka would get some quality time with the managing partner.

The woman outside the juice shop offered her a tiny cup filled with a brackish liquid. "Try a free sample of the Citrine, our Activated Charcoal Cleanser. It has lemon, lavender, and honey too."

Nikka waved her off.

"It tastes really good. Soaks up the toxins. Give it a try."

"No, thanks. I like my charcoal to stay in the barbecue."

The woman rolled her eyes and offered her tray to another passerby.

"Nikka Vaskin?" A deep voice asked, and Nikka spun toward a tiny, slight man with big ears and a long, ratty ponytail.

"Harlan Potter. Nice to meet you." The man didn't just sound like a cartoon character; he actually looked like one too. They shook hands. He had a surprisingly strong grip for such a small person.

"I hear you've made my job a little harder this afternoon. You know news spreads fast in the Springs. The locals are a pretty tight-knit group."

"So you said." She held out the restraining order. "No time to waste. The important one first."

"Gotcha." He plucked the oversized form out of her hand and glanced down at it. "Maggie's a bit of a pisser, you know. May take all my skills." He gave her a greedy look.

"I told you to call Alison." Nikka shook her head. She preferred the comedian to the letch. "You sure she's at this bakery?"

"I just told you we're a close-knit group here in the Springs. Yes, this is where she works. You want to give me the letters, too, now?"

"After this one is served. I need to make sure it's done right. Shall we go?"

The tips of Potter's large ears went red. "Lawyers don't usually come with."

"Boss's orders." Nikka shrugged. It wasn't true, but she wasn't about to admit that she was a control freak and chasing a big-time promotion.

"Whatever." He headed to the bakery with surprisingly long strides for such a short man.

Nikka followed, only to stop short.

An old, red mountain bike was chained to the rack by the bakery. She probably wouldn't have recognized it out in the streets, but with its back tire angled to her, all she saw now was a tight little butt swaying from side to side as long legs pedaled down the street away from her Outback.

Of course! Margaret Chalon was the crazy bike lady. What had she done to make Lea so mad that she slapped a restraining order on her? Never mind. That was none of her business.

But why did Ms. Chalon have to keep popping up over and over again?

Maggie yawned wide as she piped the peanut butter decorations onto the doggie cake pops. She hadn't been able to get much work done on the pops the day before, as settling back into the bakery took much longer than she had expected. So she had set her alarm before dawn in order to get an early start. What she hadn't counted on was that Lauren had moved the hide-a-key from the hiding place, and she had been locked out.

When Lauren finally showed up, Maggie had been nearly asleep on the stoop.

"You're here early." Lauren had handed her a coffee with an All Jacked Up stamp.

"Thanks. Trying to impress my boss."

"Good strategy." Lauren had smiled, and Maggie had kept quiet about freezing her butt off for over an hour.

Hours of concentrated work later, she stuck yet another completed doggie pop into the Styrofoam base. There were only two empty holes left. The idea of slipping away early to take a nap started to brew in her mind.

"Hi! Welcome to Made From Scratch. What treat can I get you today?" Lauren's shop girl, Skylar, greeted another customer.

Skylar was way too upbeat for her tastes, and her greeting made Maggie cringe every time she heard it.

"Nothing to eat, little lady. But I'll take some face time with Maggie Chalon. Get her, if you will please."

Harlan Potter? What's that little weasel doing here? She wiped the peanut butter off her hands onto the apron and marched out into the storefront, shaking a finger at the little man. "Harlan, I told you last night at the gym. Leave me alone. I don't want you following me around."

"Ah, Maggie, I'm crushed." He placed a hand on his chest in mock upset. "Sadly, this isn't pleasure, but any time you want to reconsider who lights your fire, I'm free."

"Harlan—"

He put up a hand to stop her advance. "No, seriously. This is business." He sidled over, close enough to hand her a form. "Maggie Chalon, you've been served." He snapped a picture of that very fact with his cell phone. "Thank you."

"What?" She looked down. The words *temporary restraining order* rode the top of the very official-looking form. Right under that, the name of Elizabeth Westin Walker was typed under *Section 1: Protected Person*. She had to scan down to *Section 2: Restrained Person* to find her own name, Margaret Hayden Chalon. What on earth? Surely this was some sort of joke. She raised her head to meet Harlan's gaze.

He was grinning like a flea in a dog kennel.

Maggie took in a ragged breath and glanced back down. Her name was still on the form. Not a joke.

Just then Lauren rounded the corner from her small office and took in the trio. "What's going on here?"

Skylar immediately backed up to distance herself from the situation.

Try as she might, Maggie couldn't raise her head. She didn't want to see the disappointment that would light up in Lauren's eyes.

Lauren took two steps toward Harlan, towering over him. "Look, Harlan. I don't want any trouble—"

Harlan squawked, and then a low rumble came from his mouth. "Trouble? I'm not the trouble here. But it's sure coming to the Springs. Ask Maggie. She seems to be in the thick of it."

All heads twisted to Maggie as Harlan laughed and made his way out of the shop.

"Maggie? What's going on?" Lauren asked again.

Ignoring her, Maggie watched Harlan stop at the woman standing just a few feet from the door, sticking out his hand before she unloaded several envelopes right into his palm. His fingers had nearly closed, when she snatched some back. As Harlan trotted away, she raised her head.

Maggie's breath caught in her throat as their gazes locked. A current of energy zipped between them, tugging at both ends.

She was even hotter than Maggie remembered with her big eyes, tight stomach, and high, full breasts. Now Maggie's breath was bottling up in her chest.

Too bad she was on the dark side.

The restraining order was suddenly heavy in her hand.

She rushed out the door.

Lea's assistant turned away and started tapping on her cell phone.

"Hey." Maggie trotted after her. "This is a mistake, right? All I did was peek in her room."

She sped up to get away from Maggie.

"Hey! Stop. I'm talking to you."

"I can't discuss the case with you, Ms. Chalon."

Maggie reached out and grabbed her. Her arm was taut and firm under the silk blouse, and an electric tingling ran from Maggie's fingers into her belly as soon as she made contact.

The woman stilled, looked down at her arm where Maggie's fingers still rested for a long beat, and then raised her head. Her eyes were wide and thoughtful not pinched and hostile, as Maggie had expected. They stared at each other, lost in the moment.

"Hello, Nikka?" Lea's low voice rose from the phone in the woman's hand. "What do you have for me?"

Lea's voice broke the spell. Nikka shook Maggie's hand off, brought the phone up to her ear, and began to walk away, all in one motion.

"The process server you hired did his job. Documented it as well."

Maggie stood rooted to the ground.

"Yes. I gave him some," Nikka said into the phone as she headed out of the mall. "No. Not all. I want to make sure they are done right and that everything is ready for your arrival."

With these last words, Maggie's heart sank. As usual, Harlan had it completely back-asswards. Trouble wasn't coming to the Springs. It was already here, and the restraining order was just the tip of the iceberg. This, whatever it was, was way bigger than she was.

She headed back to the bakery. Somehow in the few moments she had been gone, Justine from All Jacked Up had snuck in and was holding court. She jabbed at a piece of paper in her hand, her finger making popping noises with every stab.

"So I called the guy on the business card, and all I got was voice mail. I mean seriously, if they're going to come into my store and tell me how to run my business, the very least they can do is be there like they said they would. I mean, really...the recipes in that book are my mother's. For Christ's sake, I don't have any idea if Beth Walker even likes cinnamon."

Lauren slid the letter from her hand, so Justine's next jab hit only air. "Calm down."

Maggie stopped listening. She knew from hard experience that it would take Lauren all afternoon to achieve this goal, and even then, there would probably have to be alcohol involved. She ran her finger down the restraining order. *Nikka Vaskin* was listed as Beth Walker's lawyer. Yep, that was what Lea had called her.

"Have you seen this?" Cora from Pick of the Litter stormed into the bakery, holding out a small cell phone as if anyone could actually read it.

"Did you get a letter too?" Justine asked. "Cuz, you know, we all got one."

"Yes...Yes. But this is why they're doing it." She thrust the cell phone out. "It was just announced."

"Let me see." Lauren held out her hand and swiped the screen with her thumb and forefinger.

"Well, what is it?" Justine asked. "Read the damn thing."

"Wait a second. Bad eyes..." Lauren swooshed the screen to make it bigger.

"It's a press release from Beth Walker's publisher." Cora's eyes flashed. "You're not going to believe this."

"Kerry and Collier, an imprint of Collier Publishers," Lauren began to read, "celebrates its good luck in acquiring the rights to a newly discovered short story by Beth Walker, adored author of both *Heartwood* and the *Don't Waste Your Wishes* series. The deal was negotiated by Collier Publishers and Beth Walker via her lawyer, Lea Truman of Truman and Steinbrecker. The story titled 'The Tarot Card' will be published electronically and will be available at our webstore and on Amazon.com starting at 9 a.m. Eastern Standard Time, Friday." She stopped reading and looked at all of them. "Wow. Can you believe she wrote a new story after all this time?"

"No, I can't," Maggie said from her corner. Everyone turned to her. "From what I saw out there, she couldn't even write a grocery list."

"It did say newly discovered," Cora said. "Maybe she wrote it a long time ago."

"So why is she publishing it now?" Maggie's mind spun with this new development, with the restraining order, with the fluttering in her stomach that still hadn't died down. "She had decades to do it, if she really wanted to. The timing seems awfully suspicious."

"It sure does. How did you find this?" Justine's tone sharpened. "They contact you?"

"No. Of course not." Cora waved her hand dismissively at Justine. "Berry found it. I think it just came out, like this hour. You know she's crazy for all things Walker, and her phone is practically glued to her hand. Read the rest."

"Even more exciting news will be announced on Friday." Lauren started up again. "At a press conference at Beth Walker's house, where Walker herself, in a rare appearance, will inform the general public of yet another newly discovered manuscript, which will give great insight into Walker's own same-sex relationship with a famous movie star."

Everyone, except Maggie, started talking at once.

"Who? Who?"

"Hot damn."

"I always knew she was queer."

"Exciting, uh?"

"You're right, Cora. All this is starting to make sense," Lauren said. "They come up here and cut us off before all this. There'll be Walker mania, and we won't be able to capitalize on it."

Cora nodded. "They're banking on the fact that we'll want in on all this good fortune, and so we'll jump at any crummy deal they push in front of us."

"Except you." Justine inclined her head toward Lauren. "You don't have any Walker cupcakes or anything like that. You're fine."

"So?"

"Just saying."

"What are you suggesting? I'm not in league with them or anything."

Maggie groaned. She couldn't help it. This kind of talk was getting them nowhere. Justine's lips were pushed out, and her brow was furrowed. She was mad. Maggie got that; she was mad too. She had just been served with a restraining order for Christ's sake. But arguing with each other was getting them nowhere. The only important person in this equation was Beth. Everyone seemed to have forgotten that. Beth was the one in the middle of this shit storm.

"Look," she said to Lauren and Cora, "the doggie pops are all done." Actually, she was two short, but she would apologize later. "I'm going to take my lunch break. I'll be back." She untied her apron and flung it onto the counter on her way out the front door.

A summer breeze ran through the mall, and she swiped her hand through her bangs to get them out of her eyes. Harlan would hopefully still be on the second floor, doing Truman and Steinbrecker's dirty work. Sure enough, she met him on the stairway.

"Hello, Maggie." His leer was all teeth and lips. "Ain't got nothing more for you, babe, unless you're angling for something a little less legal and a little more manly."

"Save it, Harlan. Can you tell me where this Nikka Vaskin is staying? She's here in town, right?"

"Actually, I don't know." He jumped down the last two steps and stood by Maggie, coming up only to her shoulder. "I deal with some assistant in the office, and when they come up on my phone, both numbers are blocked."

"Okay." She bit her lip. She already knew she wasn't dealing with amateurs. "Call the assistant, will you? Find out where Nikka Vaskin is staying."

"Why? She can't take the order back. You've got to go to court in ten days, and that's when they decide for real."

"I know." She didn't, but she didn't want to give Harlan even a little edge. Maggie impatiently fingered her palm as if it were a cell phone. "Just call her."

"Oh. I get it. You want to make trouble." He whipped out his cell phone. "I can totally get on board with that."

It occurred to Maggie right then and there that he liked drama even more than money. Probably why he was so very good at his job.

"Alison, it's Harlan Potter. I need to get some documents back to Vaskin, but stupid me, I didn't write down the name of the place she was staying. It's something with *river* in it somewhere... Right. That's it. Thanks." Hanging up, he blew on his fingers and swiped them twice on his shoulder. "I'm good."

"Where is she?"

"No. Admit it. You get it, right?"

"Of course, I do. Ninety percent of the places to stay here have the word *river* in their names. Okay, it's clever, I'll admit it. So which one is it?"

"The Riverside Inn."

"Figures. The nicest place in town. I guess they don't mind spending Beth's money since they're stealing it from us." Actually, it was good. Not too far out of town. She could ride her bike. Someday, not having a car was going to bite her in the butt, but not today. "Thanks, Harlan."

Back at the bakery's door, she dropped a hand on her mountain bike. Not one to let grass grow under her feet, she could pedal out right there and then. Then she remembered the look on Lauren's face when she had cut out two days ago. She pushed the bike back against the wall. If she wanted to keep this job and, more importantly, a good friendship, she would have to hold off until quitting time.

The Riverside Inn was beautiful at sunset. Everything was awash in an orange glow, and behind the hotel, the river with the sun falling into it looked almost as if it were lit from within. Maggie, however, only had eyes for the front door and hastily crammed her bike into the crowded hotel rack.

The lobby was empty on such a pretty night. Glasses clinked from the seasonal bar on the lawn, and music and happy chatter drifted in as well. Okay, step one. She was here. She took a deep breath and shook out her hands the way she always did before a tough climb up a mountain course. How could she get Nikka Vaskin's room number? Germaine couldn't be charmed to break the law. She didn't have any of Harlan's wily tricks up her sleeve. She could hang out here, lame as it was. Nikka would have to pass through at some point.

Or—a form caught her eye—maybe she could just turn right. There, at the far end of the lobby almost completely hidden by the stone fireplace, was Nikka, tapping away on a silver laptop.

Maggie would recognize that soft, shiny hair or the curve of her neck anywhere. Boy, was she sexy, especially now that she had changed out of her work clothes and into casual jeans and a T-shirt. Maggie purposefully bit the inside of her lip. She had to stop thinking about the enemy like this.

She marched across the room and plunked down in a chair right in front of Nikka. She tried for the element of surprise.

Nikka didn't flinch.

Damn—she liked that in her women.

Instead, Nikka slowly lifted her head and once again met Maggie's look head-on. A steely glint entered her eyes, and she raised an eyebrow as if to say, *Yes, can I help you?*

Maggie settled back into the chair and held up both hands, palms out. "Okay. So why don't you tell me what the fuck is really going on here?"

Chapter 6

April 1960

"CAN WE RUN THOSE ERRANDS another day? I'm too tired." Dawn had once again opened the front door even before Beth knocked. The light normally shining in her eyes had dimmed, and her face pinched in around the edges. "Let's just go straight to your parents' house for dinner. Okay?"

"We don't have to go at all. I can call them." Beth reached out to comfort Dawn but dropped her hand at the last minute. "Let's tell them you're too tired. I'll run into town to get something for dinner, and we can just stay here?" Hope swelled inside Beth's chest. If they were alone, maybe she could bring up the only subject she wanted to discuss tonight—the kiss.

"No. We should go." Dawn slid past her and headed to the truck. "I'm sure your mother has gone to a lot of trouble over tonight, and I don't want to disappoint your father and brother either."

Beth raced ahead to open the car door for her. "Okay. If you're sure." After helping her into the car, she let her hand linger under Dawn's forearm. The skin was so soft and warm, she couldn't pull away. But mostly she wanted to see if Dawn would respond.

She didn't.

As they bounced down the road in the black Chevy, Beth stole a glance at Dawn. She sat without speaking, one hand cradling her tiny baby bump. When had that happened? It hadn't been there yesterday. Beth would've noticed when they were...

The road ahead of her blurred. The thought of the kiss was driving her crazy. What did it mean, and would it happen again? Would she be able to handle it if it did? Or worse, if it didn't?

She blinked twice, and when the road didn't come into focus, she rubbed her eyes. She had gotten almost no sleep the night before as she'd tossed and turned on her little twin bed, trying to unpack what had happened out at Fern House. Finally, around sunrise, she had drifted off and dreamed that Dawn had laughed long and hard after the kiss. It had just been a mean joke on her part. Beth had woken with her fingers on her lips and a pain piercing her heart.

With Dawn just inches from her, she was no closer to an answer. Beth was pulled in by the comforting warmth that always seemed to surround Dawn. But her head rested against the passenger window, and her eyes were closed. She was giving nothing away.

After the silent ride, Beth pulled up to her parents' house right off the main street in the center of town and tried to take in the view the way Dawn might. A ranch-style house sat on a small lot. Flowers and ivy draped over planters under the front windows, and the line on the freshly mowed lawn was so straight, it was immediately clear what her father had spent the morning doing. Beth had always thought her house pleasant and tidy, but now she only saw small and provincial. All this was a big, giant arrow to the enormous gulf that existed between her and the woman next to her.

"Ready?" Beth asked softly as she cut the engine.

Dawn nodded, and then as if a switch had been flipped, her whole face lit up. The pinched look, the tired eyes, all instantly vanished. When she stepped out of the truck, she pushed her shoulders back, and every inch of her was the glamorous movie star from Hollywood. She met Beth's surprised gaze over the flatbed of the truck and shrugged. "Showtime."

"Mom? Pop?" Beth opened her front door. "We're here."

Her father and brother already stood waiting for them in the front room. Sammy danced on the balls of his feet, buttoned into a suit a little too small for him. When Dawn walked through the door, his eyes nearly popped out of his head.

Dawn threw him a dazzling smile in return, and then, when Sammy visibly melted under its heat, she shifted the smile to Carl, who came at her with his hand outstretched.

"Mrs. Montgomery. Please come in. We are thrilled to welcome you into our humble home."

Beth jerked her head toward her father. *Humble home?* Who was this man? He sounded like the preacher on that Sunday radio show that he and her mother loved.

Carl leaned in a little too close to Dawn.

Beth bit her lip so she wouldn't laugh. She had never seen her father even a little bit anxious before.

"Oh please, call me Dawn. But if you really want to be accurate, you'd have to call me Teresa. Teresa Rusco."

"Who's that?" Sammy bounced around her like a puppy.

"Me!" Dawn waited until Beth's mother had appeared at the kitchen door and everyone's attention was riveted on her. "Teresa Rusco is my real name."

"Teresa... Rusco..." Sammy rolled the syllables around on his tongue as if it were an alien language.

"You're Italian?" Carl's eyes widened just a little.

"Very distantly, on my father's side. But, yes, you hit the nail right on the head. The studio thought the name way too ethnic."

"So they just up and changed it to Dawn Montgomery?" Sammy, unable to keep still, tugged at his collar. "They can do that?"

Dawn laughed, and music seemed to fill the air. "Well, the Montgomery part is Jimmy's last name, but there were a bunch of meetings about the first name, for sure. None of which I actually went to, of course. But if I remember right, I think they were also considering Donna and Janet. Happily, neither of those tested well."

"The name suits you," Mary said, her hand up at her neck, fingering her cross. "Very glamorous."

Dawn met her straightforward gaze and tipped her head in a greeting. "Thank you. I like it too." She stepped toward her.

Carl and Sammy backed away as if the Red Sea were parting.

Dawn linked her arm through Mary's and turned them both into the kitchen.

Sammy and Carl banged shoulders as they came together in the living room and stopped, unsure of whether to follow or not.

Beth scooted by their bumblings, only to stop and lean against the doorframe of the kitchen to watch.

Dawn stood in the center of the room, her nose up in the air. "It smells wonderful in here."

Thanks to the transformation out in the front yard, she looked lovely, as usual. Soft, loose curls framed her face, and she wore a thin green turtleneck. The material pillowed delicately under her chin and picked up the color of her eyes. The conservative plaid skirt could've come from her mother's own closet, except she would've never worn it that short. A flutter went through Beth's stomach as she followed the long line of Dawn's shapely legs all the way down to her heels.

"What can I do to help?" Dawn placed her hands on her hips as if to say she wouldn't take no as an answer. The action looked like the most natural thing in the world, but it also pulled the turtleneck tighter over her skirt at the waist, revealing the slight swelling underneath.

Both Beth's and her mother's gazes drifted to Dawn's midriff.

"Nothing, of course. You're our guest. And..." Mary did a double take. "Oh my goodness! Are you...?"

"Yes," Dawn whispered and put her forefinger up to her mouth. "Don't tell anyone. The studio hasn't released the news to the press yet."

"I won't tell a soul." She sighed. "So is that why you need our Beth out there?"

"Of course. What else did you think?"

"I don't know." Beth's mother visibly relaxed, and for the first time since Dawn entered the house, her fingers dropped off the cross around her neck. "I don't know what I thought." She smiled first at their guest and then at Beth. "Sweetheart, do your job and get Dawn into the living room and into a comfy chair. Those heels can't be comfortable in your condition."

"Thank you, Mrs. Walker."

"Oh, none of that. You must call me Mary." Her mother led Dawn by her elbow to the door and then handed her off to Beth.

Dawn met Beth's gaze and, when no one else was looking, winked at her.

"Dinner will be right up." Mary's update drifted in from the kitchen.

And it was. As if by magic, the dining room table was suddenly laden with food. A golden-brown pot roast surrounded by root vegetables and roasted new potatoes, a green bean casserole, and an entire loaf of soft white bread sat piled onto the center of the table.

Carl pulled out the chair for Dawn and then looked longingly at the empty chair next to her.

"Pop, I always sit on this side." Sammy plopped down and scooted his chair a little closer to Dawn.

Carl blushed but took his usual seat at the head of the table.

Beth sat directly across from Dawn and watched her brother and father make fools of themselves as they competed for Dawn's attention all the way through dessert.

Dawn directed the conversation between them like a champion tennis match: bouncing between Sammy's football career, what colleges he hoped to play for, Carl's managerial job at the lumberyard, and his obsession with fishing.

Beth marveled at yet another one of her talents. Every question she asked made the current topic sound like the most interesting conversation on earth, and by the time Carl had sipped the last of his instant coffee, he had loosened his tie and was all smiles. Beth had never seen him so sociable and relaxed. At the end of the evening, he clasped both of Dawn's arms, the closest he would ever get to a hug with any of them.

"You don't have to rely just on Beth, you know. You've all the Walkers here at your disposal if you need us."

"Carl, I can't tell you how much that means to me." Dawn shot Mary a look over Carl's shoulder. She placed her hands together palm to palm and gave a little bow. "And Jimmy will also be thrilled to hear that. When he calls next, it'll be the first thing I tell him."

"Maybe when James…Jimmy…is in town, you can bring him for a visit. Another dinner, perhaps."

"Absolutely." She turned to Sammy. "Get ready, you. He would love to toss around the pig skin."

"Really? You're kidding." Sammy's eyes went wide with the possibility.

"Not even a little bit. He still says that if he weren't an actor, he would play for the National Football League."

"That's where I'm going to end up. That would be a blast!"

"If you'll excuse me, I've gotten used to going to bed early. Can I ask your daughter to take me home?"

"Are you sure you can't stay a little longer?" Carl asked. "Mary can easily make more coffee."

"Let her go, Carl. She needs her sleep." Mary nodded knowingly, and Dawn returned the nod.

"Okay." Carl's face fell. "If you must."

"Thank you so much for everything. Dinner was fantastic and the company, well, I felt so welcomed by you all. Really, tonight was such a treat." She reached out her hand toward Beth, who hesitated for a moment and then swung her own out to grab Dawn's. Her fingers felt cool and soft, and they squeezed Beth's before she pulled her out the door into the front yard.

Carl and Sammy, followed by Mary, all piled out after them and were still waving good-bye as Beth pulled out of the driveway.

As soon as they were out of sight, Dawn kicked off her heels and sighed deeply. "Your mother's right. I'm going to have to find new shoes and soon."

"Oh my God, Dawn. You were fantastic. You know, I didn't want to tell you this. But my father was on the verge of making me quit. Not letting me come out to your house anymore. And now I think he would drive me over himself before he would let that happen."

"Yes, that went very well, didn't it?" The tired look was back, but Dawn still glowed from the success of her performance.

"You knew?" And then, before Dawn could answer, she added, "Of course you knew. But why didn't you say anything?"

"Oh, I don't know. I love to act. And it's been a while since I've been able to do it. And if you really want to know the truth, I enjoyed having you watch me."

She was thinking of me tonight? Beth's heart soared, and she glanced at Dawn, who was looking down at her hands, clasped in a knot on her lap. She was so small and vulnerable against the big, black seat of the truck that Beth's heart went out to her. All she wanted to do was to wrap her arms around her and take care of her. Then her heart slammed back into her chest with a sudden thought. Was this even the real Dawn? Was she still acting? Was she always acting?

The silence grew heavy inside the truck. "You know, I never had a real family growing up." Dawn's voice was soft, and Beth could barely hear it over the rumble of the engine. "When I was eight, my father left my mother or she kicked him out. I never knew what story to believe. The details always changed with how low the whiskey was in the bottle. It doesn't matter, though. The overall facts were the same. All I can remember before he left was lots of shouting, doors slamming, and my mother crying. So much crying."

"Oh, Dawn—"

"No, don't. I didn't tell you to make you feel sorry for me. I just wanted you to know that, yeah, I was acting back there. I wanted your parents and brother to like me. But I also wanted to see what it was like to be part of a real family, maybe just for a night." She sighed deeply. "You see, I'm not sure what kind of family I'm bringing this baby into, and God, you have to know, it's killing me."

"You and Jimmy will make great parents." As soon as she said it, though, Beth wasn't so sure. Jimmy seemed completely wrapped up with himself and filming his movie in Italy. She had been at the house during one phone conversation that week, and from only the side of it she could hear, he hadn't asked once how Dawn was feeling.

"Oh yeah, Jimmy will hit all his marks with the press and the photo ops. He'll take the baby to the park and to Disneyland, and for the public, you're right, he'll be an amazing father. But what I'm worried about is can you bring a child up in a house without love? It didn't work so well for me."

Beth's hands nearly slipped off the steering wheel, and she had to fight the truck for a minute before regaining control. "You don't..." When she finally spoke, her voice cracked. "You don't love Jimmy?"

Dawn turned in her seat. Her back now to the door, she was facing Beth. "No. I don't. I wasn't exactly honest with you on our first walk in the forest. Ours is a marriage of convenience. For both of us. Believe me, he doesn't love me either. That's really why I came up here."

She didn't love her husband! Something in Beth broke. Heat flooded her body and excitement, fear, hope—everything that had been building in her the last twenty-four hours—whooshed through her all at once. Possibilities opened up in front of her as if the dark road ahead of her was suddenly flooded with light. If Dawn didn't love her husband, maybe...just maybe... "Dawn, about yesterday—"

"Let's not talk about that either."

The truck swerved as the wheel jumped in Beth's hand. Tears sprang to her eyes. Dawn didn't want to talk about it, because she didn't like her in that way.

"No. That's not what I mean," Dawn said as if she had heard Beth's thoughts. "It's not like that. I've always liked both men and women."

Beth swallowed hard, pulled the truck off onto the side of the road, and turned her back to the driver's door. They were facing each other, fewer than two feet apart, but it was so dark outside of town, she could barely see Dawn. Her heart started pounding. This wasn't the way she had planned to bring up this subject, but here they were.

"What's it like, then?"

Dawn reached out and tugged Beth's hand off the seat. She intertwined their fingers one by one and then held on tight. "I don't know. But don't you see? The second we talk about it, we define whatever this is." She squeezed her hand. "And then, sadly, it defines us. Let's just see what happens. It's so much easier that way."

Beth wasn't at all sure what Dawn's little speech meant. But it did seem to suggest the kiss wasn't a mistake, which had been at the heart of all her fears. She wasn't going to push it. "Okay..." Her voice was tentative.

"Good," Dawn said softly as if everything were settled. She placed Beth's hand lightly on her belly.

Even with the wool of the skirt between them, the gesture was so intimate that Beth froze before she let her hand relax. Once she did, the soft swelling under the skirt melded to her palm, and Beth drank in the sudden tenderness that seemed to fill the cab of the truck and bind them together.

"I can't believe there's a baby in there," Beth said finally.

"Most of the time, neither can I."

They both looked down at her stomach until Dawn dropped her hand over Beth's.

"I don't know if I can do this by myself." Her voice cracked.

Beth scooted across the seat and, without thinking, gathered Dawn in her arms. "You don't have to. I'm here. I'll always be here for you."

Dawn let her head rest on Beth's shoulder until her breathing steadied. Finally, she leaned her whole weight against Beth, seemingly drawing strength from their embrace.

Beth breathed out a soft, contented sigh as she wrapped her arms tighter.

Was this really happening? Would she suddenly wake up back in her bed at home, with this wonderful dream fading away?

As if she had uttered it out loud, Dawn lifted her head and faced her. Their heads were so close, only a thin line of darkness separated them, and then without words, her lips found Dawn's, crushing into them with passion and desire.

And even though she hadn't stepped a foot outside of Steelhead, she had run away with the circus. And Dawn, for better or probably worse, was dealing her cards.

April bounded into May, and wildflowers popped up everywhere as spring beat back the dense fog of winter. Fern House took on a golden glow as it warmed with the sunlight of the season and the homey touches that they had applied here and there. Once Beth had discovered that Dawn loved tulips, she had filled the rooms with bouquets in all different colors. In a surprising display of domesticity, Dawn had sent Beth into town for yarn and crochet needles, and now the daybed in the writing room sported a handmade bedspread. Beth suggested that she hook a baby blanket, but Dawn adamantly refused, saying that it was bad luck before the baby was born and with her history, she'd be plain stupid to look for trouble.

Their afternoons were pretty much written in stone. After lunch, they took their customary walk in the woods so Dawn could say hello to her favorite tree—a young redwood at the edge of a grove with a knot at its very center. Nothing special about it, except that it was still small enough that Dawn could almost encircle it with her arms. Every day, she would bury her face in its trunk and whisper secrets into the dark red bark.

"What're you telling it?" Beth had finally asked on one walk. She was so used to being the sole focus of Dawn's days that she actually was jealous of the tree.

"Nothing."

"You know, I'm standing right here. I can see your lips moving. Are you making wishes?"

"No, seriously, it's nothing. No words, just moving my lips. I just wanted to see how long it would take you to ask."

"Really?"

"Yep." Dawn laughed and then bit her bottom lip near the edge of her mouth.

Beth had seen the gesture in her movies plenty of times when she was being coy with her love interests. But here in the wild, it seemed so natural and playful, Beth immediately felt a whoosh of desire travel down her body.

"So. How long did it take me?" The deepness of her voice surprised her.

"Twenty-two walks."

"And that means what?" She took a step toward Dawn, unable to keep away.

"Only good things." Dawn patted the tree as if it were listening. "That you respect me enough to give me privacy, but you like me enough to want to be part of my world."

Like. That wouldn't be the word she would use, but as usual Dawn had hit the nail of analysis right on its head.

"Oh, so you're playing games with me?" Beth took a little hop in her direction.

"Always." Dawn stepped up to meet her in the middle of the path. She grabbed Beth's face with both hands and drew her close until her lips were within an inch of Beth's.

She was so close. Her breath curled over Beth's lips; her ocean-breeze scent encircled her. Her eyes were dark and smoldering.

"And the sooner you realize it, the better." Her lips brushed against Beth's as she spoke.

Beth shivered and longed to take her into her arms and press their mouths and bodies fully together. But Dawn, as usual, was making up the rules to this game, and all Beth could do was stand there, her heart pounding in her chest, waiting for the next move.

"I love all this. Tell me you're having as much fun as I am."

Beth nodded.

"Tell me," Dawn said again.

"Please..." was all Beth could say.

Dawn slowly slid her hands up Beth's arms until they gripped her shoulders. She tugged her toward her, and their lips met.

Now that Dawn had made the first move, Beth leaned into the kiss, completely surrendering to her own passion. Wrapping her arms around Dawn's waist, she explored the softness of her mouth with a boldness that would've been unthinkable a few weeks ago. A swipe of her tongue over Dawn's lips and they parted. Beth slid her tongue inside. She tasted sweet and of something much headier—adventure, excitement, and a future that, up until this point, Beth thought could never exist.

Beth kissed her hungrily, and her hips slightly rocked into the body so pliant in her arms. The small bump where the baby grew was hard, but everything else was flowing and supple. Her chest brushed against Dawn's, softness against softness. In response, her breasts tightened under her shirt as her nipples constricted with desire. She could stay like this forever, body to body with her. She moaned; she couldn't help herself.

Her heart raced. What was Dawn feeling? This was so much more than the chaste kisses and comfortable hugs they had shared since the talk in the truck. Those had been great, but now the game, or whatever it was, had turned serious... for her at least. The passion felt so right on her end, but no matter how Dawn said she felt about James, she had married him and he was a man. Maybe all this was Dawn finding a way not to have to go through the pregnancy alone.

Dawn answered, sliding her hands down Beth's back to gently cup her behind. She squeezed ever so slightly, and the action pulled Beth's hips and groin up into the warmth between her legs.

The shift of their bodies sent a sharp current streaming through Beth. She trembled almost uncontrollably as all sensation flooded down below her belly. Her lips dropped off Dawn's as she struggled to come to grips with how everything down there was suddenly swelling and pushing outward. Her breathing came ragged and fast.

"Oh, God," she said, her head buried in Dawn's neck.

Dawn held her tight and whispered in her ear, "I take that as a yes. You're having as much fun as I am."

"Yes."

A rustle up the path made Beth jump. She pulled out of Dawn's arms in a flash, afraid that they might have been discovered but also driven back by the intensity of her own emotions.

"It's just a ground squirrel, silly. Look." Dawn pointed to the brownish-gray creature darting across the needles.

Still lost in the crazy cascade of emotions, Beth only saw a streaking blur. When she reached out to Dawn, she was gone, already up the path, waving her arm at four smaller squirrels on their hind legs.

"Oh, babies! Have you ever seen anything so cute?" Dawn dropped her hand to her round stomach.

Beth swallowed, forcing all her feelings back into the tight compartment from where they had come. "No," she answered, and the moment passed.

Back at the house, they climbed the stairs to the writing room. Normally, Dawn would've continued down the hall to the master bedroom to take her nap there, but one day about a week ago she followed Beth into the writing room and lay down on the daybed instead. Since then, she had moved books and magazines to the side table in that room, and as Beth settled in her chair at the desk, she propped the pillows against the side railings and drew the crocheted blanket up over her bare legs.

"What scene are you working on today?" She pulled a magazine off the table.

Beth said nothing as she fretted about how to start talking about what they were doing. What was it? Had Dawn done this before? She knew that the world would judge them, and not kindly, but she wanted so much more.

"Dawn...?" She bit her lip. How did she start?

"Oh my goodness." Dawn cried out. "She got the cover of *Time*?" She swiveled the magazine around to show Beth a woman as cute as a button. She had short red hair with blue eyes and wore an expression that announced, "Yes, I really am that good."

Dawn hit the magazine against her leg and then tossed it to the edge of the bed. "Her first picture, her very first picture, was with Hitchcock. Boy, and now, what are they calling her?" She retrieved the magazine. "*The New Girls of Hollywood—Talent in Blue Jeans.* I would've given my right arm to get a picture with Hitch five years ago, and she just walks into it."

"What movie? I don't think I saw it."

"You didn't miss much. It was some sort of comedy with a dead man, but she was good in her role. Spunky, I think they called her. Now she is on the cover of *Time*." Dawn studied the cover before tossing it away again.

Was that envy at the edges of her eyes? Beth was getting almost as good as Dawn at reading her facial expressions. And why not; she spent almost every moment looking at her when they were together.

"Do you wish you were back in Hollywood, making movies?"

"Yes. No. I don't know." She looked at Beth and smiled, but it didn't extend to her eyes. Her hand drifted to her stomach. "I think I'm ready for my next role. But I never had the cover of *Time* magazine. That would've been nice."

"It's not over."

"No, I think maybe it is. I think...I hope I'll settle into being a mother. Let's not talk about me. What did you decide about Daisy? Is she going to confront her father or not?"

"Oh, she has to. Don't you think?" Beth flipped open one of the notebooks to a blank page.

"Yes, I do. So start writing. I'm going to stew for a minute and then take a nap. When I wake up, will you read it to me?"

Beth nodded and gave her a hard look.

"I'm fine. Really. I am." And then, "Are you?"

"Yeah." Beth dropped her pencil onto the blank page. It was far easier than opening the other can of worms.

"Good. Write."

For some reason, the words came fast and furious. The story so far was about two young women who worked as secretaries at a lumberyard much like the one here in Steelhead. Daisy was from money and had taken the job to annoy her parents; Bonnie was supporting a sick aunt who had raised her. When a horrible mistake was made at the lumberyard, the management blamed it on Daisy—Dawn had come up with that idea and Beth loved it. The men at the lumberyard expected the poor little rich girl to roll over and run home to Mommy and Daddy. But she surprised them all and fought the male establishment and the injustice. Bonnie was drawn into the fight. She had the most to lose. She was actually the one who needed her job, but she couldn't stay away. Together they took on the lumberyard, the misogyny that pervaded their world, and each other.

The scene where Daisy went home to confront her father, probably the worst offender in the story, came naturally, and before she knew it, Beth was done. She swiveled in her chair to look at Dawn, who had fallen asleep half on and half off the pillow. Her neck was bent at an uncomfortable angle. Beth jumped up and gently stretched her out on the bed.

She sighed with contentment in her sleep as Beth pulled her neck straight.

She was so lovely that Beth just stared. After a while, her gaze drifted off Dawn's face and down to her chest. Dawn was breathing long and deep, and her breasts rose and sank with sleep's rhythm.

That familiar heat spread out below Beth's belly, and she had to close her fist to prevent her hand from dropping to places where she had not been invited.

Despite what Dawn said and what Beth told herself, she knew that Dawn would return to Hollywood after the baby was born, and this, whatever it was, would be over. If she were lucky, though, she had three months left, and she didn't plan to waste them. She just didn't know how to move forward.

Chapter 7

"EXCUSE ME?" HAD THE CRAZY bike lady really just asked her what the fuck was going on? Nikka wasn't a prude by anyone's standards, but she did try to refrain from starting conversations with strangers with four-letter words.

She stared into the brown eyes peeping out from under shaggy hair. Their color was rich and deep. Nikka hadn't noticed that outside the bakery. Then and now, they didn't look wild or irrational, which would have been understandable since Harlan had just served her with a restraining order. In fact, a surprising amount of intelligence shone in the tawny irises.

Maggie raised an eyebrow. "I know you heard me. What's your end game with all these legal actions? The rest of the town may roll over, but I've got nothing to lose. Well, no money anyway."

Nikka let her gaze drop to take in the whole woman, who had plopped into the chair with one foot up on the seat as if she was already thinking about a quick getaway. Her body was lean and athletic, not particularly muscular, but coiled with an almost palpable energy. Nikka scooted back in her own seat. This woman might literally spring forward at any point.

"It's a simple question. Maybe not a simple answer, though, right?" Maggie cocked her head, and her bangs fell in her eyes. She reached up to brush them back into place. The action seemed so completely unconscious, it was almost endearing.

"I'm afraid, as I said, that I can't talk about the case with you, Ms. Chalon."

"Oh, call me Maggie. You've slapped a bogus restraining order on me. Usually, women who screw me call me by my first name."

Endearing evaporated. This woman was looking to take her on—something she had no interest in and, more importantly, no time for. She had just come down to the lobby to get a better Internet connection. She slapped the laptop closed and rose from the chair. "If you'll excuse me, I'll—"

"No, it's okay. I get it. This isn't your show." Maggie got up to follow. "You're just up here as the hired help. To run interference, so when Lea Truman, who was my boss once too, you know, comes up to do a press release about Beth's new story, the path will be clear...of people like me, I guess?"

Nikka stopped dead and spun back around. "Excuse me? What new story?"

"Holy shit." Maggie rocked back on her heels. "You didn't know about the story? Interesting. They just announced that your law firm found a new story and some other revolutionary manuscript about Beth's love life that will make all of you very rich."

Nikka clenched her teeth while she rolled this new development around in her head. Why would Lea keep that from her? Maybe this woman was asking the right question to the wrong person. If Nikka was a pawn in Lea's games here, she needed to know.

"You can protect yourself and Lea and whoever else stands to make a buck out of this new story, but that's not why I'm out here. What I want to know is who's protecting Beth? Is this what she wants? Her life splashed all over the Internet for the world to see."

Don't engage. Just walk away. She's a lunatic, right?

"All this is very good for Ms. Walker." Nikka sounded surer than she felt.

"Monetarily maybe. But I'm beginning to question that too. Come on, you've seen her. I know you have. Vivienne let it slip when I was in Beth's room a couple of days ago. Does the woman lying on that bed, almost dead to the world, look like she's excited about a new release or anything else?"

Help me. Nikka heard it again, loud and clear. Over the past few days, the call for assistance or whatever it had been had faded to almost nothing in her mind. Damn this woman for stirring it all up.

"I think you saw something. You just don't want to admit it. Can you really live with yourself if you do nothing?"

"Look, Ms. Chalon. I've got a lot of work to do. If you will excuse me." She pulled the laptop close to her hip and strode to the stairs. Maggie's look seemed to bore a hole in the back of her head until Nikka rounded the bend in the stairs. Her fingers were itching to get back into her room and grab her iPad. A mind map with its key question and the radiating thoughts was already materializing in her head. Perhaps with enough circles, lines, and colors she could start to figure out Lea's end game and, more importantly, where she fit into it.

Instead, her phone buzzed just as she hit the top step. Lea Truman's name flashed across the screen. She was calling from her personal number.

"Hello, Lea." She tried to keep all emotion out of her voice.

"Alison just told me that she forgot to inform you of the press release. Sorry, it was all very hush, hush, but Kerry and Collier just announced a newly discovered Walker story and—"

"I heard." Nikka arrived at her door and entered the dark room.

"Oh, good work. I should've known you'd be on top of it. The problem is that we are planning an announcement at Walker's house in two days, and Vivienne's feeling a little like it's an invasion coming down on her. She's the physician's assistant who's taking care of Walker. You met her earlier, if you remember."

"I do."

"I'm sorry to ask you this. She's not really adept with people, and I know it's not part of your job description. But I wouldn't forget this favor if you could drive out there and interface with the people we've hired to take care of the arrangements."

"When? Tonight?" Her lower back ached from all that walking around town in high heels, and there was a blister forming on her little toe.

"Yeah, this is all coming together at the last moment. I'll be up there tomorrow to take over, but we figured to send the planning people to Fern House at night, when Beth's sleeping. I know it's a lot to ask." Her voice dropped in register.

Normally, Nikka would've enjoyed the little flirtatious show that Lea was putting on. Not that she would ever sleep with her boss, but now she didn't know what to think. How much was Lea playing her? The timing of the call, the quick apology, the new *favor*. It all seemed awfully convenient.

"No. No problem. I'll be happy to go out there," she said lightly as if she had come up with the suggestion herself. "What exactly is it you want me to do?"

"Mason, the guy from our PR firm, wants to go over logistics. Not Vivienne's strong suit. Don't worry. I've pre-approved his plan, and his firm is very good. But look at the space, listen to what he says, and fix any possible glitches. It's very important that this event goes off without a hitch."

"Right." This was totally in her wheelhouse. She'd been organizing parties since she'd gotten her first set of Barbies.

"Thanks, Nikka. It's really nice to know I have someone up there I can count on until I get there tomorrow."

"You absolutely do." Nikka played her right back.

"Excellent. Text me when you're done. You're my right-hand woman." Lea hung up.

They were just words to end the conversation on a positive note and to give her an incentive to do what Lea wanted. She knew that. But she also knew that words had power. If you said them often enough, you began to believe them.

She took her work clothes back out of the closet. Her toes cried out when she slipped off her sneakers and shoved her feet back into her heels, but she was Lea's right-hand woman. See? Just a few minutes later, and it almost sounded true.

At the bend in the stairs, she craned her head around the stairwell. Was Maggie still by the fireplace? Thankfully, the lobby was empty except for Germaine and a young woman at the checkout desk.

Nikka took in the pair as she made her way to the parking lot. The girl stood with an I've-got-nothing-to-prove attitude and pushed a black credit card over to Germaine. Obviously checking in.

There was something about her that made Nikka stop and take notice. A stunning cherry blossom tree tattoo climbed up one bare shoulder, her curly, blonde hair entwining with the twigs and branches. Nikka found herself staring; it was so delicate and finely wrought, she wouldn't have been surprised if a live blossom fell from her shoulder to the ground.

The girl turned to her.

Nikka met luminous green eyes and a sure stare. No smile from Germaine either; she barely even looked up. In fact, Nikka felt the chill from several feet away. Germaine must have gotten the scoop about what had gone down today in town.

No matter. She was here only to impress her boss, not win a popularity contest.

Driving out to Walker's she wondered why she hadn't told Lea about Maggie. The easy answer was she didn't want to look as if she couldn't handle a little opposition, especially coming on the heels of the phone number fiasco. Maggie obviously wasn't going to let this Walker situation lie. If the confrontation laced with swear words in the lobby earlier was any indication, Maggie Chalon could be unpredictable.

And yet...there was something about her. Sure, she was clearly pissed about the restraining order, but her coming out to the hotel seemed more about Walker and less about her. The concern had read sincere. Why would she take a risk for a woman she no longer worked for? And then there was the moment outside the bakery. When Maggie had touched her, she had felt...

She squirmed in her seat. This train of thought was getting her nowhere. She would mention the Maggie issue to Lea when she came up tomorrow.

That's settled. Now, I don't have to think about her anymore.

When she pulled into Walker's driveway, she was surprised by a big burly guy in a security uniform standing by the gate key post.

"Name, please." He stepped up to her car's window, holding an iPad.

"Nikka Vaskin."

"ID?"

Nikka flashed her license, and he scrolled through his device. "All right, Ms. Vaskin, you're on the list. You're good to go."

The gate swung open, and she eased the Outback down the long driveway. Wow. Security and lists. Lea was taking no chances here.

Vivienne answered the door with her usual sour face. "She sent you?"

"She did." When Vivienne didn't move to let her in, she added, "I'm her right-hand woman." It tripped off her tongue easily out loud too. She might even begin to believe that statement herself.

"Fine, come in. Make yourself useful." Vivienne led the way into the dining room where a middle-aged, sandy-haired man stood. He rushed over to her and shook her hand.

"Hi, I'm Todd Mason of Mason Public Relations."

The handshake was firm and professional. "Nikka Vaskin. Lea Truman asked me to sign off on the event."

"Excellent." He threw Vivienne a withering glance. "Finally, someone who can make a decision. Come with me." He led the way into the living room and waved his hand across the room, gorgeous even at night with the big floor-to-ceiling windows framing the dark trees of the forest.

"Imagine the press here and Ms. Truman there, standing behind a podium." He pointed to a spot right in front of the picture window. "She'll look like she could take on the whole world with that view behind her—"

A loud thumping as if a chair was being dragged around a room came from the ceiling.

Everyone jumped.

Vivienne pursed her lips, mumbled, "Excuse me," and rushed from the room.

"That's better." Todd watched her leave. "She was killing my mojo. Let's get down to business."

He spoke, almost without taking a breath, about the technical and logistical requirements of the event. Forty-eight minutes later—Nikka timed it with surreptitious glances to her cell phone—he whipped out a numbered list. Finally, he was speaking her language. He should've led with that.

"So let me get this straight." She plucked the list from him. "You've targeted businesses in town to cater this event. You do know that Truman and Steinbrecker has recently had legal actions with several of them, right? They might not be in the mood to pony up."

"Everyone's in the mood to make money." He tapped a pencil against his clipboard. "Besides, you're the only game in town, and people always want to play in the big leagues."

He was right. She was one of those people too. She studied the list and made suggestions about other items.

Todd nodded, scribbled notes onto his clipboard and said, "Yes, that's better" or "That'll work too" under his breath.

Nikka's suggestions were good, but minor. They wouldn't really affect the outcome of the press conference. Perhaps the real reason Lea had sent her out here was to give this guy face time. Make him feel important so he would turn all his attention to the event. Not to mention that the trip had put Nikka in charge, even if it was temporarily. She'd had a taste of being the boss, and she wanted more. Lea probably had plays on both fronts. Impressive.

"Okay, then," she said when they had reached the last item, "let's make tomorrow an event no one will ever forget."

"Thank you for the opportunity to put on this event. I sincerely hope this is the beginning of a wonderful relationship between our two firms." His lips closed with a pop, as if their interaction had a word limit and he had just reached it.

He snapped his folder shut and handed her his card. "In case you have any questions. Call me anytime. Is there anything else you need?"

"No. I think we're good."

"Very nice to meet you." He shook her hand again and made his way back to the front door.

"See you Friday." Nikka stood in the empty foyer, unsure of her next move. She looked up to the skylight. The stars had just come out, and their silver light flooded into the small room. There were charming details everywhere in this house; the walls probably had a thousand stories to tell.

She should inform Vivienne that she was leaving. What a change forty-eight hours made. Two days ago, she had crept up the stairs as a trespasser, and now she was Lea's stand-in.

The hallway was dark with only a soft light seeping out from under the door at the end of the hallway. Walker's room.

She tapped softly. "Vivienne?"

"Don't move. Be quiet. I'll be right back." Vivienne's tone was harsh behind the closed door.

Nikka's stomach constricted at the icy coldness.

The door opened just a sliver, throwing a yellow ribbon of light into the hallway. Vivienne squeezed through the opening to face Nikka. "Yes?" Her face had a sour expression, as if she had eaten a lemon and couldn't wash away the taste.

"I just wanted to tell you that—"

Nikka did a slight double take. Vivienne's lips twisted downward, and a vein throbbed in her neck. She had read her wrong; her expression wasn't sour. It was mean. Vivienne was nasty, and Nikka knew with a certainty that was like a hit to her gut that she was unkind to Beth Walker too.

"Yes?"

"That we're done downstairs. When Lea gets here tomorrow, she'll take over."

"Good." Vivienne slipped back into the room without another word.

Nikka stood in the darkened hallway for a moment, trying to slide this new realization into the pages of how things worked in this house. It didn't fit.

"I've told you a million times, you old bat, get away from the window." Vivienne's voice was muffled through the door, but the tone was not.

This she couldn't walk away from. She tapped softly on the door.

Scuffling came from inside and then complete silence. The door didn't open.

She knocked again, this time a little louder. "Vivienne? Is everything all right in there?"

Still nothing.

She tried the door handle.

It was locked.

Shit. This didn't feel right. Beth may be falling into dementia, that much could be true, but no one should be treated like this, especially someone as defenseless as Walker was. *Shit, shit, shit!* This turn of events did not fit into her plans.

Nikka tried the door one last time and then turned down the hallway. Her heels clicking against the wooden floor told anyone who was listening—and she would've bet her bottom dollar that Vivienne was—that she was leaving. Once outside, she pulled out her phone and Lea's number.

All's good with the event. She quickly tapped out the text message. *Vivienne seems out of sorts. Not handling Walker well. Advice?*

Okay, due diligence done. It was Lea's problem now.

At her car with her hand on the door, however, she turned to take in the house. Walker's bedroom would be in the back.

No. She forced her hand around the car's door handle. This wasn't the kind of opportunity her father was always going on about embracing. She should get into the car and drive away as fast as her Outback would take her.

Sorry, Papa. With a deep, deep sigh she scooted past her car and headed around the garage and into the backyard. Nikka expected the manicured green lawns of the suburbs where she had grown up, not the mess behind the house— thorny bushes, brambles, the forest running all the way up to the house. She fought her way through the brush, tearing her blouse on a sharp branch, until she reached what she thought was Walker's window.

It was closed. Of course. What had she expected? Bed sheets knotted into an escape rope? Beth Walker hanging from the windowsill by her fingertips? Still, there had to be a reason why Vivienne had told her to get away from the window *a million times.*

Her heels sinking into the soft ground, Nikka stood there, tossing around ideas and coming up with nothing. Until she looked right in front of her—little roundish things littered the ground under the window. What were they?

Some were yellow and oblong, others round and blue, but all of them looked like pills or some sort of medicine broken into pieces. She plucked a red oval one off a nearby leaf. It was too dark to make out the name stamped into its surface, but it was a medical-grade pharmaceutical, for sure. She grabbed a few more, just for good measure.

Nikka sucked her heels out of the dirt and fought her way through the bushes to the driveway on her tiptoes. Holding the half pill under the car's interior light, she could just make out a P-e-r on its smooth surface. Percocet? Percodan? Someone—probably Walker—was throwing bits and pieces of pain pills out the window. But why? They had to be prescribed. Hadn't Lea mentioned there was some sort of accident in Walker's past? Why wouldn't she take them if she needed them? Unless…

Three voices rose up in her mind.

"Help me." Walker's voice was full of emotion.

"You're making her upset. You need to go." Vivienne's was all about control and malice.

And then the voice of reason. "Can you really live with yourself if you do nothing?"

Nikka closed her eyes and clutched at the pill in her hand. *Dammit, that nutty woman was right. I'm going to have to do something.*

She looked at her phone. No return text or call. She rubbed her forehead, wondering what to do with this new information.

She opened her briefcase to find paper and pen for a new to-do list. Instead her thoughts ran to warm brown eyes, that touch on her arm outside the bakery, and an energy that suddenly seemed more exciting than crazy. Her stomach rose and fell, leaving a slight fluttering racing through her.

It did seem like the time to ask what the fuck was going on.

But she was thinking about a woman with shaggy bangs, not Walker...

"Yodel-ay-hee-hoo. Yodel-ay-hee-hoo."

Groaning, Maggie rolled across the bed and away from the woman's sing-songy voice belting out of her iPhone.

"Yodel-ay-hee-hoo." It had seemed funny and sweet when George had bought the ring tone for her birthday right after she had free climbed The Nose at El Capitan. Now...not so much. Way too loud for this early in the morning. Maggie opened one eye. Who was calling at the break of dawn? She dragged the phone off the bedside table. "Yodel-ay hee—"

"George, what could possibly—?"

"What the hell, Maggie. You know what just came into the office?"

"No. But I think you're going to tell me."

"Your name on a restraining order. Actually, it was reported yesterday. But Frank did me a solid and brought me into the loop. You know how serious this is?"

"Yes, I do." She sat up in bed and gave him her full attention. "It means I'm on to something. There's no other reason they'd make me stay away."

George groaned.

"Have you found anything?"

"Maggie, don't you get it? You need to give up this ridiculous conspiracy theory about Beth Walker. This is serious. This kind of stuff is not going to help you at the hearing to see if the restraining order will stand. And at that point I can't do anything to help you."

"It won't matter if you've done your job. Tell me you found something."

"No. Not one thing. Everything with the law firm is beyond reproach, and that Vivienne woman, bitch though she may be, is up to date on her licenses for custodial care."

"I'm telling you things aren't on the up and up out there."

"I couldn't find any evidence to that end."

"Keep looking, please, George. Talk to Beth, for one." When she didn't get an answer, she added, "Just give the investigation some more time, at least until your shift starts."

"What are you talking about? I'm already on the clock. It's after nine."

She swung the phone out. He wasn't lying. 9:23. Nope, now it was 9:24.

"Holy shit. I gotta go. Keep digging." She yelled the last part into the phone before hanging up. No time for a shower. Instead, she slipped a brush through her hair and swished once with some old mouthwash on the counter. Darting through the studio apartment, she grabbed a sweatshirt and her bike helmet and rushed out the door.

"Maggie's here!" Skylar chirped the moment Maggie wheeled her bike through the front door.

Maggie had visions of running her over with the front wheel of the bike.

"So you give me two good days, and then you're back to your same old—" Lauren called out before she rounded the corner from the back office. "Oh my God. Are you still in your pajamas?"

"I overslept."

"Well, we don't have time to talk about this. Right now, you need to get your butt in the kitchen. We just got an order for two hundred cupcakes, twenty each of these flavors." She handed Maggie a faxed order form. "And we need to deliver by tomorrow."

"Okay, I'll stay as long as it takes tonight." She wheeled her bike into the kitchen and leaned it up against the back wall.

"I guess that's something." Lauren followed her into the space and ran a critical gaze down to the blue polka dots on her legs. "Jesus, Maggie."

Maggie worked like a dog for the rest of the morning, even though the storefront was a madhouse and she had to listen to Skylar, the tattletale, call out her cheery greeting every few minutes. At one point, she poked her head out of the kitchen.

A line snaked all the way out the door.

"What's going on? Why's it so crowded?"

"It's happening all over town from what I hear." Lauren got up from her office to join her. "I think people are descending because of the press conference tomorrow. Crazy, huh? In twenty-four hours this place has practically become Beth-a-palooza."

They both looked at the long line.

"Whoever is putting this press conference together is pretty damn sharp." Lauren nodded.

"Lea Truman," Maggie said under her breath.

"They're sure playing up the lesbian Hollywood angle. What big-time star did Beth Walker sleep with? People are coming out of the woodwork to find out. You know how everyone wants to be a part of everything these days."

"You're not kidding. Look." Maggie pointed to a young woman at the counter with a cherry blossom tattoo on her shoulder.

"Hey, do you know where Beth Walker happens to live?" Tattoo woman grabbed her red velvet cupcake off the counter.

"Out on Fern Drive. Behind a big black gate." Skylar nodded repeatedly. "You can't miss it."

"I better put a stop to this." Lauren jumped in behind the counter.

Maggie stepped back into the kitchen and returned to the gargantuan task at hand. Two hundred cupcakes was doable. It was the ten flavors that gave her pause. She picked up the first lemon in a long, orderly line on her workstation. Her life was almost always in a state of chaos, but her stations were consistently neat and tidy, every ingredient and tool in its place. She ran the zester over the fruit, and its peel came away in long, yellow strips. The kitchen smelled like a citrus grove, and she took the fresh smell deep into her lungs. She smiled. Like her brother, she could always count on a Lemon Lover to lift her spirits, no matter what stage it was in.

"Psst."

Maggie looked around.

"Over here by the door."

Nikka Vaskin's head jutted in through the half-opened back door. "Sorry, to bother you. I know you're working."

How could anyone's hair be so shiny?

"Do you have a second?"

"Yeah, yeah." Maggie waved a hand. "Come in."

"Thanks." She scooted in through the opening, but once inside, she bit her lip and furrowed her brow.

Maggie somehow knew she was wrestling with coming at all. Normally, she liked to move forward as quickly as possible—a rolling stone, no moss and all that—but now she welcomed the pause. She was enjoying the view. Another silk blouse. This one a deep maroon, which brought out both the gray and blue of her eyes. Her black skirt, thankfully tighter than the one the day before, hugged her hips. Yesterday, Maggie would've sworn that Nikka was slim to the point of being boyish, but today, the skirt exposed the truth. She had curves in all the right places.

"It smells really good in here." Nikka broke the silence.

"Essential oils." Maggie held up the lemon still in her hand.

Nikka bit her lip again, but before the silence took over, Maggie added, "Interesting fact. There's ten times more vitamin C in the peel than there is in the juice, and you know, the peel is full of D-Limonene, which is thought to fight cancer and—"

"Can we talk?" Nikka looked around her.

"Yeah, sure."

"Maybe somewhere a little more private."

"Okay, where do you want to go?" Maggie placed the lemon carefully back into line and moved toward the back door.

"Ah, somewhere here? It might be better."

Of course. The lawyer couldn't afford to be seen with the crazy woman.

Maggie glanced around. She edged to the big metal door of the walk-in cooler and swung it open. "I guess we can talk in here."

"You're not going to lock me in there, are you?" Nikka smiled thinly, but a note of concern had entered her voice.

"You came to me, remember? The lock doesn't even engage." When Nikka didn't move, she jiggled the handle on the other side of the door. "This isn't the movies."

"Okay." Nikka made her way over with small, cautious steps.

The cooler was jammed full of the fresh ingredients for the cupcakes and looked like a study in modern art. Red strawberries, yellow lemons, and orange carrots washed the shelves in color, but the room was cold, and as soon as they entered, Nikka wrapped her arms around herself.

"You better talk quick." Maggie laughed and instantly wished she had chosen somewhere warmer so this encounter might last longer.

"You might be right." Nikka jumped right in. "I was out at Walker's last night, and something's going on. I found this outside her window in the bushes." She opened her palm and revealed something small and white. "It looked like someone was throwing them out the window."

Maggie took a closer look. One of the pills from the bedside table! Maggie did something between a hop and a dance, and she had to bite back a whoop and a "I knew it!" One look at Nikka shivering in the cold made her clamp her mouth shut. Her head was slightly downcast, and she wasn't meeting Maggie's gaze. Clearly, it had taken a lot for her to come here, and if Maggie was reading her right, even now, she wasn't too sure that it was the right decision.

"Just that one?" She marveled that her voice sounded as calm as she had hoped it would.

"No, a whole mess of them."

"She clearly didn't want to take them if she was throwing them out the window. Do you think she was being forced to and she needed to hide that she's not taking them?"

Nikka's brow furrowed. Was she always this cautious before she spoke?

"Maybe. But that sounds crazy, right?"

"She said to the woman who just had a restraining order slapped on her." Maggie had meant to be funny. She raised her eyebrows and got ready to chuckle along with Nikka, but in the cold of the room, she felt the heat rise off Nikka before she saw it spread to her face.

"Look, I'm sorry about that—"

"No. Me too. I was joking."

"I didn't come from me. It came from..." Nikka pursed her lips shut.

She was a careful one. Maggie tucked that fact away.

"I'm not even sure," Nikka continued slowly, "why I'm here. I guess... I hoped you might have some real answers. It seemed that yesterday, when you were out at the Inn..."

"I do. I've been thinking about it, and I've a theory. You want to hear it?"

Nikka stomped her feet and blew on her hands to ward off the cold. "Probably not. But go ahead."

Despite the cold, Maggie felt warm all over. Finally someone had opened the door and invited her and her theories in. Maggie wasn't a fool. She knew Nikka wasn't going to embrace what came next—no one ever did. But she was looking at her with a clear, open gaze not already filled with preconceptions, and that was good enough for her.

"Excellent." Maggie angled her body closer. "Beth has always been a recluse. No one knows why. Her brother, who never amounted to much, managed her affairs, brokered the deal for the house, which for some reason she just had to have. He was the go-between with her and the businesses here in town. Then a year ago he died. There was no other family, and somehow Lea Truman swept in. Things went on as always, or so we thought."

Maggie scanned Nikka's face. Still clear. So far so good.

"Then I became her personal chef and saw how it really was out there. Vivienne, that she-witch, practically has Beth under lock and key and never lets anyone see her. When I started asking questions, Lea fired me. I knew I was on to something. And a restraining order on top of that? It seemed a little extreme. But I couldn't figure out why."

Okay, pause. You're sounding a little hysterical.

"You think it has to do with the story and the press release?" Nikka asked.

"What else could it be? The two stories will make Lea and the publishing company very rich. I was in the way of all that, and now I'm not."

Nikka nodded. "Okay, but what makes you think Beth doesn't want this?"

"Nothing. I got nothing really. Except a gut feeling, weird timing, and now a bunch of pills thrown out a window."

Nikka sighed deeply. It wasn't the usual get-me-away-from-this-nut-job sigh that Maggie almost always heard at this point. Nikka's read more like a shit-you-may-actually-have-something-there sigh.

Maggie wanted to give her a huge bear hug. Nikka's teeth started chattering, and still she was in the cooler, listening to her.

"Lea can't be involved. Since she has power of attorney, it would be unethical." Nikka tapped her fingers against her lips. "Maybe it's just Vivienne and a misguided sense of loyalty. You should see the way she looks at Lea."

"Maybe." But Maggie believed with every fiber of her being that Lea was the mastermind here.

Stop talking. This is going well. Let her come the rest of the way on her own.

The silence dragged out between them—just a second longer than Maggie was comfortable with.

"Let's go out there," Maggie said, unable to take her own good advice. "Just you and me. We can force our way in, if we have to, and talk to Beth and see for ourselves if she's in her right mind. See if she wants this or not. She clearly doesn't want the pills."

Nikka's eyes narrowed, and she quickly dropped her gaze to her feet.

Dammit. Maggie curled her fist at her waist. She'd had her. She had totally had her, and she was too stupid to stop.

"No, I've got to meet Lea, and you can't be within a hundred feet of Beth. You do know that, right?"

Maggie nodded.

When Nikka finally raised her head, she wouldn't meet her gaze. Maggie had seen that look—of pity rolled into concern—a million times before.

"We can't go charging out there," Nikka said. "That would be suicide for both of us." She stared at the carrots on the shelf. "Tomorrow I'm going to be out there anyway. Maybe I can get Walker alone and ask her what she wants."

"That could be too late." Maggie couldn't help herself. She had to try one more time.

"For what?" Nikka asked.

"To save her."

"Only fools rush in."

"Or maybe only fools wait until it's too late to really make a difference."

Maggie stared deep into her eyes and willed her to come over to the light side.

Nikka's jaw was set. She wasn't ready to jump. In her own quiet way, Nikka was just as stubborn as she was. Maggie liked that, but they were at a stalemate. The conversation that had begun with such promise was effectively over.

Maggie swung the door open, and the heat from the bakery ovens swept over them.

"Wow, it's really cold in there." Nikka rubbed her hands together. Her voice, now light and breezy, gave nothing away about how she was feeling.

"They call it a cooler. But it's really a refrigerator."

"Thanks for listening to me." Nikka headed for the door. "I'll let you know what I find out."

"That would be great."

Nikka slid out the door without another word or even looking back.

"Who was that?" Lauren was at the kitchen door, leaning against its frame.

How long had she been there?

"The lawyer who served me the restraining order yesterday."

"I thought that was Harlan."

"She was behind it."

"So. What did she want?"

"To look in a mirror, I think."

"What?"

"She came out to run something by me, but really I think she came out here to see what it would look like if she went around the bend. If she acted on instinct and not on facts."

"Well, then, she came to the right place." Lauren came over and gave her a friendly pat on the back.

Maggie didn't feel like joking. "Yep, and she didn't like what she saw."

They both continued to stare at the closed door.

"She's very pretty." Lauren handed Maggie the peeler and pushed her gently back to her workstation.

"Really? I hadn't noticed." Maggie grabbed the fruit at the end, and another burst of fresh lemon filled the air.

Chapter 8

May 1960

"So, Miss Walker. How does it feel to be done with your first novel?" Dawn grabbed a celery stick from the picnic basket and thrust it out like a microphone.

"Amazing. Terrifying. Miraculous. There aren't even enough words."

"Well, you better get a handle on it, because next we need to get it to a publisher and on the bookshelves."

"Like it would be that easy. Have you forgotten what it's about? It's not exactly a best-seller in the making. Like *Auntie Mame* or anything."

Dawn swung the celery back under her own mouth. "There's where you're wrong, Miss Walker. *Heartwood* is just as good as any book on the best-seller list, maybe better. It's fun to read and raises real social issues that will resonate with a lot of people for a long time."

"You're kidding, right? It's about two women taking on the male establishment at a lumberyard, all with some pretty strong undertones, if you know what I mean." What was wrong with her? She couldn't even say that part out loud. What had she been thinking—to have spent months writing something that would never see the light of day? "No one's going to get on board with it." She looked at Dawn. Suddenly, she was talking about more than just the book.

"I know some people who know some people." Dawn tossed the celery stick into the nearby brush. "When you're ready to send it out, you let me know, and then we'll see who's right."

Beth shook her head at Dawn, who didn't even wait for her answer before she leaned back on the blanket and clearly moved on to other thoughts. She took her weight off her swollen belly by resting on her elbows and raised her face to the afternoon sun.

Beth ran her hand down the turquoise stripe of the Mexican blanket they were sitting on. Where did Dawn find this? Or the picnic basket? She was always full of surprises like organizing this celebration right under her nose.

It should be so romantic—just the two of them, sitting at her favorite beach, just far enough from town that they wouldn't have to share it with anyone. But there were a dozen stripes between them. They weren't even sharing the blanket with each other.

"Is that the Tall Tree?" Dawn pointed to a splash of green towering over the forest rooftop in the distance.

"Yep." She marveled how Dawn could flit from one subject to another in a heartbeat.

"How old is it supposed to be?"

"I don't know." She spread out a wrinkle in the red stripe. "Two thousand years, I guess?"

"As old as the Pantheon, more or less." Dawn craned her neck as if that would give her a better view of the tree on the horizon. "Jimmy told me when he had a break last week, he visited the Pantheon. I'd like to go to Rome someday. Would you?"

Irritation bubbled up in her the second Dawn mentioned Jimmy's name. She got up off the blanket and stepped into the edge of the stream. Freezing-cold water rushed around her bare feet, sending a shiver up her body. "Like that's ever going to happen. I'll never get out of Steelhead."

Silence hung between them for a moment, and then Dawn said, "What's wrong? You should be happy. You've finished your book, we're on an amazing picnic, and it's a wonderful day."

Beth longed to turn around to see Dawn's expression, but as childish as it was, she kept her back to her. She had had enough of Dawn's games and the passionate kisses that led nowhere. The book was just another one of Dawn's amusements. She had worked Beth up into a frenzy of excitement over it, and now what? Even if she did agree to send it out, no one was going to publish it. She didn't have a shot.

"Come over here."

Beth shook her head. A painful tingling ran through her numb feet. She was going to have to move sooner than later.

"Don't be like that. Please come here."

"What's the point?"

Again the silence stretched out.

Beth pressed her mouth closed and pushed her focus to her feet. She couldn't feel them at all.

"Do you really think you're ready?" Dawn jumped into her thoughts.

Beth said nothing.

"You know that once we go down that path, it changes everything. We can't come back. I know you think I've been leading you on, teasing you, but I've been holding back only because I'm worried that you don't know what you're getting into, and I'm scared too. The world does not like people like us."

Finally! They were talking about them—their relationship or whatever the Sam Hill it was. She swiveled out of the river to face Dawn, who lay on her side with her head resting on a crooked arm.

Beth met her gaze evenly. "Don't you get it? I'm already in so deep, I don't know which way is up." The calmness of her voice surprised her.

"I do get it. But this is so much more than us or that moment you're longing for. You've no idea how this can play out on the larger stage. You're so young."

"I'm not a child." She realized a second too late that was exactly what a child would have said.

"No, I know that." Dawn licked her lips and then sighed deeply. "I meant to say inexperienced although I'm not sure you'll think that's any better. It's just that these things never have a way of staying private once you cross that line, and no one's happy about two women being together. Believe me." Her gaze traveled down Beth's body to flowing water and stayed there. "Are you really ready for that—all of it?"

"From the moment I saw you at Hank's!" All her pent up frustration flowed out in her voice.

Dawn's attention jerked back to her face.

"No, before that. All my life, probably. I just didn't know it until now."

"You're sure? It's a high price to pay."

Beth's breath caught in her throat. Was this it? What she had been dreaming about for months. How high could the price be? They could manage it all as long as they had each other. She nodded, unable to speak.

"Okay, then." Dawn patted the blanket with her free hand. "Come here." This time her voice was low and throaty.

Those two words ignited a heat below Beth's belly, slowly sweeping through her. She stumbled clumsily on her numb feet across the bank to finally fall on the blanket right next to Dawn. Shy now that the moment was actually here, she searched the cool, green eyes, not knowing what to do next. Dawn had always been the one to make the first move. Why was she just lying there, giving nothing away?

She should just come clean. Knowing Dawn, she probably had already guessed anyway. "I've never done this before."

"It's not hard. Don't worry. Do what feels good."

Beth reached out with shaking fingers to push a loose curl behind Dawn's ear. She took a deep breath and then traced a line down Dawn's chin and into the opening of her blouse. The heat, the softness of her skin, the swell of her breasts were almost too much for Beth. Her hand stilled, unsure. And then she felt Dawn's heart pounding hard in her chest. Unbelievably, Dawn must want this too.

With almost a mind of their own, her hands unbuttoned the blouse, and she pulled it eagerly off Dawn's shoulders. Her gaze dipped down to Dawn's breasts, so full and beautiful they made her heart skip a beat. After all these months of sneaking furtive looks when she thought Dawn wasn't paying attention, staring straight at them was heady and so exciting.

Beth slid her hand around Dawn's back to find the hook, and with a lucky tug, the bra swung off and landed near the blouse.

Free from her clothes, Dawn rolled over and arched her back.

So much better than she had imagined. Beth reached out to cup what was finally right there for her taking. The warm flesh filled her whole hand, and she was surprised how heavy they were. Suddenly, she remembered Dawn's condition and pulled back as if she'd been burned. "Are you sure this is okay?"

"Oh yes. I need this. Just be gentle. I'm very sensitive right now."

Beth returned her hand and caressed her breast with featherlight touches, exploring its curves and smoothness as she built up her confidence. Almost by accident, she brushed a thumb over Dawn's nipple, which hardened instantly at the touch.

Dawn gasped, and Beth's breath caught in her throat. Encouraged, she squeezed ever so slightly and was rewarded with a soft moan. Electricity sparked through her. She had never heard anything so wonderful until...

"Kiss me."

Beth dipped her head to Dawn's mouth, but Dawn thrust her chest out instead. Son of a gun. She wasn't talking about her mouth. As she brushed her lips down her neck, Dawn's scent enveloped her. She smelled like the summer afternoon and her own heady smell. Beth couldn't get enough and buried her head in Dawn's chest for several heartbeats before running a trail of kisses lower. When her lips brushed the swell of her breast, she hesitated.

Dawn slid a hand up Beth's side.

Encouraged, Beth skimmed over to her nipple and lightly took the hard nub between her lips.

Another low moan, and Dawn arched upward again, this time thrusting her breast deep into Beth's mouth.

Instinct took over. Beth sucked harder, flicked her tongue back and forth, and then brazenly nibbled with her teeth—all the while slowly increasing the intensity.

Dawn slid her fingers into her hair and squeezed. "Oh yes. That's good. Touch me lower." She leaned back on the blanket.

Beth took in the swollen stomach and the long legs stretched out and open on the blanket. "I won't hurt the baby, will I?" Usually, the baby was just an abstract idea in her mind, but now it seemed far too real.

"No. But you're going to hurt me if you don't get to it." Her laugh was low and sexy. It was intoxicating.

Beth eagerly moved closer and ran a hand up Dawn's leg to the edge of her skirt. Her fingers slid under the cotton hem and up to panties that were already moist to the touch.

"Pull them down," Dawn said even before Beth formed the question in her head.

Her fingers brushed her sex as she did, and Dawn moaned at even that slightest touch. It emboldened Beth to go further, and she hiked the skirt up around Dawn's hips so she could see what she was stroking. Beth drew a sharp breath. Dawn was beautiful everywhere, and when she spread her legs for Beth, she felt her world open up.

Dawn was hot and wet and swollen.

"Just touch me here." She drew Beth's hand to the top of her sex. "I'm so sensitive right now, I think it is all I can take."

Beth slid her fingers into Dawn's slickness and touched her slowly at first.

Dawn raised her hips, pushing into Beth's hand, and together, they found a rhythm that seemed to grow and intensify as they moved as one.

"Oh, Beth." Her name floated on Dawn's lips. She clenched her legs around Beth's hand as her whole body began to shake. Dawn moaned deeply, and her body shuddered in one surge after another.

"Wow!" The last tremble faded from her body, and her hips sank back to the blanket. "Your fingers can sure do a lot more than write."

Beth sat back on her haunches.

Dawn pulled the skirt down but otherwise hadn't moved. Was it over? It had been better than her wildest dreams, but unspoken needs still swirled in her. She closed her eyes as she tried to push back the mounting tension between her legs.

"Don't worry. We're not close to being done."

Beth opened her eyes to stare into Dawn's—the green irises swirled with passion and desire. Their lips met, and she had no thoughts except how good it felt, how full her lips were, and how much passion simmered in the kiss.

Suddenly, Beth's blouse and bra slipped off her shoulders. She didn't have any recollection of Dawn pulling at the buttons or the hook in the back, her focus was so keyed on the gorgeous woman in front of her, but with Dawn's hands seeking her breasts she couldn't deny the fact that she was half-naked.

There was nothing tentative about the way Dawn touched her. She cupped one breast with her entire palm and rolled the other between her thumb and forefinger until all feeling rushed to Beth's chest, where everything was hard and erect. Beth groaned with more pleasure than she had ever known. And then Dawn took her into her mouth. She had to slide around Beth's body so the baby bump didn't get in the way, but since her mouth was the only contact point, all sensations intensified. A deep trembling began inside her.

"Lie back."

She did as she was told, and when Dawn fluttered kisses down her stomach, the quivering roared into an ache.

"I know you've never been with a woman." Hot breath sailed over Beth's stomach. "Have you been with a man?"

"No." The answer was little more than a ragged breath.

Dawn skimmed a finger up her thigh. "Have you ever pleasured yourself?" She traced slow circles around Beth's sex.

"Yes," she breathed. "But it was nothing like this." She tingled with anticipation.

"Well, I hope not." Dawn's fingers dipped and finally cupped her sex.

Her touch sent the ache rushing through Beth's body, and she reeled up, seeking even more contact.

Dawn rocked back and forth, hitting her in places that she had never reached herself. When Beth thought she couldn't take it anymore, Dawn slid her fingers inside and then plunged them deep into her.

Beth cried out with a pleasure she had never known as their lovemaking filled her completely. For the first time in her life, there was no longing, no feeling that she didn't belong. Just her and Dawn and this incredible feeling that raced everywhere.

Her release caught her by surprise, cascading through her with a surge so strong that it drove everything else from her mind. Dawn's snuggling into her side barely registered. She held her close as the last of the shivers subsided.

"Feels good, doesn't it?" Dawn's voice floated to her from far away. All she could hear was the echoes of her orgasm still roaring in her ears and the love overflowing from her heart. No one had told her it was going to be like this.

Whatever the price, she was willing to pay it.

"Pop. Can I talk to you?" Her father had just stepped through the front door from a day at the lumberyard. He had that haggard look after a tough day, and Beth knew she should wait until at least after his first drink, but the excitement of how the day might end wouldn't let her.

"Now? Can it wait?"

"Mom's already in the living room." Beth grabbed his arm and dragged him toward the couch, where Mary sat, her arms crossed over her chest. She took a seat across from them and pointed to the highball on the coffee table. "I just poured the soda, so it should still be good."

She waited until he took a sip and nodded his approval. "Okay, young lady, we're here because..."

After a deep breath, she leapt. "So, you know Dawn's pregnant, and the studio's publicity department is all set to write up a press release."

"That's wonderful news." Her mother pressed a palm to her chest. "The baby will be here in a couple of months."

"Sure, that makes sense," her father said.

"Yeah, and Dawn is afraid that when they do, the photojournalists and the street photographers might show up. And she's kind of nervous about living out at Fern House all by herself." She clenched her fist; Dawn had told her to get to that last part more slowly.

Both her parents reacted at the same time. "No one like that is going to come up to Steelhead," Carl said.

"What about her husband?" Mary raised a finger to the cross at her neck.

Beth looked from one to the other and decided to take the easy question first. "Well, Jimmy would be here. But he's stuck in Italy. There was bad weather on the set, and the shoot had to be extended. He's trying to get back as soon as he can, but he's not going to make it until after the news is out." The production lingo rolled off her tongue as they had practiced.

Mary nodded, but her hand didn't drop from around her neck.

Beth turned to her father. "Dawn says we're going to be surprised about what happens next. She says that the studio will actually set most of the publicity up. But there are some people who will show up when they aren't invited and take pictures that aren't authorized."

"If people want to see pictures of Mrs. Montgomery, they should just go to the movie theaters."

"Yes, Pop, that's the way it should work, but it doesn't always. There are a bunch of terrible magazines out there that need stories." She shuddered as she remembered that she had been one of their biggest fans before Dawn arrived.

"So what are you telling us?"

"Dawn was hoping that I could move in out there for a while." The words tumbled out in an awkward rush. Beth immediately wished she could bite them back and start again. She eyed her parents, waiting for their reaction.

Silence filled the room.

"Dawn was hoping…" Her mother repeated, her tone doubtful.

"Yes." Beth prayed she wasn't blushing. "She's lonely out there and, with the baby only a few months away, a little scared."

Mary let out a deep sigh on the couch.

Now was the moment to roll out the line she had rehearsed all the way home in the truck. "She misses Jimmy so much."

"Well, of course she does." Her father knocked back his drink and looked longingly at the sideboard, where the whiskey bottle stood.

"You should see how sad she is whenever she hangs up the phone from his calls."

"He calls all the way from Italy? That must cost a fortune."

"They're very much in love, Pop."

"Well, dear, what do you think?" Her father turned to her mother. "We can't leave Mrs. Montgomery out there alone."

Beth bit back a smile. One down, one more to go.

"I don't know..."

Shoot. Her mother wasn't going to make this easy. Beth cast around for something else to say, but Dawn had made her promise that she would stop after the *they're very much in love* line and let the situation take over.

Mary shook her head repeatedly, and a coldness rose in Beth's chest. For the very first time, Dawn might actually be wrong.

Carl leaned in to her. "I know what you're thinking, Mary. It makes me a little nervous too, but they're adults, and I could swing by after work to check up on them." Another sort of longing altogether washed over his face.

Holy smoke! Her father had a thing for Dawn. Beth sat back in her chair. She couldn't beat back the small smile that leapt to her lips. Dawn had been right all along, of course. Her father was going to do the rest of the work for them.

"They'll be fine. If Mrs. Montgomery...Dawn needs our daughter, who are we to say no?"

Mary's eyes narrowed. With a tiny pop, the chain snapped at her neck. She pulled away the cross in her clenched hand. Opening her fist, she looked first at the simple silver amulet and then at her husband. "It just doesn't seem right, dear. Not any of it."

"Oh nonsense. This actually seems more right than Beth working as a...housekeeper or whatever she does out there. I think it is far better that they've become friends."

Her mother opened her mouth and then closed it again without speaking.

"At least I'll know what to tell the guys down at the yard. I think it's a good idea."

Mary dropped the cross and its chain to the coffee table. "I'll have to get that over to Brent's to have it fixed. Actually, can you drop it off on the way home from work, before you stop off at Fern House?" She slid the necklace across the glass. There was a sharp scraping noise until her father picked it up.

"I certainly will."

Her mother didn't even look at her as she left the room. Beth knew she should be upset, maybe even afraid—her mother had never actually agreed to the move—but the knowledge that she would sleep in Dawn's arms tonight gave her such joy, any misgivings were swept away.

"All right, Pop." Beth bounced up from her seat before he changed his mind. "See you tomorrow, then?"

"Yes, dear. Be safe."

"I will."

Freedom enveloped her the minute she closed her front door. *No, not my door. I don't live here anymore.* The smile became a grin that lasted so long that when she turned up Fern House's drive, her mouth hurt.

Dawn was waiting for her on the front stoop, sitting with her head back in that classic movie star pose. Give her a cigarette and she could've been on a set. As soon as Beth got out of the truck, she cocked her head and raised her hands.

"Oh my gosh, you were absolutely right."

"Did you doubt me?" Dawn laughed in that low, throaty way that made Beth quiver.

"Maybe for a minute." Beth grabbed the arm that Dawn offered. "But then I remembered who I was dealing with, and I stopped exactly when you told me to."

"And then your father took over?"

"Yes. How did you know he would?"

"I hoped he would, that's all. Come inside. I've a little surprise."

They moved upstairs into the master bedroom. Candle light flickered from almost every surface, and somewhere, without her knowing it, Dawn had gotten roses and spread their petals on the bed.

"Oh my."

"Let's see how many times I can make you say that tonight." Dawn dragged her to the bed.

After their lovemaking, Beth snuggled into Dawn's arms, feeling the last waves of her pleasure wash over her. She had never been so content in all her life, and all she had to do was close her eyes and fall asleep in the arms of the woman she loved. When she had almost drifted off, her mother's voice echoed in her ear. "Dawn was hoping..." She tried to push the question away and find the comfort that had been hers just seconds before.

"Dawn?" She could hear the hesitation in her own voice. Not the time. But her own doubts couldn't be swept under the carpet again.

"Mmm." She sounded almost asleep too.

"Why me?"

"Just lucky, I guess."

"No, seriously. You could have anyone, anywhere." She raised herself on one elbow. Dawn shone with the afterglow of their night together. "Seriously, why me?"

Dawn opened one eye and then the other. "Are you worried?"

"Maybe a little." Her whole body tingled, but it felt good to have the question out in the open. If it went badly, though, the drive back to her parents would be an awfully long one.

"Don't be, my sweet. We're good. We're perfect."

"I love you." Her heart was pounding so loudly that it drowned out her voice in her own ears.

"I know." Dawn slid a hand around Beth's neck and pulled her down for a gentle, quick kiss.

Beth slid off her lips to gaze into her eyes. She hoped to hear Dawn say those four magical words: *I love you, too.* Surely Dawn, who knew things, even before she did, would see what she wanted.

Instead she pulled Beth's head down to her shoulder and snuggled into her. "You wore me out."

That was enough for now and for many days afterwards. Beth was learning to live in the moment, and what moments they were. The two of them—and it still was just the two of them even though the baby bump was growing daily—always seemed to be laughing at one thing or another. Dawn's silly sketches, Beth's burnt pot roast, the boisterous charade games after dinner. Then there was the lovemaking. Beth had never known anything so tender and sweet.

Her father had dropped by a couple times, but he was so nervous around them that he slapped Beth on the back as if she were a buddy at the lumberyard and drove away fast enough to stir up the dust in the driveway.

They stood on the front stoop, measuring his getaway. When he rounded the corner, Beth dropped her hand into Dawn's. She felt as if their world in Fern House stood outside of everything and was protected by the same crazy magic that had brought them together.

The call that brought it all crashing down came two weeks later. The studio was sending up Courtland Hyland, one of their publicity executives, to manage the first set of interviews and pictures that would introduce Dawn's new and grandest role to the world.

"I wish it weren't Courtland." Dawn sighed as she put down the phone.

"Why not?"

"He's nosey and not in a good way. Rumors have it that he sells the really juicy information to the highest bidder on the side. We'll need to be careful."

"We can do that. Easy-peasy."

Even so, when Dawn introduced her to Courtland as her personal assistant, it cut Beth to the quick. She let her gaze drop off Beth as if she wasn't worth a dime.

She's an actress. It doesn't mean anything. This is her acting.

Beth wished Dawn wasn't so good at it—turning her feelings on and off so easily. Either she should have twenty-five Academy Awards statuettes on the mantelpiece, or there was a core of truth in the actions.

When anyone needed coffee or when someone left paperwork in the other room, he or she would turn to Beth. She wasn't stupid. She hadn't expected to be welcomed with open arms like a Hollywood insider, but she hadn't really understood the strict hierarchy either. She rushed from room to room on errands, relegated completely to the sidelines. After so long in the sun, the cold there was almost frigid.

After the interview, Courtland had them all troop out to the redwood grove behind the house to shoot the publicity stills.

"Arch your back a little, dear," the thin man with the camera said.

"No." Courtland waved him off. "We want more Doris Day than Jayne Mansfield. We are sending this to *Good Housekeeping*, not *Playboy*."

"What about *Time* and *Vogue*?" Dawn asked.

Beth sighed. Despite what Dawn had said weeks ago in the writing room, she was still chasing that *Time* cover.

"Yes, of course. But we need Jimmy in the shot if we want to get coverage in the biggies. The new and best role for James Montgomery. We need the baby, too. Especially if it comes out cute."

Beth knew Dawn well enough by now. She was fighting to keep the smile on her lips.

"I guess I know where I stand." Dawn paced the living room floor after Courtland had left. "It's always about Jimmy. No matter what I do. It always has been, and it always will be."

Beth stood off to the side and wrapped her arms around her own chest. She had never seen Dawn like this. "They were talking about the cover of *Good Housekeeping*. That's good, isn't it?" she said softly, not sure which way to take this conversation.

"Great." She stopped pacing and focused all her attention on Beth, her eyes blazing with ferocity. "My condition will be the subject of coffee klatches all over the Midwest."

"People will be talking about it. That's what important. At least that's what Courtland said."

"Courtland doesn't know his ass from a hole in the wall."

Beth flinched. Dawn didn't use language like that. Who was this woman in front of her? Beth took a step back, even deeper into the corner. "You said you were good...with this new role."

"How can I be?" Dawn threw up her hands. "Everything is spinning away from me. I've absolutely no control anymore, and I've given up almost everything. Who could be good with that?" She spat the last few words out and looked to Beth searchingly.

She needed to say something. Anything. Dawn needed to be talked down off this ledge as soon as possible. But she had nothing. Dawn almost never talked about the baby, except to Jimmy, and that was only to relay what the doctor had said. Why hadn't she noticed that before?

Dawn raised her eyebrows, waiting, and still Beth couldn't find a response. As the silence dragged out, a hardness seeped into Dawn's expression. She shook her head and spun back to her pacing.

Tears sprang to Beth's eyes. For so many reasons, she wanted to be the one Dawn could turn to when her back was up against the wall, the one who knew what to say to keep them together. But at the heart of it all was the fact that she wasn't in control either. In fact, the truth had hit her hard. She had way less control than Dawn did, since a curt shake of her head had the ability to cut Beth to the quick.

She backed out of the room, wiping her eyes. The hall was dark and cool and gave her a minute to think. Maybe she couldn't say anything with words, but she might be able to speak with actions. To remind Dawn of all the roles, the one with her was the best. She raced upstairs, through the master bedroom and into the walk-in closet.

Before Courtland and his team descended, they had whirled through the house to eradicate all clues of their secret life. Everything was packed neatly into the back closet. She swiped the clothes out of the way to get to the boxes. If she could restore their house to the way it had been before the interview, maybe she could bring Dawn back to that point too. Ridiculous and probably stupidly ineffectual, but all she had.

She opened the first box to find crocheted squares with white Bs and Ds in red hearts. Another was full of Dawn's sketchbooks. She flipped through the pages as she pulled them out. Beth in every pose, planting flowers in the garden, writing at her desk, reclining, half-naked after lovemaking at the river. The box near the back held Beth's writing notebooks. Her first story, *The Tarot Card*, sat on top. She hadn't seen it since that day she had left it on the coffee table after their first kiss. But Dawn had.

Dawn had taken a simple, childish story and turned it into a work of art. On the cover was an intricate rendition of a lover's tarot card. The traditional angel on top was pushed way to the background so the lovers, two naked women, were the first shapes that jumped out at the viewer. Their hands reached across the width of the card to just barely touch—the chemistry between them sparking, almost alive.

Beth looked closer and realized that the woman on the left had short hair, brown eyes, and a smaller stature while the one on the right was taller, with blonde hair and green eyes. It was them! They were the lovers. Dawn had, from the first reading, seen right through the story, and here was the proof that she accepted, even celebrated, them as a couple.

All that churning in Beth's stomach, which had followed her upstairs and only grown as she unpacked the boxes, subsided. It was going to be okay. No one could draw a picture like that and not feel something. Beth couldn't expect Dawn to switch gears so drastically without a few hiccups along the way.

No. This was actually good. She could use the cover to start the only discussion they should have. What would come next for them?

Dawn's footsteps came up the stairs. "Beth? Sweetheart?" She turned into the room. Concern sounded in her voice, and regret played over her face. "Can we talk? I don't know what happened down there. I—"

"We don't need to talk about that." She held up the cover of the story and waved the picture in Dawn's direction. Suddenly, she felt so strong and sure. "You love me, don't you?"

Dawn met her gaze as if considering her next move carefully and nodded slowly. "I do."

Beth let the joy of this moment sink in. Dawn loved her. She had said it at last. Finally.

"I love you too. So much." Beth had the cover off the last box, one shoved way into the back. She didn't remember packing that one. Her hand dipped inside for more proof of their love.

"Don't." Dawn jumped toward her. "That's private."

But it was too late. Beth's heart that had been so full just seconds before ran dry. At the bottom of the box were only three things, but they spoke to the true role for Dawn: rolls of cash tied up with rubber bands, a brand-new passport, and a letter written in Dawn's own hand.

"What's this?" Beth asked so softly she almost couldn't hear the sound of her own voice.

"Please don't," Dawn said just as softly. "Just leave it. Close the box."

Beth wished she could. Close the box and go back to just moments before, when she had been so sure of Dawn's love. Instead, she fingered the passport and finally flipped it open.

It was Dawn, but a Dawn and a name she didn't recognize at first. Dark hair, a puffed-out face, a dull expression she had never seen in her eyes. She flicked it closed and drew out the letter.

Courtland, I can't tell you how horrible my life here at Fern House has been these past months. The shame at what I have done, here. What I have become. You're a friend, and so I know I can trust you—

Beth dropped the letter as if it had burst into flames. Pain like she had never known ripped through her. It started in her heart with the word *shame* and radiated out to the tips of her fingers and toes. It seemed to tear right through her and fill the closet with her sorrow.

"Beth! Stop! It's not what you think. Let me explain."

Something snapped in Beth with those words. Her heart broke, and the rose-colored glasses she had worn from the first day dropped right off her face. For good. She didn't even reach out to try to find them again.

"I don't know. Can you explain? Or are you always acting?"

Chapter 9

LEA, IN A CREAM LINEN pantsuit free of wrinkles, strode down the middle of the sidewalk heading to All Jacked Up.

Nikka glanced at her iPhone. Her boss was right on time, not a minute early or a second late. Any other day, she would marvel about how much control Lea had over herself and her environment. At the moment, however, she was still shivering and fretting over her unsettling conversation with Maggie in the cooler.

Nikka closed her eyes at the memory. The whole visit had been such a bad call. She had gone to the bakery just to work a few things out in her own head, including why she couldn't stop thinking about Maggie. Suddenly, she was risking frostbite and being roped into a black-ops mission to free Walker from a hostage situation. There had to be other ways to handle such a delicate situation.

Lea sought Nikka's glance and smiled broadly. She came right up and ran a hand lightly down Nikka's arm in greeting. More intimate than a handshake, but still professional. Lea held her arm until Nikka focused completely on her boss's face.

"Thanks for the text last night," Lea said. "I'm going to be completely honest with you. I'm not too sure about Vivienne either."

Nikka's shoulders dropped. See? Maggie was wrong about Lea. She didn't know what was going on with Walker. "I'm so glad to hear you say that. Last night I—"

"Wait, we need to get through today and tomorrow, and then you and I can take a hard look at what's going on out there together. Yes?"

Nikka nodded. She could live with that. Again, exactly what she had told Maggie. One day shouldn't matter, and Lea had said *together*. Here was the better way. "Yes, let's do that."

"Good." She squeezed her arm and let Nikka go. "Why are you so cold? And why are you waiting out here instead of inside?"

"I didn't want to contaminate the water." Nikka chose to ignore the first question. "I'm persona non grata in there."

"Oh, that's right. She was the difficult one."

"Yeah, a little angry to say the least."

"All right, then, this is how we are going to handle our meeting. I'm going to throw you under the bus, play her side of the game, and with a little luck we should get what we want. You up for a little acting?"

"Sure. If that's what it takes."

"Just go with it. Show me what you're made of. Shall we?" Lea opened the door for Nikka, and they both walked into the coffee house to face Justine Cammelle, who was coming at them fast with a finger waving in the air.

"This is private property, ladies, and you aren't welcome in this establishment."

"First, let me apologize. I'm so sorry about yesterday, Justine." Lea darted ahead of Nikka to meet her with a slight bow. "May I call you Justine?"

Lea's cordial greeting threw Justine for a loop, and she stopped dead near the empty space on the counter where the *Creative Coffees* cookbook had stood the day before. "Ah, yeah. I guess so."

"Great, and you must call me Lea." She clasped Justine's hand in a shake and simultaneously directed her to a more private table in the back. "Perhaps we can start again as friends this time?"

Nikka shook her head as she joined them. Lea was like a surgeon, her moves so precise they had already cut Justine out of the equation without her even knowing it.

"And that friendship has to start with a true apology. You see, I stupidly sent my assistant out here to do a job that I should've done myself. She's new to this case and wasn't as prepared as I had hoped." Lea glared at Nikka.

"I'm sorry." Nikka had to remind herself that they were acting. She hoped. Lea's irritation felt very real.

Lea directed them all to a nearby table and sat down between Justine and Nikka. "What Nikka should have done," Lea scooted her chair closer to Justine, "was offer you a new deal. An exclusive that will bring you a lot of business."

Justine shook a finger at Nikka. "She was very rude."

"S...Sorry." Nikka glanced down at her feet. She hoped she wasn't overdoing it.

"Well, now you're talking to someone who makes the decisions." Lea tapped the table with her forefinger, shifting Justine's attention back to her. "As you probably already know, tomorrow morning Beth Walker's story, 'The Tarot Card,' drops on Amazon."

Lea paused until Justine nodded.

"So just a thought... What if it also drops here? My office could upload it to your website just for the day. People could come here, buy a cup of coffee, maybe a cinnamon roll, and log into your Wi-Fi. They could sit and read the story for free while they're here."

Justine's eyes widened. Nikka could almost see the dollar signs pushing up her eyelids.

"It would only be for the day, of course. Otherwise, we risk other online bookstores price-matching, and we don't want to make the story permanently free. And you'd have to jump all over the marketing since it's tomorrow. I think you could turn a tidy profit, but the real benefit is that you'd set yourself up as the ultimate Beth Walker connection here in the Springs. And to sweeten the deal we could guarantee at least two more exclusive days with Walker releases in the next few months."

"Interesting." Justine leaned back in her seat.

Nikka studied her. Justine was trying to play it cool, but she was way out of her league.

Lea already had a contract out of her workbag and was sliding it across the table. "Providing, of course, that we can come to a new agreement tonight about the points that Nikka raised so rudely yesterday."

Justine glanced at the paper that had almost magically appeared right under her nose.

Nikka did too. She couldn't see the fine print, but the numbers and percentages on the paper gave the advantage to Walker and Truman and Steinbrecker in a big way. The story here was the ticking clock. If Justine didn't sign, she would lose the exclusive.

Justine licked her lips as she stared down at the contract. "I should probably have my lawyer look at this." Her voice was hesitant. Nikka could clearly read that she wanted to be talked out of that move. And if she could see that, it would've been a clarion call to Lea.

"That's always a good move," Lea said, "but it all needs to be in place before we can upload the story."

Justine dug around in her back pocket and pulled out her phone.

"There are, of course, intangibles here as there are with most deals. True, you'd have to pay compensation to the Walker estate, but it would be business as usual after that, and we'd look to you to be our liaison with the other businesses here in the Springs. This once-in-a-lifetime opportunity would, of course, come with reparation…"

Lea let the words trail off into silence. Justine didn't react.

"…and power…"

Here she got a bite. Justine leaned forward slightly.

Lea moved in for the kill. "You could influence your friends and the entire community about how we move forward. They would look to you for guidance and your expertise."

Nikka shifted in her seat. Lea was laying it on pretty thick.

"Really?"

"Yes, absolutely." Lea pulled a black pen out of her bag. Truman and Steinbrecker was etched on it in silver script. She nudged the pen toward Justine's hand. "The contract is completely boiler plate, standard through and through. You can have your lawyer look at it any time."

"I don't know…" But Justine already had the pen poised over the empty line at the bottom of the contract.

Hours later, Nikka eased into a back booth at The Lumberyard across from Lea. Her feet throbbed painfully in her heels, so she kicked off her shoes under the table and rubbed at the blister, now fully formed, on her little toe. That afternoon they had hit almost all of the businesses that had been on Lea's original list, and Lea's briefcase was stuffed with the signed contracts to prove it.

"We're celebrating." Lea handed Nikka the drinks menu from the back of the table. "And order a real drink. Don't get a flight of craft beers or anything."

"Okay."

"Tomorrow has to go off without a hitch. We didn't invite a ton of people, only those who were eager for the story." Lea picked up an advertisement for a hamburger, gooey with cheese and mushrooms, from the edge of the table. *World-Famous Truffle Burger* ran across the top in big, glossy letters. "I wonder what makes it world-famous."

Lea looked as if nothing that fatty or delicious ever passed over her lips. Just the way she was sitting with her suit jacket off and the top few buttons of her blouse open screamed *I am hot; look at me.* So Nikka did. She let her gaze linger on the swell of one breast and the edge of a lacy bra for just a second. She was hot. There was no denying it.

"Oh thank God," she said as the waiter appeared.

"We'll have two of these." Lea waved the burger advertisement at him. "And I'll have a Greyhound, please, with Grey Goose vodka. If you don't have Grey Goose, come back and I'll order something different. I don't want a substitution. "

"Yes, ma'am."

"Good. Nikka, what are you drinking?"

"I'll have a Greyhound too." She had no idea what she'd just ordered. She didn't drink much. She liked to stay completely in control so she left that Russian stereotype to her father and brother. She did, at least, recognize that Grey

Goose was a step up from the Smirnoff that her father had at home.

"Can I suggest you start with an appetizer? Our spinach-artichoke dip is our best-seller or the—"

"No. Just the drinks and the hamburgers."

A few minutes later, as soon as the cocktail was dropped onto the table, Lea circled the rim of the glass with one finger. She took a long sip and visibly relaxed against the back cushion of the booth. For the first time all day, she really looked at Nikka, studying her.

"You picked up the cues well back at the coffee store. What was it? Theater in an after-school program? Improv in college?

"Slam poetry in high school."

"I knew it was something. Doesn't really matter. They're all good training for a lawyer. "

Nikka took a small sip of the drink in front of her. *Ah, thank goodness...grapefruit.* Fortunately, nothing more than spiked juice, but the expensive vodka made it very smooth. She would have to keep her wits about her. She looked up. All of Lea's attention was still on her.

"So what's your story? Girlfriend, boyfriend, something in between?"

"Not interested in boys. No girlfriend for a while. Trying to get ahead in my job." She drew her lips into half a smile—sophisticated, she prayed, not sucking up.

"Sitting with the managing partner at dinner in the middle of a big case. I think you can check that off your to-do list."

Nikka's smile broadened.

"The relationships will come too. When work takes up so much of your time, it's really hard." Here she met Nikka's gaze. Her blue eyes softened as she looked at her.

This was just casual dinner banter, right? Surely Lea wasn't flirting with her. That would be crazy.

"It's a good thing you're not involved with anyone. This kind of case doesn't come along often."

"I know. I'm very grateful—"

"When I was just starting out, I was involved in a very big case myself." Lea swirled the ice around in her drink with the rosemary sprig. "It was Peter Robertson's first book, *Cold Crush*."

Nikka took a quick breath. "You were involved with *Cold Crush*?" She had studied the case at Stanford.

"Well, not in any real way. I was just an associate with Kendel, Mattern, and Braun at the time, but I did get to see the inner workings of IP law at its very best."

Lea smiled a sophisticated half smile that left Nikka wondering what would conjure up the whole smile. That was how it was done, though. Nikka was sure she had looked dopey with her attempt.

"You know I'll flat-out deny it if you repeat this to anyone. But Robertson told me he willfully stole the central theme and architecture for his book from those historians. He was trying to get into my pants at the time, unsuccessfully, of course. Consequently, he let a lot of stuff slip in the attempt."

"Really?" Nikka leaned in. This had certainly not been in the law books at Stanford.

"Yep. Point for point, he told me. He said that they had already done all the heavy lifting in developing the theory that Jack the Ripper was actually Jackie the Ripper. A woman and a midwife. He knew all he had to do was add the vengeful lesbian angle, and he could get away with it." Lea raised her eyebrows playfully as she handed over that tidbit.

Nikka took a sip of her Greyhound. It was suddenly more sour than smooth. The courts had called the Robertson case a victory for common sense and a triumph for the expression of ideas, not the ideas themselves. To know for sure that Robertson had maliciously stolen the material did put a new spin on those law school lectures.

"Adam Braun is one of the best lawyers I've ever seen in action. And that's the take-away, Nikka. The ability to spin things, how you put them together is so much more important that the intention beneath them."

Was it, Nikka wondered, but then quickly pushed that thought away.

Lea knocked back the last sip of her Greyhound and held the empty glass out to the waiter, who was at the next table. "One more. You want another?"

Nikka shook her head.

"There are cases that define us as lawyers. More than one if you're lucky. And, Nikka, this could be yours. Walker's, of course, is night and day different than Robertson's. But it's just as high-profile. We're going to need a point person on Walker. To keep everything organized. We'll have to pull you out of the cubicles and into an office of your own to give you more space."

Bam! There it was: the opportunity that her father had always told her would come her way. All she had to do was grab it like the brass ring it was.

"An office? Of my own?" It seemed too good to be true.

"A small one, but yes, it's the first step."

"Lea, I don't know what to say."

"Nothing. You've earned it. But you better keep on earning it. No one can rest on her laurels in this business."

The waiter slid the hamburgers onto the table. They were huge, bulging with mushrooms and cheese, and accompanied by a mound of fries.

"Ketchup? Mustard?"

"No, thank you," Lea said for them both.

Nikka studied the plate. The thick patty was slipping right off the bun. What had looked delectable on the advertisement looked completely unmanageable in reality. "How are we supposed to eat this?"

As a reply, Lea flipped the top bun off onto the side and pulled two forks and knives out of the kitschy wooden log holder. She handed one set to Nikka.

"Yes, it's going to be a lot of managerial work. Making sure we dot our i's and cross our t's. But you've got a knack for that, and you won't believe what you can learn seeing a case from this angle." Lea carved out a bite of her burger. "This is good. Maybe not world-famous, but good. We can leave right after the press conference tomorrow. I didn't like the new car service that Alison booked for me on the way up, so you and I can drive back to the City together."

Nikka remembered the wordless ride up the 101 Highway at the beginning of the week.

"I'll sit in the front seat, and we can hammer out how to put the best offense in place for Walker."

"Absolutely. I'm all in." Nikka flipped off the top bun just as Lea had done and plunged her fork into the burger's heart.

Maggie yawned and stretched her arms over her head. Her lower back howled in protest. Knots were tied up inside other knots, and she could barely stand upright she was so exhausted. Two hundred cupcakes—ten different flavors— baked, frosted, decorated, boxed, and ready to go. She had done it all in one day. She glanced at her watch. Well, two days, technically, but the important thing was it was done, and she could look Lauren in the eyes again. She grabbed her phone.

Finished, she texted. *They look great. I'll put them on the delivery shelves in the cooler so Skylar can load them in the van when she gets in. I'm going home to sleep!*

All she could think about was a shower and crawling into bed for at least twelve hours. Then, when she awoke, she would figure out what to do about Beth.

She grabbed the first set of boxes and carried them to the shelf in the cooler. She slid them in right next to the sign that said *deliveries.* Damn. There wasn't going to be enough room. She glanced around. There was plenty of room on the shelves across the cooler, where they kept all the cupcakes for the store. She would have to leave a note for Skylar so she wouldn't miss the overflow.

She had taped clear and careful instructions onto the shelf when the paper, too heavy for the tape, dropped to the floor and disappeared under the unit. Man, good thing she had been here.

She could hear Lauren's frantic phone call from Fern House as she stared in the bakery van the next morning. "Where are the Lemon Lovers?"

Her muscles groaning, Maggie stiffly bent to retrieve the note but then froze. An idea tugged at the edge of her mind. What if she hadn't seen the note fall? It would've lain forgotten under the shelving unit. Skylar wouldn't have known about the extra boxes, and there actually would be a hysterical phone call.

Then someone could locate the missing cupcakes and rush them out to the event. And that someone, if she played her cards right, might be able to do a little snooping at Fern House without being seen.

Guilt pulled at her as she stood back up without the note. The last thing she wanted was for Lauren or Skylar to get in trouble—especially since Lauren had handed her job back to her on a silver cupcake platter. On the other hand, a chance like this wasn't likely to present itself again. The crowd at the press conference could easily hide someone who was violating a restraining order.

Maggie took one last look around. The note was out of sight. The Lemon Lovers for the conference looked like ordinary bakery stock. And Skylar, cheery as she was, would panic at the first sign of trouble. Lauren would have to turn to Maggie.

Yeah. This plan will work. Easy-peasy. She flicked off the kitchen lights and went home.

Maggie's phone yodeled at ten thirty the next morning. She had slept through her alarm, so the confusion when she answered was real.

"Oh my God!" Lauren's voice was shrill on the other end. "I don't know what the hell happened, but there are no Lemon Lovers in the van. Skylar said that she loaded everything on the delivery shelf. Did you make them?"

"Of course I did."

"Maggie, listen to me. Skylar's losing it. Get your ass over to the bakery, and find out what happened to those cupcakes. Call me back!"

The line went dead, and Maggie looked at the phone for a moment. The die had been cast.

At the bakery, Skylar was nearly in tears. "I don't know how this could've happened. I loaded everything that was on the shelf. Look, it's empty."

Maggie tried to infuse calmness into her voice. "You didn't see the note?"

"What note?"

"On the shelf. I left it right here." She touched the metal rung where the instructions had once been. "It said that I put the Lemon Lovers over there." She pointed to where the boxes sat.

"No, I didn't." Skylar's voice cracked. "When I came in this morning, there was nothing on that shelf except the boxes. I swear."

"Hmmm. I wonder." Maggie flipped the brakes of the rolling shelf down with one foot and pulled the empty unit into the middle of the room. Sure enough, the note sat in the vacant space. "Oh, shit. It must have fallen off."

"I didn't see it. How could I have?" Skylar was actually crying now.

This was harder than she thought it would be. "Don't cry. This isn't your fault. I'll just run the cupcakes out to the event, and it will be like it never happened."

"Really? You'd do that for me?"

Maggie could only nod.

Skylar wiped her eyes. The tears stopped as quickly as they had started. "Do you think Lauren will fire me?"

"No. I won't let her."

Skylar threw her arms around her and squeezed tight. "Thank you."

Lauren wasn't nearly as grateful when Maggie called over to Fern House to explain what had happened. "There's always something with you, Maggie, isn't there?"

"This wasn't my fault, you know." She stepped to one side in case lightning or an act of God blew through the bakery roof to strike her. When it didn't, she added, "The paper just fell to the floor."

"Whatever. Just get them out here ASAP."

"Ah, Lauren...? You know I don't have a car."

"Oh, for Christ's sake. Take mine. The keys are in the top drawer in my office, where they usually are."

"See you soon," she said to no one. The line was dead; Lauren had hung up on her for the second time that morning.

Maggie wound her way through town with the cupcake boxes tucked carefully into Lauren's backseat. The last thing she needed was a real accident to add to the chaos of the fake one. Once she eased onto the straightaway of Fern Drive, she gave the Saab a little more gas. A smile tugged at her lips, and her hands relaxed against the steering wheel. Wouldn't it be a hoot if one of her hare-brained schemes actually worked?

The commotion at the big black gate at Beth's house told her she had congratulated herself way too soon. Several men, all wearing official-looking security jackets, stood guard at every access point. They tapped on iPads, talked into walkie-talkies, and scurried around, looking imposing. Waving the lucky few that were on the list down the long driveway, they turned away twice as many. One tall man stood over two women and simply shook his head as he jabbed his finger down the street.

She didn't know what she had expected—obviously not to pull right up to her usual parking space, but not this circus. Maggie took a deep breath. It was a good sign. It told her loud and clear that Lea was going to great expense to protect something...or someone.

She pulled onto the shoulder of the road just beyond the gate and ran her hand through her bangs. She could drive down a couple of miles to the old service road. But it was in such bad shape that no one used it. Lauren's car might not make it all the way to the house, and the clock on the dash said eleven fifteen. The press conference should have already started. Lauren was probably having a shit fit. If she were to have any time to snoop around, she needed to get the cupcakes up there immediately. She picked up her cell phone and dialed.

"Where are you?" Lauren's voice was thin.

"Right outside."

"Do you have them?"

"Of course, I do. Can you call down to the guards and get my name on the list? I'll bring them—"

"No." Lauren's voice rose an octave. "I already tried, but you're on another list. A bad list. They're not letting you in. I can come down myself or get someone else—"

Maggie's mind went into overdrive. Her whole plan hinged on getting past that gate. "Wait. Hang on."

She rolled down the window and zeroed in on the first person she saw—a tall young woman walking away from the gate, alone, head down.

"Hey," Maggie called out. The woman turned to her. "Couldn't get in?"

"Maggie? What on earth are you doing?" Lauren asked over the phone.

"Hang on," she said again and turned back to the girl on the shoulder. "What's your name? I can get us in if you just give me your name."

"Josie Williams." She didn't vacillate. Didn't ask why. Just jumped in with her name.

Maggie liked her immediately. She waved her over as she returned to Lauren. "Put Josie Williams on the list. We're driving up to the gate right now." She killed the call without giving Lauren even a second to back out.

She gave her full attention to the young woman who was already at the car window. Up close she looked younger than she had from across the street. Several piercings—nose, ears, and one eyebrow—worked against the classic beauty of her fine features. A curious gaze and large green eyes met Maggie's scrutiny head-on.

"You got a picture ID, Josie Williams?"

"I do." She patted a pocket on the backpack she was wearing.

"Then hop in." Maggie inclined her head to the passenger side of the car.

Again, Josie didn't hesitate as she rounded the car and slid into the front seat. "Wow. It smells good in here." As she reached for the seat belt, the short sleeve on her right arm rode up enough to expose the delicate trunk of a tree tattoo.

"Hey, weren't you at the bakery the other day? Made From Scratch. Asking for directions? To here, right?"

"I was. But I made a big mistake."

Maggie raised an eyebrow.

"I should have ordered whatever's in the backseat. I got red velvet."

Maggie snorted as she spun the car off the shoulder and back onto the road. "You're going to have to do all the talking. Okay?"

"Sure."

As soon as they pulled up, the security guard leaned down to the car window. "Name, please."

Maggie looked over to Josie, who met the man's stare with indifference. "Josie Williams," she said.

He tapped on the iPad and ran his finger up and down the screen. "Sorry, I don't see you."

Don't panic. Let it play out. Lauren may need a moment. Maggie opened her mouth to buy them time when Josie jumped right in.

"Look again. I was just put on the list."

The guard sighed. They both sat as still as mice while he scrolled again through the names on his screen. "Oops. Yep. Here you are. May I see some ID, Ms. Williams?"

"Sure." Josie pulled out a California driver's license and showed the man a cleaner-cut version of herself—only one piercing, her curly blonde hair tamed by a headband.

He took a long look at the ID, switching from picture to real person several times. "Thank you." He moved to the car behind them.

Maggie blew out a long breath and eased up the driveway. "Wow. You're good. No panicking."

"So are you."

"Huh?"

"You don't have to cop to it. But it's clear you're up to something." When Maggie said nothing, she added, "It's all good. I don't care. I'm not here to bust anybody."

Maggie glanced at her. Josie sat with her hands folded neatly in her lap and her gaze fixed on the road ahead.

"You're not coming up here to do something stupid, are you?" Maggie asked. The last thing she needed was competition in that arena.

"No. I love Beth Walker. I just want to see her in person, maybe get a selfie with her for Snapchat or Instagram. How cool would that be?"

"Pretty cool," she said, although she had the distinct feeling that the girl was still acting. Whatever. She didn't have time for what Josie Williams might have up her sleeve. She had to worry about parking.

The driveway, normally so empty, was crammed with news vans, cars, porta-potties. Nearly running the Saab into a bush, Maggie squeezed Lauren's car past the Made

From Scratch van and into a tiny space right next to a white Subaru. She gasped as she recognized the car. Of course, Lea would bring her right-hand woman. After the talk in the cooler yesterday, she would have to avoid Nikka like the plague. She had practically given her a blueprint of the plan even before she devised it, and Nikka's hasty exit the day before made clear whose side she was on.

"Where are they?" Lauren, normally so composed, had flown down the steps of the house to the car before it had even come to a stop. Her eyes were wide and her face pinched.

"Here." Josie slid out of the car and tugged the front seat up to reveal the neat stack of boxes in the back.

"Thank God." Lauren pushed past Josie. "Maggie, you better take off before anyone realizes you're here."

"You don't need any more help?" Maggie jumped out of the car as well.

"No. Not from you."

Maggie cringed. Lauren wasn't usually so harsh.

"Jeez. I'm sorry. I just don't want either of us getting into trouble. Besides, I'm just going to get these Lemon Lovers on the table and head back to the bakery myself. This event is crazy. Nothing's going right. You wouldn't believe how stressed out people are in there."

"Okay," Maggie said.

When Lauren was halfway up the steps, juggling the boxes with both hands, she turned back. "Promise me. No funny tricks. You'll disappear. I don't want any trouble."

"I promise." She forced herself to meet Lauren's gaze even though her stomach roiled.

Lauren nodded and vanished into the house.

Maggie stared after her. When she was sure Lauren wasn't going to pop out again, she tapped Lauren's keys. With a single beep, the car's locks slid down. She glanced toward the back of the house. Luckily, there were no security guards roaming around. They all seemed concentrated at the front gate. But she had no idea how everything was set up inside, so she figured her best bet was to sneak in from the back. That way it would look as if she had disappeared, as Lauren had demanded.

Wait a second! Speaking of disappearing... Where was Josie Williams?

Chapter 10

June 1960

THE DEEP DARKNESS OF MIDNIGHT crept into the den at Fern House. Beth sat on the couch, her back rigid against the pillows and her feet firmly on the floor. Dawn, as usual, was curled up in the wing-tip chair by the fireplace, small and forlorn. Beth dropped her gaze. She didn't want to feel pity for the woman who was tearing her heart into little pieces.

"I know I should have told you all this ages ago. In the truck on the way home from your parents probably or maybe even before. But the last thing I wanted was for you to feel sorry for me." Dawn paused.

Beth didn't look up. She wasn't going to be played... again.

"And after that, there never was a good time. You know how when you miss the right time, it just gets harder and harder to actually say it out loud."

Another pause. Dawn obsessively rubbed one bare foot against the other.

Beth closed her eyes to block out the image.

"Jimmy's not a nice man." Dawn started up again. "In the beginning, I had no idea. It was fine, fun actually. We both like playing games, and so we played them together. Then he began to think that his needs and wants were more important than anything else. He's beyond self-centered and narcissistic. That's probably why he's found so much success in Hollywood, but at home he made a two-year-old throwing a tantrum look like a saint."

Dawn swallowed so hard that Beth heard it across the room. "Believe me, it was exhausting listening to him go off on some executive or reviewer who didn't get him. I felt like my mother, figuring out ways to beat off the storm in my own house. You see, I needed him for my career, and when I think back, it was crazy. But I guess when you're in something, you can't always see it clearly. Right?"

Beth bit her bottom lip and then nodded slightly.

"The yelling and tantrums were bad enough. And if that's all it were, I would probably still be down there. But there were drugs, and finally he directed all his anger at me. Telling me how lucky I was to have him, how my career was dependent on him, how I'd be nothing without him. And then I got pregnant."

This time the pause stretched out into the night.

Finally, after losing the battle with herself, Beth looked up.

Dawn met her gaze, and even the darkness couldn't hide her vulnerability. Tears welled up in her eyes.

"You got pregnant..." Beth prompted.

"He came home from a meeting at the studio. They were trying to block his participation deal with *Conqueror of the World*. He was furious. Actors all over are making these lucrative deals where they get paid on the back end, and his was going up in flames. Even now he's lying when he says he's getting ten percent of the profits. They wouldn't even give him a minimum guarantee. I tried to talk him down. He didn't care enough to listen to me. He lashed out."

A coldness dropped through Beth. She had no idea whether Dawn was telling the truth, but she knew what was coming next. And if it was true, now her heart was breaking for two reasons.

"He raised his fist." Dawn curled her hand and pushed it into the air. "It never went further than that. I got angry. He backed down." She dropped her fist. "But I knew he was testing the waters, so to speak, and if I stayed there long enough, he would find a way to get in the deep end. I couldn't stop thinking what if next time, it was the baby?"

She sighed deeply, and when she spoke again, her voice had a steely reserve. "I had to get out of the marriage. So I put it into his head that we needed a house away from it all. He jumped all over that. He doesn't trust anyone in Hollywood—or me for that matter. We were on a press tour in San Francisco, and I actually don't know how we ended up in Steelhead, but it didn't really matter. All I needed was a place to disappear from, and Steelhead isn't on anyone's radar. No one would be watching. I could just be here one day, take the money and passport upstairs, and be gone the next." She waved her hand as if she were ending an elaborate magic trick.

"That's not what happened. How did I get involved?"

"You were going to help me. I saw how you looked at me that first day at Hank's. I knew you were already in love with me even before you knew you liked women."

Darting pains ran down her torso. Of course she had known, but why did the truth have to hurt so much?

"In the beginning, I saw you as someone who would help me. I thought if I threw you a bone every so often, you would lie for me when I vanished. You might even..."

Suddenly, the writing room, the kisses that lead nowhere...everything made complete sense.

"I would what?"

"Take on Jimmy. Fall on your sword. I don't know what I thought. Destroy yourself to save me if that's what it took. Oh God, Beth. I'm so sorry."

"So you were playing me."

"In the beginning. Yes."

The only way to combat the pain was to take a deep breath. It filled her lungs and squeezed a tiny bit of the hurt out.

"But then the day came, and I didn't go," Dawn added quickly. "I just couldn't. There's an unused ticket up there somewhere if you're looking for proof. But I realized I didn't want to run, and I told myself I still had plenty of time to change my mind again."

Beth opened her mouth, and Dawn put up a hand before she could start.

"Yes, you're right. Part of it is that I didn't want to give up my career, but you got to believe me. I didn't want to give you up either."

"That's not what the letter upstairs says."

Dawn bunched both of her hands into tight fists. "Beth, that was a lie!"

"Really? Because it doesn't look that way. It's addressed to Courtland. The man you said would sell anything to the tabloids. It looks like you're going public with...us. How could you?"

"Exactly!" She unclenched her hands and raised them, palms out, to Beth. "Don't you see? That was the new plan."

Beth's brows furrowed. What was she missing?

"I was never going to send the letter to Courtland. He was here all day, and it would've been so easy, especially for me, to let something slip or give you a look that I had to immediately cover up to make him suspicious and set up the letter. But you were here today. Never once did I give him any indication that you were anything more than an assistant to me."

That much was true; indifference as cold as ice had flowed off her all day long.

"You see, all I was going to do is threaten Jimmy with a scandal. You don't know him. He's like a dog with a bone—and not in a good way. Unless it was in his best interest to dump me, he would drag me along with him forever, just because he could. He doesn't love me. I hear the girls in Italy revolve faster than a spinning door and that on a two-week hiatus from the film, a time he could've come home, he took the flavor of the week up to Lake Como. His career comes first, second, and third, so he'd do anything to save it. If I threaten to destroy his career with a baritone babe scandal, he will give me and his baby up." Dawn tilted her head.

"What's a baritone babe scandal?" Beth asked, her voice surprisingly monotone.

"You know. Us." Dawn shrugged.

Beth chewed on her bottom lip. Dawn's confession answered a lot of questions. Mostly why someone like Dawn could fall for a nobody like her. And why she had been so quick with the writing room on that first day and everything else later.

I can't forget she is an actress. This whole thing could be a movie script; the story's so tidy and romantic.

"So if you really fell for me, why not tell me? Why not let me in on the plan? Why keep it a secret?"

"To avoid a scene like this. I know I waited too long to tell you I love you. I don't even know when it happened. Maybe when I heard 'The Tarot Card' for the first time…

maybe when I see how you look at me... All I know is that when I thought I was pretending to fall in love, I really did." A sad smile played at her lips. "Believe me, it surprised the hell out of me too."

Did Dawn really love her? Beth's heart had quickened with those three little words, *I love you.* Dawn had never said it out loud except for now, when it was in her best interest to do so.

"I don't know." Beth shook her head. "You've been in complete control since day one."

"Sweetheart, look at me. This isn't what complete control looks like." A tear finally spilled over and slid down her cheek. "You think it's easy to sit here and open up to you after a lifetime of protecting myself from everyone I've ever met?"

"No, of course not. If that's true, I'm so sorry your life has been like that. But I can't stop thinking that you always write the script. You told me what to say to my parents and exactly when to stop. How to act with Courtland..." Her voice turned shrill as all her emotion poured into her words.

"I've had to write my own scripts my whole life. Why do you think I'm so good at reading people and hiding who I am? Now that all this is out, we get to write our own script. Together, if you'll have me."

Beth took in a deep breath and held it until her lungs screamed for air. She shook her head uncertainly.

"Listen. We already have our first act." Dawn raced from the room. "I'll be right back."

Here was her chance. To get into her truck and drive away for good. Dawn was trouble; that much was clear, and she, herself, was already in so far over her head that staying put would probably pull her completely under. She tried to get off the couch. Her legs were wobbly and wouldn't hold her weight. She fell back into the cushions and into indecision.

Did she really want to leave? Dawn had said she loved her. But, surely as she was sitting here, there had to be another angle.

Dawn returned to the room, waving a white envelope. "Look, this came in yesterday. I wanted to wait until Courtland left before I showed it to you. Actually, I wanted to go back to the river with another picnic but... Oh well, you need to see it now." She flapped the letter in the air.

Beth just sat up straight and lifted her hand, making Dawn walk all the way to the couch to give it to her. It looked official. Titanium Pages and a New York address were printed in silver in the upper left-hand side. Dawn's name and her Steelhead address were typed across the front.

"Open it," Dawn said.

Beth slid her finger under the back flap and then realized that it had already been opened. Whatever was inside, Dawn, of course, already knew. A thick piece of paper slid out easily. She unfolded it and took in the information all at once.

Unbelievably, Titanium Pages was very interested in publishing *Heartwood* by the unknown author Beth Walker.

"It's a tiny publishing house, but they specialize in literature like this, and I think if they push it right... Oh Beth this is the beginning for you...and for us. Our new script together."

Beth fell back into the cushions. Her whole body went numb. She didn't know what to feel.

"This is good news," Dawn said.

"When...When...?"

Dawn plopped beside her on the couch and let her leg brush against Beth's. "I sent it in right after our day at the river. I knew you'd come round to submitting eventually, and I thought it would be a wonderful surprise if I could take you somewhere and whip the letter out."

"So you did it all without telling me...or asking me?" Coming on the heels of the previous conversation, the miraculous appearance of this letter jabbed hard at her.

"Yes. I was trying to protect you. I mean, there was a chance that they'd reject it, and I didn't want you to get hurt or lose your nerve. I know you're going to be great someday. I'm sure of it in that way I know things. But if they didn't accept it, I didn't want you to quit before you even got started."

Dawn always knew just when to pull out the writing card. Beth glanced down at the letter. She held it so tightly that the edge was crumpled, but the words leapt up at her. *Far better than pulp fiction. Underground hit. A new, astonishing voice in the secret lives of women.* She wanted what the letter promised with an almost visceral need, but it was addressed to Dawn, not to her. She was the contact person.

"Have you gotten back to them?"

"No. I was waiting for you."

A hundred thoughts swirled in her brain and crashed into each other. Did Dawn only stay to control *Heartwood*? Or had she thrown away her own future for one they could share? Would she ever know what Dawn's real rationale was? She clenched her fists on her lap as the rush of emotions from the whole day threatened to overwhelm her.

"You're happy about this, right?" Dawn's voice was husky with feeling.

When she looked at Dawn, it was as if the veil had been rent. Beth saw her as if for the first time. She was still lovely beyond measure, but a wariness sat at the edges of her eyes.

It had probably always been there; Beth just hadn't noticed until now. At some point since they had walked downstairs, the power had shifted, and now she held some of it in her own hands.

Her fists uncurled on her lap. The palms held angry red marks from her nails digging into them.

She had sold her novel!

A calmness like heavy water spread over her. If she had to grow up and sell her soul a little to grab success, where was the harm? Especially since the price bought her a front seat in this relationship.

"Well, are you happy?" Dawn asked.

"Yes. I am." The answer felt right rolling off her tongue; her voice carried with it a new maturity.

Dawn dropped her head on Beth's shoulder. "We should write back to Titanium Pages in the morning. Let them know and start this ball rolling."

"Okay," Beth said. Exhaustion spread through her. Suddenly, she was tired beyond words. "Come on." She got up from the couch. "We should go to bed. It's been a long day...for both of us."

Later that night, Beth woke up shivering and searched for the covers. She found them at the foot of the bed and pulled them up to her chin only to realize that she and Dawn were on opposite sides of the mattress. Normally, she snuggled up to Dawn, her front to Dawn's back. The warmth that their togetherness generated was enough to keep them toasty all night long. But tonight there was at least a foot of space between them.

Dawn reached out and interlaced her fingers with Beth's. Even in sleep, she seemed to know what Beth was thinking. Dawn's hand was soft and warm, and despite the dark thoughts that still swirled in her mind, Beth squeezed it before she drifted back to sleep.

In the morning, Beth was the first one up. She slid from the bed as not to wake Dawn and headed downstairs. The letter still sat on the coffee table, and she read it again, this time savoring the praise and letting the excitement finally take root. This could be the beginning for her. She had so many stories in her head, and who knew what might happen?

Dawn moved around in the bedroom upstairs, and Beth made her way into the kitchen to put the kettle on for coffee.

A shrill ring pierced the air. The phone in the den echoed all the way into the kitchen. It could only be Jimmy this early; Dawn's footsteps took the stairs two at a time to catch the call.

"Hello?" Dawn's voice was breathless from the trot down the steps.

Yesterday, Beth would've hurriedly made the coffee, run a cup in to Dawn, and hung out by the door so she could eavesdrop. Today that story had changed. She pulled out two mugs as well as the milk and sugar for Dawn and escaped to the back porch while the water boiled.

A cool morning breeze drifted through the trees, and she turned toward it, letting the air dance around her face as she waited.

Dawn eventually slid the screen door open and joined her on the porch. "That was Jimmy."

"I gathered." The space between them was at least a couple of feet. Lovers or strangers who didn't really know each other? It was still unclear.

"They've three weeks left on set, and then he's coming back."

"That's two weeks shy of when the baby's due."

"Yes, he says he wants to be here when his son is born."

"And if it's a girl?" The baby rose up before her for the first time as an actual future person.

"I'm not sure if that would be better or worse." Dawn drummed her fingers on the porch railing. "Look, we need to talk."

"Yeah, we do," Beth said.

"If we want to stay together, we should figure out a plan."

"Is that what you want?"

"I do, Beth. You got to believe me." Dawn slid toward her.

Beth fought the urge to slide even closer. "Why?"

"A thousand reasons, no reasons at all. I just do." Another one of her non-answers.

"We can't just take off. There's the baby."

"Yeah, I know. I'm too recognizable to have a baby in some out-of-the-way hospital, and Jimmy will have the law and public opinion on his side if he wants to take the baby after it's born." Dawn's fingers flicked restlessly on the railing.

"I'm not moving down to LA to hide as your assistant, if that's what you're thinking," Beth said. "I hated it yesterday, and we can't weather any more secrets, I don't think."

"Oh…okay." Dawn wrapped her arms around her chest, either to protect herself from the chill or the conversation; Beth couldn't tell.

They both stared out into the forest for a moment.

"I just thought… Maybe…" Dawn started slowly, clearly thinking out loud. "You could take all that money upstairs.

Move somewhere as a writer. That should keep you going for a while. I could come visit you."

"On what? Quickie vacations when you don't have a movie or press tour?" Beth asked.

"Or even better I could come with you."

"To live? With the baby?"

"I have to get away from Jimmy. You have a better idea?" Dawn looked at her for a real answer. This wouldn't have happened twenty-four hours ago. Everything had changed.

"Where were you going to go with the passport upstairs?"

"Somewhere in South America, Brazil maybe. Where it would be easier to hide. But that ship has sailed now that I am so close to delivery."

"I know. I was just wondering. I'm not sure there's a good answer."

"You don't want to call it quits, do you?"

Dawn had finally been brave enough to say it out loud. They had been circling around the simplest answer since the moment Beth had found Dawn's stash upstairs. Now that the question had been thrown in Beth's court, a weight lifted from her shoulders. It would be so much easier to go their separate ways. Not deal with a baby or a relationship that was as much pain as pleasure.

She could run away to New York and Titanium Pages and truly find herself there. There had to be real estate offices in the Big Apple. She could plod along in a day job and write at night. It actually sounded romantic in a starving artist kind of way.

"No." The answer surprised her. It came from her heart, not her head. "There has got to be some other way."

Dawn's deep sigh was better than any answer she could've actually voiced. Or maybe it was an answer Beth could read what she wanted into. Most, though not all, of the doubt melted away, and she draped an arm around Dawn's shoulders. She was freezing.

"Let's go back inside. I'm sure the water's boiling by now." She turned Dawn back into the house. It felt good to be driving the relationship even in this small way.

They spent all morning at the kitchen table. The answer they finally came up with was the one that had already been in play. They would hold their relationship over Jimmy's head. Threaten to go public as a couple if he didn't give Dawn her freedom, at least behind the scenes.

"That's a big chance to take," Beth said. "What if it backfires? What if he says no?"

"If we play it right, it shouldn't." Dawn sat clutching her coffee mug, but the sparkle had crept back into her eyes. "Jimmy's public image is as a man's man, an all-around beefcake. What if it comes out that he can't even keep his wife satisfied? Or maybe…we can threaten to tell the press that this really is a marriage of convenience. And that he likes men…and we're married to keep each other's secrets." She tapped the empty mug against the table. "Oh yes. That's better. We should go with that."

"Are you sure? I don't think we should go that far. There's an awful lot that can go wrong with just the first part. I mean, this relationship is true after all. And what would this truth do to your career?"

"We wouldn't have to worry about this. Not if we play it right!" Dawn nodded as she revved up. "Jimmy is a terrified little kid inside. All we've got to do is get the jump on him. He's only any good when he's in control. All we got to do is make him think we're going to do it. Acting 101."

"I don't know if I can—"

Dawn slapped her hand on the table, oddly reminiscent of Jimmy that first night. "What if we both move to New York? You would be closer to your publishing house, and I could pursue Broadway. No, wait. Live television. You know how many shows they film out there? I could totally reinvent myself." She looked at Beth and added quickly, "And you could write. Not as my assistant. As an artist in your own right."

Despite herself, Beth got caught up in Dawn's excitement. "That I could do. If I really want to be someone, I would have to write a different type of book, not about the secret lives of women." God, was she really considering this?

"You could absolutely do that! Publish *Heartwood* under a different name, and write more mainstream books on the side under your real name." Dawn's whole face lit up as if the plan had already proven to be a wild success.

"Like what?" Beth took in a quick breath. For goodness's sake. She *was* considering it.

"Whatever you want. What about those kids' books you're always going on about with the tiger and the magic cabinet?"

"It's a lion and a wardrobe."

"Whatever. It's all make-believe anyway. You could make up whatever world you want."

"I do like fantasy. But I can't compete with those books."

"Then don't. Go for a younger age group. Before they reach those books."

"That's actually not a bad idea." Beth nodded as the notion sank in.

"I really think this could work. And when you're done writing the kids' fantasy world, you could write one for us. Where women get their happily ever after—together. Imagine that. It's about time."

Beth reached across the table to grab her hand. "I'd rather live it than write it."

"We'd still have to be careful. And we'd have to get the studio to create a new story. Maybe a love affair on the set for Jimmy—like Elizabeth Taylor and Richard Burton. He could ride it all the way to the bank. Oh yes, Beth. I'd rather live it too!"

Dawn got up from the kitchen table and pulled Beth with her. "Come on, then. Let's go call Titanium and tell them the good news. It's nearly noon in New York, and we have a lot of work to do."

The phone was practically glued to Dawn's ear for the next week. She made calls first to Titanium Pages, then her agent and finally her friends in New York. Things fell into place surprisingly fast. Within days, a contract for Elizabeth T. Rusco came from Titanium Pages. Just for show, Beth took Dawn out to the beach at the river where they first made love to sign it. Beth insisted on a name that combined all their various names, real and imaginary, and even made Dawn sign the T onto the contract herself.

Dawn somehow found an available sublet on the Upper East Side of Manhattan with three bedrooms—one for each of them, to keep the story kosher—and wired money for the deposit. Her agent had a lead on a new comedy for NBC that shot at Uptown Studios. The role was another zany housewife with a heart of gold. Now that advertisers were coming out of the woodwork to get her to sponsor diapers and baby bottles, he was sure it would be perfect for her. Dawn told Beth about each offer with increasing confidence. Beth completely fell into Dawn's mood, kicking away that little voice that was telling her to still watch out.

They made one last trip into San Francisco to the baby doctor, throwing out baby names the whole way.

"It's going to be a girl," Dawn said.

"How can you possibly know that?"

"I just know. What about Patricia or Mabel?" Dawn asked.

"Or we could do flower names. Like Violet or Poppy."

"Or Rhododendron. When you came to dinner that first night, that was the flower you brought. Right?"

"Yes." Beth reached across the bench seat to rest a hand on Dawn's leg. "You remembered."

"Of course I remember. We can call her Rhoda to commemorate that night." She squeezed Beth's hand.

"We can't name her after a fast-growing shrub. It's silly."

They shared a laugh. "I don't care what we call her," Dawn said, "Just as long as it isn't some form of James."

At the appointment, Dr. Hoffman stroked his white beard. "Two more weeks and you should move closer to the hospital here in town. Just to be safe."

"Do we need to be worried?" Beth barged into the conversation. Usually, she just hovered in the background.

"No. The birth should all be very routine. Don't worry. You're not having the baby." He chuckled, his belly shaking with his laugh.

Beth packed up all her writing books and other possessions into boxes and dumped them into the back of her truck. She meant to take them back to her parents' house so she would still have access to them if the baby came early and the house was no longer open to her. But she never seemed to find the time, and they just sat in the bed of the truck. She did keep one notebook, though, by her at all times. The pages were filling up fast about Ameliah, a girl who wrote her secret wishes into a magic composition book at night and woke up the next morning to find them playing out in real life not at all how she expected.

She read Dawn to sleep every night with Ameliah's latest adventure.

"Don't stop." Her voice was light with laughter. "That's adorable."

"That's all I wrote today."

"Rhoda wants more."

"We're not calling the baby Rhoda."

"It's actually kind of growing on me." Dawn smiled, and Beth's heart melted.

"Do you really think this will work?" Beth asked. "Us? A baby? New York?"

"I do."

Dawn flipped over, and Beth snuggled up, spreading her arms around Dawn's stomach. Something tapped at her hand.

"Oh my God. Did you feel that?"

"Of course. You should feel it from the inside."

"Hello, not Rhoda." She buried her face into Dawn's hair. That little voice telling her to be careful was barely audible anymore. Was it possible that they had weathered the storm? "I love you," she said into Dawn's curls.

"I love you back."

Maybe the storm had rolled through and done its worst but hadn't broken them. Maybe Dawn was right. The future was theirs for the taking.

One morning a couple of days later, a loud pounding jolted them out of bed. It came from downstairs, the front door, and they threw on bathrobes and rushed down the stairs.

Dawn pulled open the door. "What the hell—" She stopped dead.

There on the front stoop was James Montgomery, as cool, calm, and collected as a Hollywood superstar should be. He smiled like a snake that had slithered out of the grass.

"You know, I didn't believe it," he said. "When that woman called and told me what was going on out here, I didn't believe it. I told her not my Dawn."

Beth took a step back. What woman?

"Nope. I told her my Dawn, if she knew what was good for her, would never disrespect me like that. But clearly..." He let the words hang in the air so the venom could drip off them.

"Jimmy!" Dawn stiffened. "What are you doing here? Shouldn't you still be on the set?"

"We wrapped. It's in the can. Dailies look good. Especially yours truly. It's going to be a big, big hit."

"But you said on the phone..."

"You're up to something. I said what I needed to keep you put."

Dawn staggered back, and Beth instinctively put out an arm to catch her. She pulled it back at the last second before it grazed the back of Dawn's robe. Too late. James had caught the action.

"Looks like your mother knew what she was talking about."

His words registered with a blow. "My mother?" Beth asked.

"Yeah, she got a message to me all the way in Italy. How I don't know. She's got some follow-through, that woman. I should get her on my publicity team. I called her back. We had a nice chat, although what we were talking about was truly abhorrent."

Now it was Beth's turn to stagger back. What did he mean? Her mother was the cause of this horrible moment? Surely not.

He turned his attention to Dawn. "I thought we were done with all this."

"Jimmy, stop—"

"She does this all the time. Goes off on little dalliances. Men, normally. There have been some babes. I guess now it's whoever's at hand, really. All she needs is to be adored." He threw out his arm as if to discount everything that had happened in the last seven months. "She didn't tell you that part, did she? Well, managing people and their expectations is a huge part of the excitement for her. I should know."

"Don't believe him. I told you he enjoys being cruel."

Cruel or not, if what Jimmy was saying was true, he already knew about Dawn's tendencies. Dawn had never told her that part. Omissions were as bad as lies. The plan was never going to work. How could Dawn not have seen that?

"We enjoy being cruel to each other," he said. "That's our thing. But, you know, she must actually like you on some level. Usually, this is where she walks away."

"Beth, don't listen. It's not true. He's just stirring up trouble between us. Don't you see? This is how he wins."

James, as if he didn't have a care in the world, ambled back to the Corvette in the driveway, opened the door, and rooted around in the car.

"It's like a game of chicken," Dawn said. "We can't be the first to back down or give up. Jimmy's bluffing."

"Gotcha." James pulled out a magazine with a bright red cover. He set the keys on the hood of the car while he flipped through the pages.

"Beth, come back inside. Don't listen to him. He will ruin everything." Dawn reached out a hand, but Beth took a step across the threshold to the front stoop and shuddered. She literally stood in between husband and wife, a position that she had been in since the beginning. Every single doubt about Dawn and their relationship came rushing back and dug in tight.

"Oh, here it is." James held the magazine open to a story for Beth. "Look."

She hesitated so long that he thrust it into her hands. Even so, she held it just with her fingertips. Dawn with her hair up and big, glittery earrings jumped off the page. She was in a party dress, at a premiere Beth gathered, but the headline read: *The Lowdown on Dawn Montgomery's Night Out... Without Her Husband.*

Beth scanned the article. It spoke to Dawn carousing at a club downtown.

"See, you probably thought you were special. Nope. You're just a new kind of fun."

"That's not true." Dawn snatched the magazine out of her hands. "For Christ's sake, Jimmy, we both know that we went to that club to pick up your grass and God knows what else. Have you forgotten that I'm the discreet one?"

Beth flashed on herself dumping all the magazines in the outside bin at home. "Is that why you wanted me to get rid of everything months ago? Because you didn't want me to see stories like that? What, you thought I'd be an easier target that way?"

"I told you it was all different in the beginning." Dawn's voice cracked with emotion. "Besides, it's not true. The studio threw me at that rag in order to save him. They thought Jimmy, who can't act his way out of a paper bag, was the bigger star."

"That's good, baby. Really good. But save the acting for the cameras. Fun time's over. Come home to LA and have my son."

"Jimmy, shut up. I'll fight you if I have to, in the courts, in the magazines, but I'm staying here. With her. And if you try to take this baby from me when it's born, I'll go public with how you treat me and a thousand other things. I will lie through my teeth if I have to. No studio head will be able to get you out of the hot water this time. And no court will award you this child."

James's whole body went rigid, and his fist curled into a ball at his side. "Dawn. Don't do this. You'll be sorry. You're really going to throw your career away?"

Dawn said nothing. Her hands were balled up against her side in a weird mirror image of his fists.

"Over this short, little nothing of a chick?"

"Yes."

But Beth had seen what Dawn hadn't said. The brief look of uncertainty that slid over her face before she opened her mouth. The slight shuffle in her feet after she had closed it. Beth screwed her eyes shut so she couldn't see anything else. The doubts raged in her like a whirlwind.

What it came down to was she had no idea whether Dawn really loved her. Dawn for sure hated Jimmy, but that wasn't at all the same thing. She loved Dawn; she really did. She probably would never love anyone else the way she loved this woman standing two feet away from her. But was love supposed to turn your family against you? Rip you apart and shatter you into tiny pieces?

She opened her eyes. "I can't be a pawn in this game between you anymore."

Dawn's mouth dropped open. James grinned, showing each of his perfect teeth.

Beth licked her lips, trying to find the words to explain, but nothing came.

"Beth, please. You can't possibly think—"

"I don't know what to think anymore. That's the problem. You need to figure this out." She darted inside to the side table in the foyer, where they kept the car keys. One set for her truck and another for the El Dorado still in the garage. Fumbling, she knocked all the keys to the ground and then bent over to grab hers.

"What are you doing? You can't leave me."

"I can't stay either." Tears flooded her eyes as she looked at Dawn. "I just need time to think."

"Don't leave me with him. I need you to stay strong. For me. For us." Dawn's breath quickened.

Beth needed to get out of there. Now. If Dawn started crying, her resolve would vanish. She dashed for her truck.

Dawn grabbed for her arm as she slid by her, but Beth, for the first time in their relationship, twisted away from her touch.

James laughed at the show in front of him. His cackle came at her as she slid the key into the ignition and threw the car into reverse. She just barely slammed on the brakes before she backed into the Corvette. He had completely boxed her in.

"Beth! Stop," Dawn cried out.

She shifted the car into drive and pulled onto the unpaved service road right off the driveway. She had no idea where it led or if it was even passable, but this was her only out. Gunning the engine, she flew down the road. The truck careened over potholes and through low-hanging branches before finally hitting the main road.

A right-hand turn took her away from town and everything she knew. At some point she would have to deal with the betrayal from her mother and from Dawn, but that was way in the future. Now she was just running.

As luck would have it, her boxes still bounced around in the truck's bed. She had her notebooks, a stash of clothes, and all that money rolled up in rubber bands. She would use it to set up a new life and then pay Dawn back.

The road stretched out ahead of her, winding in and out of the forest and eventually ending at the Pacific Ocean. She took the first turn too hard and slid sideways into the dirt. Her wheels spun out of control for an instant before they grabbed the road again.

Slow down. Slow down. She had to make it to the coast in one piece. What then?

There was that inn right on the coast. She could stop there, change out of her pajamas, and make a plan that went beyond remembering to breathe. She lifted her foot off the accelerator, and the trees around her returned to solid forms. She drove on slowly, trying not to think about anything but the road ahead of her and putting distance between her and what she had left behind at Fern House. She was having a hard time voicing Dawn's name even in her own head.

Out of nowhere a streak of blue came at her in the rearview mirror. James's Corvette zoomed down the road, slipping erratically into the dirt bank on the edge of the street with every turn.

What the hell? Were they coming after her?

The Corvette started honking.

Beth dropped her foot back onto the accelerator and sped away.

The sports car was thrown into another gear—badly, the whine of the transmission so loud it echoed in the cab of her truck.

Beth watched it in the rearview mirror. It was swerving all over the road. The person at its wheel was in imminent danger of losing all control.

Another car, this one bright red, rounded a curve behind the Corvette. She would recognize the big fins anywhere. The El Dorado from the garage. Two cars. Two drivers.

Dawn was driving? But James had said she couldn't drive. No. The conversation flooded back into Beth's mind. She had said later that she was a terrible driver. *A car crash waiting to happen.*

The Corvette slid dangerously near a redwood on the shoulder.

No! Beth pumped her brakes. She had to slow down, to help her.

The Corvette slowed as well, righting itself to the road.

The El Dorado took advantage and pulled alongside the Corvette. James was honking, and Beth could see in the rearview mirror that he was motioning for Dawn to pull over.

Dawn gunned her engine, and the Corvette charged ahead.

James swerved toward her, trying to cut her off.

Dawn must have jerked at the wheel to get away from him, because the Corvette veered one way and then the other.

A loud skidding noise filled the air. Beth hit her brakes hard, and her truck slid to a stop. She craned her head around.

The Corvette was up on two wheels, careening dangerously toward a tree on the side of the road. With a deafening smack, the car crashed into the tree, unbelievably righted itself, and swung back onto the road, still moving out of control.

Beth swung her door open, leapt out of the car, and began to run back up to Dawn.

James jammed on his brakes, sliding down the road. He skidded past the moving Corvette and right into Beth's path.

Holy shit! She jumped out of the way, and the car slid by. It missed her only by inches. She came down hard on her ankle. Pain shot through her as she twisted and fell.

The Corvette ran across the road and smashed hard into another tree. Glass flew in the air. A wrenching sound of metal being torn off the car filled the air. The front of the Corvette crumpled as if it were made of paper.

"Dawn!" Beth struggled to her feet. Her ankle screamed in response, and the pain ran all the way up her body. She dropped back down to the ground and began to crawl, trailing James, who was also on the move. A burning smell like acid assaulted her nose as she came closer. And then the worst noise imaginable drifted over.

A moan—full of pain and agony…and regret. It was soft, but it cut right through the chaos.

Beth dragged herself to the car and pulled herself up on a door handle, using it like a crutch. Empty. The moaning rose again. She spun, fighting another jolt of pain, to find its source.

Dawn, thrown from the convertible during the crash, lay on the ground, her leg jutting out at an unnatural angle.

She took a step toward Dawn, but her ankle wouldn't hold. She crumpled to the ground.

James was already by her side, bending down to her. "Get away." His voice was a low hiss. "See what you've done to her!"

Beth fought to breathe as panic surged over the pain in her body. Oh my God! If she hadn't jumped out of the way, he would have killed her.

Dawn's eyes fluttered open, and she raised a hand. "Beth?"

James slid his arms under Dawn's body, staggered to his feet, and began to carry his wife to the El Dorado.

As they passed, Dawn reached out toward her.

But Beth couldn't move, rooted to the ground by the stabbing pain in her ankle and the crushing weight of the guilt pushing down on her.

James slipped Dawn into the back of the Cadillac and, without even a backward glance, sped off down the road back toward town.

All she could manage was a half crawl, more like a drag to the side of the road. Her whole leg contorted in pain, but the rest of her was numb. Her heart and her head had both balled into little leaden weights that would not crack.

She sat in the dirt, how long she had no idea, watching her ankle swell up to three times its size; black and blue marks spread like ink under the skin.

At some point, a man pulled his van right up to her and rushed out. "Oh my goodness, miss. Are you all right?" He bent down to her. The briny scent of the ocean clung to him.

"No," she said so quietly he had to tilt closer. "I shouldn't have left her with him."

Chapter 11

"I GOT THEM! THEY'RE HERE!" The big woman from the bakery flew gracefully between the people coming in the front door and standing by the stairs.

Nikka jumped back to avoid the collision.

The woman slid to a stop and thrust the set of boxes at Todd Mason, who waited in front of the dining room. His face was so red, he looked as if he would explode.

"About time."

When Nikka rounded the corner, reporters, bloggers, and other invited guests mingled in the living room. Their grumblings were getting louder by the minute.

Things had gone from bad to worse this morning. She had no idea what was happening with the cupcakes or, more importantly, the microphone and a badly wired mot-box on the podium, whatever that was. Thankfully, the culinary and audio issues were out of her hands. What was firmly in them, however, were Lea's problems. The press conference should have already started; there wasn't adequate parking, and the reporters' deadlines loomed large on this Friday afternoon.

And where was Lea? Not in the hallway that connected the living room to the foyer. The half-bath on the far side of the foyer was taped off and also empty.

Alison, Lea's assistant, bolted from her post at the stairway and rushed up to Nikka. "Oh my God. The executive from KPAC just stormed out."

"Shit! Go see how close we are to starting." Nikka steered Alison toward the dining room at the end of the hallway, opposite the living room, where Todd stood still fuming. "I'll find Lea to see why she's not at the podium."

"Lea said not to leave the stairs or the front door unattended."

"Forget the front door. I'm going upstairs. I'll keep watch."

Alison furrowed her brow.

"We have got to get this show on the road. Go."

Alison trotted down the hallway as Nikka took the stairs two at a time. At the extraordinary sight that greeted her, she skidded to a stop.

In the middle of the hallway, Lea stood with her back to Nikka and held Vivienne tightly in her arms. The older woman had her head nestled in the crook of Lea's neck, trying to catch her breath.

"Look. Don't panic," Lea said. "She just has to stand there."

Nikka couldn't make out Vivienne's response.

"Just find a way," Lea said. "I'll read the statement first."

Nikka darted into the first open door—an office with a daybed. She stood still as a mouse to hear every word being said out in the hallway.

"Take a deep breath, and I'll take you back in there myself. I know it's hard, but we can do it. We're a team."

"Promise?" Vivienne's response was more sniffling than words.

"I do."

Fabric rustled. More hugging? Stroking? Surely not kissing. Nikka shivered at the thought of any part of her own body touching Vivienne's. The sniffling grew softer until a door opened and closed. After creeping out into the hallway, she stood there alone for a moment and tried to process what she had just seen and heard. Before she could, the door to Beth's room opened, and Lea slipped out.

"Ah." She locked on to Nikka. "Are we ready downstairs?"

"Alison is finding out. But the natives are getting restless."

"Okay. Let's go." Lea pulled down on the hem of her suit jacket, yanking out the wrinkles where Vivienne's head had been.

"Is everything okay in there?" Nikka motioned to the door.

"I hope so." She leaned in to Nikka as she passed. "Vivienne's gone round the bend. We need to find a replacement for her as soon as we can."

What the hell? Either she or Vivienne was being played here. She was pretty sure it was Vivienne. In fact, she would bet her salary for a lifetime that there would be beach weather in Siberia before Vivienne and Lea were a couple. Lea was probably just telling Vivienne what she needed to get through the day. This was her business after all.

Alison and Todd Mason waited for them at the bottom of the stairs. "Ms. Truman. I'm so sorry, but we are finally ready."

Lea turned to Nikka. "How do I look?"

Nikka ran an appraising glance up and down her boss. Black skirt and jacket with a lacy camisole underneath. Professional, sexy, in control.

"Great."

"All right, then. Showtime." Lea strode into the hallway, only to turn around and stretch a hand back to Nikka. "Stand up there with me."

Nikka hesitated. What would Lea gain with Nikka up there?

"Opportunities like this don't come up every day." Lea seemed to channel Nikka's father.

She was right. Nikka could figure out why Lea wanted to share the podium later. She dropped her hand into Lea's. It was soft and warm and fit perfectly.

Lea squeezed her fingers and met Nikka's gaze with a half smile. "Come on. This can be your moment too. Our moment." She let go and strode toward the living room with a bounce in her step.

Nikka rushed after her to grab her future beside her boss.

Maggie needed to get into the house without being caught by Lea or Nikka. The back of the house was a perfect entry point. She could scale the deck off the kitchen that cantilevered into the forest. That way, she could peek into the kitchen without being seen, making sure she could slip inside without running into anyone who knew her. First, however, she made a quick detour to the bakery van and pulled a wrinkled Made From Scratch T-shirt out of the glove compartment. Her stash in case she ever forgot her work uniform for events, which happened more than she cared to admit. After yanking it over her head, she jogged to the back deck. She judged the climb. A foothold on the pier footing, a handhold on the joist and she could leap over the top rail. She was already in motion when a loud "stop!" cut through the air.

No! She couldn't be caught before she even got started!

Hanging off the joist, she looked down and saw, of all people, Josie Williams.

"I knew you were up to something." Josie crossed her arms.

"You're wrong. I'm not." Although swinging by one hand from the bottom of the deck clearly said otherwise.

"Bullshit. We both know they're checking press IDs at the front door. This is your way in."

"Okay," Maggie said. "You got me. What do you want?"

"I want to talk to Beth Walker."

"I can help you with that. But first you got to help me."

"With what?" Josie's tone turned cautious.

"This is a rescue. They're keeping her here against her will."

"For real?"

"Would I go to all this trouble if it weren't?" Maggie nodded up to her hand still clutching the joist.

"You could be crazy."

"But I'm not. For God's sake. You want in or not?"

"I do."

This Josie Williams was her kind of gal.

Polite applause filled the living room. Nikka radiated with pride as Lea stepped to the podium.

Lea looked out at her audience and met as many gazes as she could. "I still love you," she said softly, but the microphone, finally working, carried the words to every part of the room. "God knows I've tried to stop. Tried to cut you out of my heart, but every time I look around or fall asleep, I see you. Still with me, like a ghost, haunting me with your betrayal."

Lea paused dramatically; the audience, so restless only minutes earlier, leaned in as one to hear what she would say next. Who knew she was such a great actress?

"Obviously not my words. I'm very fond of you all, but we'll have to get to know each other better before we can call it love."

The audience chuckled. She had them.

"No surprise here, those were Beth Walker's words, written to the love of her life in letters that she never sent. But now, thankfully, we all can read them." Lea held out her hand.

A tall librarian-looking woman stood up from the first row and handed Lea a pair of old, tattered composition notebooks.

A unified gasp came from the people in the room.

"Sorry." Lea laughed. "These aren't the real notebooks from *Don't Waste Your Wishes* although we're still looking for those. That's the next press conference, we hope."

More laughter from the audience.

"This is... Let me first thank Lynne Davis from Kerry and Collier for an amazing partnership on this venture. This is *Beth Walker Revealed*."

She nodded at the woman who had handed her the books. "A couple of months ago, we found these documents at a local bank in a safe-deposit box that had come up for renewal. As legal representative of the Walker estate, Truman and Steinbrecker opened the box, expecting nothing, and instead found a treasure beyond belief. These are the originals of the love letters to a Hollywood starlet who died in a mysterious car crash only a few miles from where we are right now. We've all speculated about who Beth Walker drew on as the basis of her *Heartwood* couple, Daisy and Bonnie, and whether there was inside knowledge, if you get my drift. And now, after all this time, we finally have our answer."

She paused to let the drama build. "Yes, tell everyone you heard it here first, folks. Beth was madly, passionately in love with Dawn Montgomery, the breathtakingly beautiful star of such movies as *Drop in the Bucket* and *Summer's Day*, wife to superstar James Montgomery, who lost his battle with cancer last year, and as these letters will chronicle in exciting...and intimate detail, lover to a young Beth Walker."

Once on the deck, Maggie peeked in the kitchen.

Only the catering staff bustled around inside, so Maggie buzzed through the kitchen porch doors as if she owned the house. The staff froze until Maggie tapped the bakery logo on her chest. "Made From Scratch. We did the cupcakes. These the extras?" She pointed to a three-tier stand on the counter, filled with cupcakes.

"Ah...yeah," a woman in a white chef's coat answered.

Maggie edged by her, grabbed a small plate out of a cabinet by the fridge, and then snatched a Lemon Lover off the stand. "Thanks. I just need one." Her motions were so confident in a kitchen she knew like the back of her hand, the staff immediately scooted out of her way.

Yes, she was in!

Everyone was crammed into the living room, listening to Lea, except one young woman posted by the stairs.

Maggie winced. Of course, Lea would have that base covered.

She scurried by the living room door and eased up to her with the cupcake. "Hi. Lea Truman told me to take this up to Ms. Walker before she comes down."

"Sorry, no one gets up the stairs."

Maggie shrugged. "Ms. Truman's orders."

"She would've told me. I'm her assistant, after all." The girl rose up on her tiptoes, clearly searching for someone in charge.

Maggie's throat constricted. If she even made eye contact with anyone who had power, there would only be two seconds until total implosion.

Think. Think. Think. Maggie had nothing. *Wait a minute... Assistant? Yes! Thank you, Harlan.* "Yeah, I know. Alison, right? Look, go talk to Ms. Truman if you want." She motioned in the direction of Lea's voice, knowing fully well that Alison wouldn't dare interrupt her boss now. "I'll just be at the bedroom at the end of the hall." Maggie didn't wait for an answer. She started up the stairs, hoping that Alison would crumble in the face of all her inside knowledge.

No shout called her back as she bounded up the stairs.

Adrenaline rushed through her body. She could get used to success like this.

"What the hell are you doing here?"

She had celebrated too soon. Maggie took in the situation with one glance.

Vivienne, holding Beth by the arm, loomed before her in the hallway. When Beth saw Maggie, she tried to pivot out of Vivienne's grasp, but Vivienne was clutching her way too tightly.

"What am I doing here? What I should have done the last time we were in this position." Maggie set the cupcake and plate on a side table and made straight for Vivienne. She grabbed her thumb in the perfect self-defense move, yanked her hand away from Beth, and twisted her wrist and arm up behind her back in one smooth motion.

"Hey!"

"Hush. Not a word." She yanked up Vivienne's arm, and Vivienne whimpered in pain. "You don't want to mess with me. I'm probably already on my way to jail, so I've got nothing to lose."

Beth grabbed a nearby door handle to steady herself as Maggie strong-armed Vivienne back down the hall toward Beth's room.

Maggie shoved her through the doorway and held out her hand. "Keys?"

Vivienne's look went to a nearby table. The keys sat on its surface. She lunged, both hands out, but Maggie, who had followed her gaze, was faster. She snatched the keys first, and Vivienne's fingers curled over empty air.

Quickly, Maggie shut the door in Vivienne's face. "Payback's a bitch." With a grim smile, she locked her in and spun to Beth.

"They lock me in. Make me take drugs," Beth said, her voice shaking. "Are you here to help me?"

"Yes." Maggie laced her arm through Beth's and directed her to the stairs. "I'm sorry it took me so long."

At the landing, she peeked down the stairs.

Alison was still guarding her post, but she wasn't facing them or the front door. Her attention was directed to the living room and Lea's speech. She was edging closer toward it with Lea's every word.

The front door opened a few inches.

Maggie froze on the top step, her arm around Beth.

If a guard or reporter stepped through that door, they would discover her and Beth in an instant.

But instead, Josie peered through the gap and flicked her head up in acknowledgment.

Maggie released the breath she'd been holding. She crept from stair to stair, guiding Beth in what became an excruciating trip. One creaking step and they would be caught.

Seconds seemed to stretch into years. Would they ever make it down?

Lea picked up a paper that was already on the podium. "In a statement that Ms. Walker wrote when she heard we were having the press conference, she states, 'I believed that these letters and all my early notebooks in fact were gone or misplaced, and since the events portrayed here are of such a personal nature, I finally asked people I depend on and have faith in...'" Lea smiled broadly and pointed to herself. "That's me. 'And they assured me that people might be interested to see what such an emotional time was like for me.'"

A murmur went through the room.

Lea glanced first at Nikka and then to her audience. "Interesting to say the least. Aren't we all thrilled beyond belief that something new by Beth Walker is about to hit the stands?"

Nikka looked out at the sea of nodding people in the audience.

Lea placed the statement back onto the podium and ran her hands over it, giving the reporters a moment to digest the news.

Nikka watched her, taking careful note of everything she did.

Lea met her gaze and raised her eyebrows in an unspoken sign of victory.

Nikka couldn't help it; she smiled. Everyone stared at them, waiting for Lea's next words. Someday, it would be her standing at the podium—her father was right—as a managing partner in Truman, Steinbrecker, and Vaskin.

"Let me bring in the author herself for a brief photo opportunity only. Ms. Walker is not up to answering any questions at this time. Lynne Davis and I will be happy to take your questions once Ms. Walker retires."

Lea looked to the doorway of the living room. Her eyes narrowed.

Nikka followed her gaze.

The threshold to the hallway was completely empty.

Nikka started. Where the hell were Vivienne and Walker?

Lea's hand covered the microphone as she leaned toward Nikka. "Get Walker down here. Now!"

"I'm on it." Nikka casually made her way to the back of the room, looking as if she were out for an evening stroll. Last thing she wanted to do was capture anyone's attention. Fat chance. She wasn't even out of the living room before a reporter grabbed her sleeve.

He fixed her with a probing stare. "Where is Beth Walker?"

Crap.

Maggie blew out a breath as Beth's foot finally hit the bottom landing. Just a few more yards until they were out the door and she would have pulled off a rescue for the record books.

"Is there a reason why Ms. Walker isn't here?" A man's voice reached her, followed by footsteps.

Josie, eyes wide, quickly pulled her head back and closed the front door.

Maggie half carried and half dragged Beth into the tiny bathroom at the edge of the foyer. She closed the door just in time, but not before Nikka, followed by several reporters, turned into the hallway. Had she seen them?

Three steps out of the living room, Nikka nearly slammed into Alison. "Why aren't you by the stairs?" She barreled around her. "Never mind. Just don't let anyone up after me."

The door at the end of the hallway was locked. She pounded on it as loudly as she dared. "Vivienne. Are you in there? Open up!" she said in a stage whisper.

"I can't." Vivienne's words were two loud sobs. "The keys are gone. And so is Beth."

Nikka's mouth went dry. "What do you mean *gone?*"

Maggie pressed her ear to the closed bathroom door. Voices filled the foyer.

Beth brought a shaky hand to her forehead; Maggie circled her arm tighter around Beth's waist. She was holding up more than half the woman's weight now.

Come on, Josie. Come on!

"Oh my God," Josie cried out. "There is a bee on me. I'm allergic! Get it off! Get it off!"

Yes. Good girl. Maggie took a chance and opened the door a sliver to see what was going on.

Josie was in the foyer, spinning around as if looking for the culprit.

Two men and a woman rushed over to help.

She flapped her hands and dragged them away from the bathroom. "It's gone. I think it's gone. Did it sting me?" She pulled her top down off her shoulder, giving everyone a wonderful view of her cherry blossom tattoo, especially its branches that disappeared into her cleavage. "Is that something here?" She ran a hand down from her neck to her chest. "It feels like it's stinging."

Everyone stepped in closer. Even Alison came off her post to check her out.

In the bathroom, Maggie bit back her smile. The classic sexy girl as a distraction. And an impressive rendition at that. The girl had the chops to pull it off.

Maggie cinched Beth to her, eased out of the bathroom, and made her escape under the noses of all Josie's good Samaritans.

Once outside, she dug into her pocket for the keys to the Saab still parked at the edge of the driveway.

Two beeps and the locks popped open. Maggie let out a long breath. They were going to make it.

"Come again?" Nikka asked. "I can't hear you. Something's going on downstairs." The commotion was probably connected to Beth. That was where she needed to be. She turned down the hallway.

"Maggie took her."

Nikka stopped dead. "Maggie Chalon? The woman who used to work here?"

"Yes," Vivienne said behind the closed door.

How could she have been so stupid? She should have known Maggie was behind all this the second Beth wasn't where she was supposed to be.

She raced down the stairs.

Several people were crowded around a blonde girl with a tattoo.

What is she doing here? A question for another day. Nikka rushed out the front door and blinked hard. What the hell?

Beth Walker, all alone, wove her way through the parked cars in the driveway. Her steps were unsteady, but determined as she headed to the far side of the driveway.

"Stop!" Nikka called out as she dashed to her.

At the call, Beth picked up her pace.

Now Nikka saw where she was going. A beat-up Saab was trying, unsuccessfully, to back out of the gridlock in the driveway.

"Ms. Walker." Nikka grabbed her arm as much to steady her as to take possession of her. "They're expecting you inside. Please come with me."

"I will not." Beth's voice was hoarse; her body shook with a slight tremor.

The front door of the house opened. Alison popped her head out for a second, took in the situation, and then pulled back sharply.

"Let her go!" A voice rang out.

Nikka recognized it instantly.

Maggie Chalon burst out of the Saab, clearly breaking the restraining order. Was she going through with her plan to kidnap Beth Walker? Under all of their noses? Surely, she couldn't be that stupid.

"You shouldn't be here," Nikka said.

"I was right!" Maggie rushed over and got right in Nikka's face. "They lock her inside the bedroom, and they make her take drugs she doesn't want."

"Shit." Nikka shook her head even though she had direct evidence that both claims were one hundred percent true.

"Come on. I know you wanted to help when you came to see me the other day. Here's your chance." Maggie glanced over to the front door. "We don't have much time."

As if on cue, Lea, followed by Alison, Lynne Davis, and a dozen reporters, poured out of the house. Lea threw out both arms, preventing them from descending into the driveway. "Nikka," she said calmly, "Ms. Walker should come in for her photographs now."

Everyone focused on Beth, who was trying to pull herself out of Nikka's grasp.

Raising her free hand in the air, Nikka acknowledged Lea and the others on the stoop. "She's a little confused. She's coming." If she could convince the author to return to the press conference, she could come out the hero of this situation and embrace all sorts of opportunities.

Maggie was on her in an instant. "That's the wrong choice. They're bad people. Criminal, even."

"We can leave. There's a road over there." Beth shakily pointed a finger across the driveway. "Beyond that white car."

Nikka's Outback sat with its nose to what barely looked like a dirt path.

"Yes, but it's in terrible shape."

"I made it through once," Beth said.

"And you've got four-wheel drive, right? Let's go!" Maggie yanked on Nikka's blouse and inclined her head to the Subaru.

"Whoa! I'm not going anywhere." Nikka waved to the house and Lea. "Ms. Walker, please just come back inside. We can sort out whatever is bothering you."

"Not while Lea and Vivienne are there. Never again."

Nikka met Beth's gaze head-on. Panic, pain, and sheer determination shone from the older woman's eyes, but not an ounce of confusion or dementia. "I…I…" She tried to say *can't*, but the word simply wouldn't come out. Beth wasn't crazy, and whatever was going on here wasn't as simple as she had thought. The clues had been laid out for her. She just hadn't wanted to see them.

Breaking from Beth's stare, she looked back over to Lea, who was still holding back the reporters, while that tattoo girl was edging around the group. Lea's raised eyebrows and pursed lips said it all. *What are you doing? Get that woman over here.*

Nikka bit her lip. If she did that, she would move into an office right around from Lea's once they were back at work. Was she really going to throw a shiny future away on a knee-jerk reaction and an old woman's plea?

Everything around her seemed to freeze as if waiting for the answer. The people on the stoop, Lea, and Beth had fallen quiet; even the birds had stopped chirping. She had no answer.

"Nikka." Lea's voice cut through the silence like a knife. "We're a team."

And that was all it took. The same words she had said to Vivienne in the hallway upstairs, spoken in the same calculated and controlling tone.

She had been played. Not completely, she had a part in it too. She wanted what Lea offered almost more than anything, but not at the risk of losing her ethics, her decency, herself. The outside world came rushing back: the chatter from the people on the stoop, Lea calling out for her to come back, and the sound of birds in the trees.

"Please." Beth's soft plea pushed her over the edge.

Nikka reached into her suit pocket. The Outback's lights flashed yellow, and the door locks popped up.

"Yes!" Maggie slid her arm under Beth's elbow, led her to the passenger side, and carefully deposited her on the backseat.

On the stoop, Lea shouted into a walkie-talkie, probably for security.

Nikka only had a few minutes before the guards came pounding down the driveway and things got really crazy.

"Get in. Get in!" Maggie called from within the car. "They're coming!"

With a sinking heart, Nikka dropped into the driver's seat. Her finger hovered next to the *engine start/stop* button for one last moment. Man, start or stop. Could her choice be any clearer?

The thumping of heavy boots struck the driveway. There would be no way she could ever come back from this moment.

Nikka hit the button. The car's engine roared to life just as the passenger door was yanked open. Nikka swiveled in her seat. Was she too late?

It wasn't the guard. The tattoo girl jumped in beside Beth, breathing heavily from a sprint across the drive. "Hey. You're not leaving without me. We had a deal." She yanked the seat belt down and buckled in all in one motion. "Go, go, go! Boss lady is right behind me."

Nikka gunned the engine and left behind in shambles everything she had worked for her entire life.

How on earth was she going to break this to her father?

Maggie let out a deep breath and pressed her palm to her heart. They were okay now.

Barely.

The road was in worse shape than she remembered from her lunch-time bike rides. The car bounced around as if they were on a thrill ride, and Nikka gripped the steering wheel ferociously, cringing whenever a branch scraped against the car.

Beth whimpered from the backseat.

Maggie had been so focused on the forward progress down the road, she hadn't turned to see how Beth was doing.

Beth sat facing Josie with her eyes screwed shut. After a beat, she opened them, stared, wide-eyed, at the girl in front of her, and then shook her head several times.

"Beth," Maggie said, "you okay?"

Ignoring her, Beth raised a hand to touch Josie's cheek. "Are you...? You can't be..." She looked at the girl as if she had seen a ghost.

"Do you know her?" Maggie asked Josie.

"No," Josie said. "But she knew my grandmother."

Beth cupped Josie's face with both hands. "Dawn..."

Maggie pressed a finger to her temple. Did Beth actually think the reincarnation or the ghost of a woman dead for over fifty years was sitting in the backseat with her? Shit, maybe their problems were just starting after all.

"You're not Dawn, are you?" Beth said, pulling their foreheads together. "You look so much like her."

Before either Josie or Maggie could answer, the car lurched onto the main road and skidded to a stop.

"Which way?" Nikka's voice was so thin, Maggie almost didn't recognize it.

"I don't know." Maggie turned back and peered through the windshield to the paved road.

Nikka groaned deeply.

"I mean, I haven't... I didn't get this far in the plan."

"Well, I sure don't know what the hell I'm doing." Nikka glared at her.

"We need to go somewhere safe." The voice of reason came from the backseat. "Where no one will look for us." Maggie marveled how sure of herself Josie sounded. "And then we can figure it all out."

Ignoring her, Nikka spun the steering wheel to the left, toward the town. "No. We should go to the police. If we get there before Lea, maybe we can—"

"No police." Beth's shrill voice filled the car.

Both Maggie and Nikka pivoted toward the backseat.

Beth had grabbed Josie's hand so hard her knuckles whitened. Her jaw was set.

"Look, Ms. Walker," Nikka said. "If they really were locking you in and drugging you, you need to file charges as soon as possible. The longer you—"

"I won't do anything until I'm free and clear."

"Of what?" Nikka asked.

"Of those pills. The Oxycodone, the Percocet."

"It's a mistake to wait. You should—"

"No. I'm almost there. I've been throwing most of them out the window." A slight tremor ran through Beth. "Next time I meet the world, I don't want to be beholden to nothing or nobody. Let me finish this."

"She's detoxing?" Nikka turned to Maggie.

"Apparently."

"By herself?"

Maggie nodded. "I guess so."

Nikka dropped her head against her headrest. "This is crazy."

Beth was struggling, her fingers pulling at a cloth napkin tied into a knot.

"Here, let me." Josie took it from her and opened it to reveal pills of all colors and shapes.

"I just need a half of a pill. No, make it a quarter."

"For Christ's sake, we should take her to a hospital!" Nikka said.

"Let's give her a chance to do this her way." Josie handed Beth the napkin to let her choose.

With shaking fingers, she took a small one and pushed it into her mouth. "No hospital. I've been through the worst part already. You saw me then. I'm much better than I was."

"I had a friend who weaned herself off like this," Josie added. "She's doing great now."

Maggie resisted the urge to grab the wheel and spin it to the right herself. If this scheme was going to work, they needed Nikka to climb on board with them. Her jaw was as set as Beth's, her teeth clenched in what looked like a vise lock, and the blood had rushed from her hands she was gripping the wheel so tightly. It didn't look good.

"I was right before. Trust me I'm right now." She pushed Nikka as far as she thought she could.

Exhaling deeply, Nikka spun the steering wheel to the right. "Fine. So where does this way take us?"

"Make this right and then your first right again up into the mountains."

Nikka's wheels grabbed the asphalt of the main road as she followed Maggie's instructions, and they were back to smooth sailing—at least as far as the driving was concerned. "What's there?"

"A cabin about an hour from here. It's safe and empty. Perfect for her...and us until we can figure out what to do next."

"I'm not sure about this. But I don't feel good that I waited so long to help. Karma's a bitch, right?" Nikka hit the gas, and the car surged forward.

They rode in silence for fewer than ten minutes before passing a tree with a faded slash, markings from some cataclysmic event long ago. Beth turned to stare at it until she couldn't see it anymore and then buried her head on Josie's shoulder.

Maggie met Nikka's questioning stare.

She shrugged in response.

A half hour later, the Subaru was chugging up the mountain. Redwoods had given way to sugar and knobcone pines, and even on this summer day, the air this high up had a chill to it. Maggie flipped down the visor and opened the mirror.

Beth was sound asleep on Josie's shoulder, with Josie's head resting on top of hers. The perfect contrast of young and old, blonde and silver. They both looked so innocent in sleep. Without the drool pooling on Beth's lips, it could've been a Rockwell painting.

"Look," Maggie said softly as to not wake them up.

Nikka angled the rearview mirror and took a quick peek at the pair.

"How old do you think she is? She looks— Oh God, if she's under eighteen, this just got a whole lot worse."

"I saw her driver's license. There were no blue or red boxes, so she is probably over twenty-one."

"Thank goodness."

"Unless it's a fake." Nikka gasped, so Maggie quickly added, "Don't worry. It probably isn't."

"I should just drop you off and head back to the police station in town anyway."

"Beth isn't going to like it."

"Well, Beth isn't the one having criminal charges filed against her as we speak. And you... Breaking a restraining order can also be really serious."

"Let's just get up there and then figure it out. The four of us."

"Really? How can you stand to be without a plan?"

"And how can you be boxed in by one all the time?"

They fell silent. Just like in the walk-in cooler. When their life philosophies collided, their conversation had screeched to a halt. Maggie stole a quick glance.

Nikka didn't look mad, though. Actually, she was even prettier than she had been in the cooler. The heated conversation had brought a glow to her cheeks, and sometime during the morning, her blouse had untucked from her pants. The corporate vibe was long gone. The whole adventure had given her a slightly disheveled appearance, which softened her edges. Spontaneous and rash was a good look for her. All Maggie had to do was convince Nikka of that.

And Nikka was right in her own way too. They would need a plan sooner than later.

The silence lasted until Maggie pointed to a driveway carved into the road on their left. "Turn there."

Nikka brought the car to a stop in front of a log cabin tucked into a clearing surrounded by pines and firs.

"Whose place is this?"

"My family's. We've owned it for ages. My great-grandfather invested in all sorts of property around the Springs. This one he kept so his descendants would always have a place to come."

"Just a little place in the woods to bring the people they abduct?"

"Funny." Maggie grinned and glanced at Nikka so they could share the joke.

A hint of a smile darted across Nikka's face before she tapped the LED screen beyond the steering wheel. "I'm out of gas. I can't go back until I get more."

Josie stirred in the backseat and repositioned Beth from her shoulder. "Man, she's heavy for a little thing. Can we get her inside?"

"Yeah, there's a bedroom in the back," Maggie said. "We can put her there for now."

After jumping from the car, Maggie walked the length of the front porch and pulled the hide-a-key from a chink in one of the logs at the end.

Nikka dumped her briefcase on the front porch and helped Josie ease Beth out of the backseat. She woke enough to walk but was still groggy, so each of them slid an arm around her to help her inside.

They half-carried Beth past the stone fireplace, nearly bumping into one of the worn couches. Maggie hastily pushed an abandoned game of Monopoly on the floor out of the way.

"You know, this is how a lot of horror stories start." Josie stumbled beneath Beth's weight. "A bunch of women alone in a cabin in the woods. You know, the lesbians are always the first to go."

"I'm afraid in this horror film, we were dead before we got here." Nikka's tone was back to being grim.

"Bring her right back here." Maggie led the way to a small bedroom off the hall. Once inside, they pulled Beth onto the bed. She fell back asleep as soon as her head hit the pillow.

"Wow, you're right. She's surprisingly heavy." Nikka shook her arms that had supported Beth down the hall.

"I told you so." Josie dragged out the words, sounding a lot like a teenager, but when she sat down by Beth's side to ease her shoes off, her actions were more like a mother's. "I'll stay with her. I don't want her to wake up and not know where she is."

Alone with Nikka in the living room, Maggie was at loose ends. For the first time since Lauren had woken her up that morning, she didn't know what to do. She had a big hand in rescuing Beth, picked up a proven asset in Josie, and even managed to drag Nikka along—surprise, surprise. She should be basking in the glory, but the ribbons of worry that spooled off Nikka reached out to wind around her too.

"You want a soda or something?" Maggie attempted to break the tension. "This place is always stocked. That's one of the rules if you use it."

"Yeah, sure." Nikka rubbed her temple and then added, "Thanks."

In the kitchen, Maggie pulled out her cell phone and, with a battery that was about to die, spent her last connected minutes trying to make Nikka feel better. She walked back into the living room with two sodas.

Nikka also had her nose buried in her phone. As she tapped and swiped across the screen, her brow furrowed.

"Everything okay?"

"No." Nikka bit her lip. "I was sure there'd be a million texts or calls from Lea. But there's nothing."

"So, that's good news, right?" Maggie held out both a Coke and a Diet Coke.

Surprisingly, Nikka took the sugary Coke.

"I'm not sure." Worry crept into her voice. "There's no way that Lea's going to let this drop. She's up to something, and she's not tipping her hand to tell us what." Nikka dropped the Coke to the table and started swiping her finger across the screen again. "I should go back. I'll call the auto club."

"They won't come out here I'm afraid," Maggie said. "The cabin is on a service road."

"Great." Nikka's face fell as she glanced around the room, eyeing the door as if she were an inmate planning a prison break. Finally, she settled her gaze on Maggie, her eyes dark and stormy. She plopped onto the couch and sank into the cushions, her shoulders slumping against their flowered prints. The pop of her Coke tab sounded overly loud in the silent room.

Maggie's heart went out to her. It couldn't be easy—to start the day on top of the corporate ladder and end it on the bottom rung. She could tell Nikka that she had thrown her career away for truth and justice and all the things the law was supposed to be. But if Nikka didn't know that already, nothing Maggie could say would sway her.

Besides, truth be told, Maggie was glad she was stuck here. Beth would need a lawyer, and Lea wouldn't have brought her to the Springs if she weren't the best. And last but not least, Maggie had her all to herself up here.

She plopped down beside her, her shoulder just inches from Nikka's. "Look. It says here on House Call MD"— Maggie read off her phone, trying to lighten the mood— "that the symptoms of opioid drug withdrawal are very uncomfortable but are not life-threatening. That's got to make you feel a little better."

Nikka circled her head back and forth, saying yes and no at the same time.

"Seriously. Not even a little bit?"

"Maybe a little bit." Nikka didn't smile, but her shoulders straightened just a bit. "I mean, we're crazy to take this on, for sure, but at least Beth is out of that place."

"Yeah, it's a good start." Maggie stretched her legs out on the coffee table and marveled that for the first time they had gotten through a conversation in agreement.

Chapter 12

BETH'S EYES FLUTTERED OPEN; SHE felt good. The warm and fuzzy haze from the Percocet comforted her like a thin blanket, but for the first time in ages, the relief was not the first thing on her mind. Instead, her thoughts turned to the future. *I can do this. I can survive without the pills. Without...*

Soft light from a golden sunset streamed in through the open window across from the bed. Wait a second... The window was usually to the side of the bed. She turned to take in her surroundings, and there, perched on a chair barely a foot away, was a profile so familiar, she gasped out loud.

"Oh, good. You're awake."

No, of course, it wasn't her. They had gone through all this in the car. The mistake wasn't completely crazy, though. The eyes were almost exactly the same, the slant and the color, the hair and the chin too. The nose was a little longer, and a tiny golden stud and hoop caught the light from the window. "What's your name, dear?"

"Josie."

Well at least it wasn't Rhoda. Beth held out a hand, and Josie set down a sketchpad and a charcoal pencil and moved over to the bed.

"Where are we?" Beth asked.

"A cabin in the woods." Josie smiled. "No one followed us."

Beth dropped her head back on the pillow, and tears welled up in her eyes. She had escaped. The ordeal was finally over.

Josie was watching her with familiar green eyes as if she could tell the exact thoughts that were running around in her head. Beth hadn't seen that look in over half a century. An all too familiar pain stabbed at her breast.

Josie reached out to pat her hand. "This is Maggie's place, the woman who got you out."

"Yes, I know. The cook who makes flowers out of vegetables." Beth pulled herself into a sitting position and wiped a tear away. She pointed to the sketchpad lying open on the bed. "That yours?"

"It is."

"Will you show me?"

"I'd love to." Josie flipped the pad toward her.

Studies of the nature outside the window filled the page: an intricate pine cone, a fir tree with spiraling branches, a falcon soaring on the breeze.

"That's my favorite." Beth tapped three snow-peaked mountain tops, so delicate that the lines at the edges seemed to fade into the paper. "What are they?"

"Ideas for tattoos."

"For your body?"

"You bet. Like this one." Josie pulled up the sleeve of her shirt to reveal the cherry blossom tree on her arm.

"Oh my goodness." Beth reached out to touch one of the flowers before pulling her hand back. "May I?"

Josie nodded.

Beth ran a finger across one branch. "That's breathtaking."

"Thank you. I designed it."

"You know…" Beth swallowed. She was going to have to take the plunge sometime, no matter how much it hurt.

"Your grandmother was an amazing artist too." A sharp stab lanced through her breast.

Still so bad after all this time.

Her mouth went dry, and her throat constricted. She craved another pill. Desperately.

No.

She would fight hard not to fall into that spiral of agony again. She knew from experience it was a bottomless pit. She focused on what Josie was saying. Her happy tone pulled her back from the edge.

"—I have some of her sketchbooks at home. Actually, that's how I started drawing. I would get paper and copy some of the pictures I found in there. There was this tree, a redwood, I think. I drew it so many times, I'm sure I could recognize if I ever saw it in person."

"A little knot in the trunk about this high." Beth sliced her hand through the air above her head. Boy, she hadn't thought it would be this hard.

"You've seen the picture too?" Josie clapped with delight—just like Dawn would have.

"And the original as well." Beth forced herself to take another breath. "I can show it to you, if you'd like... If we ever get through this mess."

"I'd like that very much. I—"

A soft tap on the door cut into the conversation.

"Come in." Beth's heart settled into a more comfortable rhythm as Maggie entered with a sandwich on a plate and a steaming mug.

"I heard talking, and I thought you might be hungry."

"You know, I am. But if you don't mind, I think I might like to try to get up and eat at the table like a regular person, if you'll have me."

Twenty minutes later after official introductions, they sat at the table, sandwiches all around. Maggie poured red wine into a tumbler in front of her plate and then offered some to Nikka, who shook her head. When Josie raised her glass, Nikka put her hand out to stop Maggie. "How old are you anyway?"

"Twenty- two."

"You look younger," Nikka said but dropped her hand.

"Her grandmother was ageless too." The pain in her breast radiated down her rib cage. Not good. She had relived her moments with Dawn so often since the accident, but never out loud and never with Dawn's spitting image staring her in the face.

"Thank God you brought it up. I'm terrible at walking on egg shells." Maggie laughed. "So, you're Dawn Montgomery's granddaughter?"

Josie nodded.

Nikka studied her. "You know, I can totally see it now. You look just like her."

"Is it true?" Maggie leaned toward Beth. "You and Dawn Montgomery?"

Heat flooded Beth's face and moved down her neck onto her chest. She had never been at ease with all the attention focused on her, and her relationship with Dawn was something she had adamantly denied to her public and compartmentalized in herself for decades. With all eyes on her, Beth hesitated. Dawn's tragic death and hiding both their relationship and her grief had made her susceptible to the pills and people like her brother and Lea taking control of her life. She didn't want that anymore, but coming clean after hiding the truth for so long wasn't easy. She forced herself to nod.

"I'll be damned," Maggie said.

"Wow," Nikka said.

"And so when I saw you on the street." Maggie turned to Josie. "You had...what...tried to get in to see Beth?"

"And failed." Josie took a deep breath and big sip of her wine. "I knew about Beth and my grandmother, but not about anything else. I just wanted to talk to her and get the scoop."

Beth leaned in. Was this her way back to Dawn?

"When I was a kid, I found those sketchbooks I told you about. They were in my grandfather's attic with a bunch of other boxes and stuff." Josie paused and searched Beth's face as if weighing something but then quickly continued. "I don't know where they came from. Grandpa would never talk about Dawn with anyone. When my mom was touring with some third-rate play one summer, I stayed with Grandpa and Kristabel, his fourth wife. I found them then. The books were full of nature studies, but every so often there would be a picture of the same woman. Doing stuff. Like writing or planting flowers. There was one of her..." Josie turned to Beth. "You sleeping by a riverbank half-naked. They all had stuff written underneath them. BW in the garden, BW writing, BW after the first time..."

More heat ran across Beth's cheeks.

"I never knew who it was. I never read your books. I'm sorry. Was never much of a reader, but then I saw your picture on Twitter with the announcement about the story—"

"What story?" Beth asked.

"'The Tarot Card.'" Nikka met her gaze. "Your publisher just released it. They want to drum up a renewed interest in *Heartwood*. Introduce the real moneymaker to a whole new younger audience. Didn't you know?"

Beth shook her head. "They told me the press conference was about new covers for the *Wishes* books."

"I'm pretty sure you signed a contract."

"I may have. There're a lot of things that I'm not as clear about as I should be in the past year or so, since my brother died, I'm afraid." Beth took a deep breath as everyone at the table fell silent. She couldn't find a way to end that thought. Addiction and losing control of your life was hardly casual dinner conversation.

After a moment, Nikka reached across the table to pour herself half a glass of wine. "I can look into all that if you want."

"You could? You'd do that for me?"

Nikka studied the wine in her hand. "Yeah, I would." She finally looked up to slide her gaze past Beth and gave Maggie a slight shrug, who was beaming from ear to ear and trying to fight the smile all at the same time.

The real question staring Beth in the face was could she do it? Could she bring back memories and stories that had nearly drowned her? She wasn't sure she could keep her head above water, even with these wonderful women supporting her.

Beth glanced around the table, first at Josie and then at Maggie and Nikka.

Holy moly.

She had been so concerned with herself that the obvious had escaped her. Nikka and Maggie. They had a thing for each other. It was written all over Maggie's face. Nikka, on the other hand, wasn't aware of it yet, but Beth knew how that went. It was the same for her in the beginning with Dawn.

Nikka would realize soon enough. When you found the one, there was no fighting fate.

The wine tasted almost bitter on Nikka's tongue. Why on earth had she made that offer? A couple of hours ago, she had wanted to run away from this situation as fast as she could. And now, she had just offered to dig around in a field of legal land mines that were sure to blow up in her face.

What had changed? She conjured three notecards in her mind and started filling in the blank lines.

Was it Beth? Her name in bold topped one of the notecards in her head. Since the moment she had punched Beth's address into her GPS, she had been dreaming about meeting the author. Now she was sitting down to a meal with her, privy to her secrets with a famous movie star. Her ten-year-old self would've shouted with sheer delight if she could've jumped into a time machine to tell her that someday she would have dinner with the author of *Don't Waste Your Wishes.*

Was it Josie? The first notecard flipped to the back of the pile. They had just met, but it touched her how protective the young woman was of Beth. Sure, they had a ton of connections with that sketchbook and Dawn, but still, at twenty-two, Nikka had only been consumed by her own selfish goals—getting on Stanford Law Review and graduating high in her class. She had always thought that people with piercings and tattoos were somehow less evolved. Obviously, she had to rethink that narrow point of view.

Was it Maggie? The third blank index card slid into view, and Maggie's name popped up. There was something about the woman sitting across from her that was both maddening and strangely alluring. She was energy coiled into human form, beyond exhausting, and she flew by the seat of her pants so fast that Nikka was forced to play catch-up most of the time. Yet it was charming how quick she was to laugh at herself and smile with others. Maggie had been clucking around her all day like a mother hen. And the way she ran her fingers through her bangs when she was thinking was awfully cute.

Or was it all of them? A fourth card materialized on top of the other three. Even with Lea up to God knows what, a sure shit storm brewing back at the Springs and in her career, there had been a lightness to the meal that was sorely missing from her life in the City. Maybe she just wanted to climb inside that feeling for as long as she could. It wasn't as if she had anything else going at the moment.

Then it hit her. There was no definitive answer, no matter how many imaginary notecards she filled up in her head, and much to her surprise, that was okay. She mentally ripped the cards in two and tossed them out of her brain. For the first time in her life, she settled back in her chair and just let the worry go. It was surprisingly easy.

Josie was in the middle of an answer to a question she had missed. Her hands waved in the air as she accentuated a point, and Maggie had a big, broad grin on her face as she listened.

"It was all my grandfather's money, and I was of age, so my mom really couldn't say anything. But she was totally judgmental. I mean, everyone is when you tell people that you're a tattoo artist. When I bought the studio, though, she really blew a gasket. I thought it would've changed when *Wallpaper* came out and did a story on me—"

"What's *Wallpaper*?" Beth asked.

"Probably the best art magazine in the country," Maggie said. "You really were in *Wallpaper*?"

Josie nodded. "I know. Crazy, huh? They usually only do fine artists. *Dynamic visual style, bold colors that are an experience in and of itself and ultra-delicate line work. Her women and flowers are as perfect as they come.*"

"They're right." Beth reached out toward her shoulder. "It's like fine art."

"I have over one hundred fifty thousand followers on Instagram and a two-month wait list." Josie puffed up with pride that on her, Nikka realized, read more like delight.

Maggie whistled through her teeth. "Impressive."

"You would think so, but not so much for my mom. She is never happy with anyone's success but her own."

"Mothers are hard to figure out." Beth curled her hands in her lap. "I never got mine. We were estranged too...until the end."

They shared a sad smile.

"We would have been fine." Josie started up again. "If I had just gone into the family business."

"Which was? Not acting?" Nikka couldn't imagine her father pushing her into such a foolish and unreliable profession.

"Sure, what else? I mean, she grew up in the shadow of my grandfather, and supposedly, he never loved her. To hear her tell it, the only thing he ever gave her was his name: Jamison, Jamie for short. When I was born, he insisted that mine began with a J too. He was pretty selfish and egotistical, although he always had a soft spot for me."

Beth clenched her hands in her lap with the mention of James Montgomery.

That's right. She must have had had a history with him too, and from the white spreading across her knuckles, it wasn't a good one. Nikka reached out and slid a comforting hand across her back.

Beth smiled at her and stretched out her fists.

"So my mom thought that if she could become successful, Grandpa would love her. And when she couldn't, it was my turn."

Beth had to clear her throat before she spoke. "You acted too?"

"A little. I didn't like it. But some casting director said I was a natural, and that was enough for my mom. She wanted it for herself, not me. I got three national commercials, and when I was up for my fourth, I convinced my best friend to do this." She pointed to the curved barbell at the end of her eyebrow. "I showed up to the callback with a big bruise and this gross yellow stuff oozing everywhere. Needless to say, I didn't get the part."

They all laughed. Nikka took another sip of her wine. The bitterness had mellowed.

"The funny thing is," Josie said, "that she did put me on a career path. My grandfather, just to piss my mom off, took me to a tattoo parlor to fix the piercing—she thought he was taking me to a doctor to get rid of it—and there I saw these gorgeous designs covering the walls. I knew what I wanted to do."

"That simple?" Maggie asked.

"That simple. Never looked back."

Could it really be that simple? Nikka's brows furrowed. No double-and triple-thinking involved. It would free up a lot of time, if she didn't have to chart out every single move.

Blue and red lights flashed through the room.

Everyone swiveled to the big picture window. Nikka froze, seemingly rooted to the seat of her chair.

A sheriff's car rolled up on the dirt driveway outside.

No, it was never that simple.

"Shit. The cops." Josie jumped up. "I'll get her in back. Come on, Beth."

Beth immediately started shaking as she pushed herself out of her seat. "Don't let them take me."

"Don't worry. I'll fix this." Maggie sprung to the door, leaving Nikka all alone at the table.

Her stomach flipped and went sour. *No good deed ever goes unpunished.*

Loud knocking shook the door. "Come on, Maggie. Open up. We know you're in there."

Nikka, trembling as much as Beth had, stood up from the table. She never in a million years thought she would be on this side of the law.

Maggie waited until Beth had cleared the room to swing the door open.

An incredibly fit man with a huge scowl on his face filled up the entire threshold. "Maggie Chalon, you are under arrest."

"Sorry you had to drive all the way out here, George, but thank you for coming." Maggie stepped back to wave him in as if it were a social call. She peered into the driveway. "You too, Frank."

Nikka took a step back as two, not one, uniformed men strode into the cabin. They moved with an official swagger, their hands on their gear belts. The one in back had even flipped open the latch on his gun holster as he entered.

Her heart pounding, Nikka fought to take a breath. Maggie, on the other hand, crossed her arms over her chest and rocked back on her heels as if she didn't have a care in the world. What was going on?

Damn this woman. Nikka ground her teeth; she hated playing catch-up.

Her brother stood straight-backed in the doorway, seemingly trying to wipe all emotion from his face. Two splashes of red appeared in the middle of his cheeks as he lost the battle. He was whopping mad and trying to protect her all at the same time. Growing up, Maggie had seen that look countless times. Nine times out of ten, their father had called them on the carpet for things that she had set in motion.

"Maggie. I'm here officially. You need to tell us where Ms. Walker is and then come with me down to the station. I'll pull in all the favors I can, but you've crossed a line here, and there's only so much I can do."

"Seriously, George. You really think I'm a criminal?"

"There were over a dozen witnesses at Fern House who saw you violate a restraining order, and every reporter there filed a story. And yes, some are even calling you a kidnapper."

Maggie felt rather than saw Nikka begin to crumble at the mere mention of the criminal offense. When she threw her an encouraging glance, Nikka was staring at George and Frank like a feral cat who might dart off at any moment.

"I'm famous?"

"More like infamous," George said, his annoyance surging to the forefront. "It was quite the public getaway."

Frank moved toward her.

George put up an arm, stopping his advance. "Please, get Ms. Walker."

"Okay, okay. I will. But, George, this truly is one time where I got it right. Completely right. And I wanted to prove it to you. That's why I came here. I knew you'd figure it out, and you'd be the one to show up."

George closed his eyes, groaned, and dropped his head back. "Just go get her, Maggie."

Maggie threw her hands up as if she was surrendering before walking out. She thought it a nice touch, but the tension was too heavy, and no one smiled.

"And you are?" Her brother asked Nikka as Maggie walked down the hall.

"Nikka Vaskin. I work for... Well, I guess I should say I used to work for Lea Truman."

"How did my sister turn you? Wait. Don't answer. It's her superpower. She's like a character from the Marvel Universe."

"Did Lea file any charges?"

"No. Should she have?"

Maggie fought the urge to spin around to help Nikka with her brother.

"Not at all." Nikka's voice was low and calm.

A warm sensation spread through her. Nikka could totally take care of herself.

She knocked on Beth's door. "Beth, can you come out here for a moment?"

Josie must have been right there since the door creaked open and her face appeared in the small crack. "Are they gone?" she asked.

"No. They will be, though. All Beth has to do is come out and tell them the truth. Is she up for it?"

Josie swung the door open the rest of the way.

Beth stood in the middle of the room, rubbing her hands obsessively. "I can't do it." She shook her head repeatedly. "I'm sorry. It's too much all at once."

An unfamiliar panic rose in Maggie as she met Josie's gaze with her own questioning stare. House Call MD had said that anxiety and agitation were sure signs of withdrawal. Not the time for these particular symptoms.

"We'll be with you, Beth." Josie put a comforting arm around the older woman.

She was so good with her. Maggie thanked her lucky stars that she hadn't pulled farther down the road and grabbed some other woman this morning.

"They think we've kidnapped you," Maggie said. "Just come out to tell them that we haven't."

"Then we can come right back," Josie added.

Beth rubbed her neck. "You think I can do it?"

"I do." Josie reached for her arm.

"Okay. I'll try."

Maggie rushed ahead to size up the room. Nikka's grim face and the chill swirling around in gusts told Maggie all she needed to know. It was up to her to lighten the mood.

"Here she is. And look, no duct tape or rope or—" She bit her lip. She didn't want to spook Beth, who had stopped at the edge of the room at the sight of the two men. "Beth, this is my brother, George. Please talk to him. He's a good man."

"Ms. Walker." George approached and gently stilled her hands that were still moving around in circles. "Are you okay?"

Beth looked around the room, taking it in as if she had never seen it before. To Maggie, the woman laughing at the table earlier seemed long gone and someone confused and not at all in charge had taken her place. Beth's revolving gaze finally stopped on her.

She nodded encouragingly.

"Let her answer for herself, Maggie. Ms. Walker, are you okay?" George asked again.

Beth shifted her gaze onto him. She looked slight and tired. Small wonder after the day's events, but her confusion wasn't helping their cause.

"No," she said simply.

Maggie's stomach dropped. Had she really said no?

"I'm not okay."

Frank relocated to Maggie's side and gripped her arm as if she were going to make a run for it. Maggie tried to shake him off as wisps of dread rolled around in her stomach.

"Hey. No need for that," Nikka said, stepping to Maggie's side and gave her a reassuring nod.

Despite everything, a soft fluttering hit her belly. Nikka had come to her rescue.

"Did they hurt you, Ms. Walker?" George kept his voice soft and nonthreatening.

"Of course we didn't—"

Her brother flashed her a warning look. "Ms. Walker?"

"They did."

Frank's grip tightened.

George sighed deeply.

Beth closed her eyes and nodded her head up and down for what looked like a count of ten. "Please arrest them." When opened, Beth's eyes flashed, and she stood a little taller. "Vivienne and Lea Truman. And you, young man." She turned to Frank, her voice gaining a little strength as she spoke "Let that woman go. Make her a deputy in fact. She's the only one who fought for me all this time."

Maggie jerked her arm away from Frank just as Beth reached over to pat her other one. "I heard you arguing in the driveway with Lea the other day. I never said thank you for that and for today."

"You're welcome." Maggie smiled down at Beth.

"So you're saying that everything my sister's been telling us is true?"

"I'm not sure what she's been telling you, but yes, Vivienne and Lea are the ones that have been keeping me captive out there... giving me pills I didn't want... signing papers that they had no right to." Beth looked as if she might start to crumble as the accusations tumbled out one by one.

Josie squeezed her tight as George backed off.

"I'll be damned," he said.

"Don't sound so surprised, George. I was bound to be right sooner or later."

"Don't celebrate too soon, sis. Ms. Walker, we'll need you to come to the station to make a statement officially."

"She's not well, and she can't travel all that way until she is," Josie said. Beth leaned heavily against her.

George scratched his head. "I don't know."

"What about a video statement?" Nikka jumped in. Now that things had turned, Nikka's color had brightened. Good thing too. George never could resist a pretty woman. They had always had that in common.

"What exactly are you suggesting, Ms. Vaskin?"

"Video statements are admissible. All you need is a witness with legal authority. You don't need to do it at the station."

"Like you?" Maggie asked.

"No, like a policeman or a judge...or, in this case, a sheriff."

"That might work," George said.

Even Frank was nodding.

"I would feel better about it if you had a lawyer and he were present," George said.

"She is." Maggie pointed at Nikka.

"Ms. Walker?" George clearly wasn't convinced.

"Yes," Beth said simply.

"She engaged me over dinner," Nikka added.

"Okay, then." George shrugged. "Let's get started."

They sat Beth down on the couch in the living room, scooping the Monopoly game back into its box, and Frank positioned himself in front with his cell phone. George directed the session. Beth patted the seat next to her for Josie and took one deep breath after another. Finally, after a few false starts, she began.

"When I was younger, I tore all the ligaments in my ankle. If the weather changes or I've been on it too long, it still gives me trouble. So Sammy got me some pills for the discomfort, and when he passed, I was taking them regularly, maybe even too often. They helped with all the pain, not just the physical kind." She looked around the room, Maggie felt, to try to find an empathetic response. This was clearly more than a statement to the police. "Anyway, my brother had already hired Lea's firm to control my interests. Vivienne came and took over for Sammy, and then it just got bad. I... I..."

Beth took a ragged breath.

Maggie shuffled in place; she wanted to help, but she didn't know what to do.

"They can't hurt you, now or ever again," Josie said softly.

"Vivienne was... She made me take pills when I didn't want to. She kept me asleep a lot of the time... And when I wouldn't do what she wanted, she would...do this." Beth rolled up her sleeve and revealed a purple bruise on her forearm. The handprint was so obvious, it looked almost like movie makeup.

"This happened yesterday when I wouldn't take my pills." She yanked up her sleeve beyond her upper arm, where an angry red mark had already started to swell. "And this was from today. When Vivienne was taking me downstairs."

Maggie's heart broke. If she had only acted sooner, there might not be a bruise or a mark on that arm. A quick look at Nikka, whose eyes were tearing up, told her she wasn't the only one feeling this way. She reached out and squeezed Nikka's arm.

"I hate to ask you…" George took a deep breath. "…but were there any witnesses to this alleged abuse?"

"I didn't see the physical abuse, but I certainly witnessed the verbal abuse," Nikka said softly.

"Maggie?"

"No, they restricted my exposure to her. I did see her asleep once. It didn't look natural, as you know."

Beth's head dropped against the back of the couch as exhaustion consumed her.

"Let me get her to bed." Josie gently helped Beth up.

"I'll come too." Nikka made a detour to Maggie first. "She really should be seen by a doctor. Her health is paramount, but we may need some sort of medical statement if Beth really does want to take this any further. There's clearly more here than just stealing some manuscripts."

"I'm on it." In this light, Nikka's eyes reflected the smoky grays of the stone in the room. Maggie searched the irises for the caution that was usually there. She couldn't find it. Her eyes were clear, staring right back at her. They were in this together. Both of them would fight as hard as they could for Beth. A shiver traveled all the way down her body.

Tearing herself away, she walked with her brother to his cruiser and waited until Frank got in to pull George off to the side.

"Now you can really investigate Vivienne, right?"

"Yes. We will look more closely into how those prescriptions were filled, for a start, and certainly the physical evidence speaks for itself."

"Good. And we need Dr. Harvey to come up here tomorrow. As soon as he can. In the morning?"

"Yes, that would be a good idea."

"You'll arrange it? Can you send him up with a container of gas? Not much. All we need is enough to make it to that Chevron on the highway. Oh, and can we get some food? Maybe a chicken and some fresh squash and green beans? They're just coming into season."

"Okay. Anything else?" Her brother's tone revealed he'd had just about enough.

"Yeah. Sorry. Can you leave your phone charger?"

He rolled his eyes but nodded.

She wrapped her arms around him and held him tight. "Thank you. I know this wasn't easy for you. Beth needs us, and I think I really did have this one under control."

He squeezed back. "Be careful, Mags. This is far from over."

"I can handle it." She thought about the three women, especially Nikka, waiting for her inside. "We can handle it."

"I hope so. I truly do. But please, think of this as a wake-up call. You may get lucky this time, but you can't keep doing this."

"Doing what?"

He rubbed his forehead. "Jumping into everything with both feet and pulling everyone in after you. Jesus, you're thirty-two years old, and you move through life like you're a teenager."

She frowned. Where was this coming from? He should be congratulating her on a job well done. "Gee, when did you turn into Dad?"

"Low blow. You always tell yourself you're on some righteous cause, but you forget most of us don't live like that."

She answered with a deep sigh. His words cut at her. She had heard this talk before, from her parents and past girlfriends, but never from her brother. They just stared at each other for a moment.

"You know Lauren was at the station too today."

"Really?"

"Yeah. I've never seen her so mad. Did you steal her car?"

"No, of course I didn't. Her car is..." She cocked her head. "Well, technically, I just stole her keys. That's hardly the same thing."

George rolled his eyes.

"Let me go get them."

A minute later, she dropped Lauren's keys into his outstretched hand. As his fingers curled over them, she said, "Tell her I'm sorry."

"You should tell her yourself."

Maggie nodded. She didn't want to admit it, but he was right on some level.

"Think about what I said. You're one of the most amazing people I've ever met. And that's without sibling bias. But it's time to grow up and decide what kind of adult you're going to be."

Chapter 13

NIKKA SHUT THE DOOR TO Beth's room and headed back into the den. She almost missed Maggie sitting alone on the couch, looking small and forlorn crammed into the cushions. The energy that usually swirled around her in gusts had dissipated.

"You okay?" she asked.

Maggie nodded. "Yeah."

Nikka had the distinct impression, though, that she was trying to convince herself of that very fact.

"Josie's going to stay with Beth. She found a sleeping bag and mat in a closet. I hope that's okay."

"Sure. That's good. I'm glad she's doing that."

Silence echoed around the room.

"All right, I'm going to…" Something made Nikka pause. Maybe the way Maggie's bangs hung in her eyes—she wasn't sweeping them back the way she usually did—or the way she had pulled her legs up under her. Whatever it was, all her defenses were down.

Normally, Nikka shied away from weak and vulnerable. She had no room for either of those qualities in her busy life. In fact, the moment Alexis had told her how much she needed her was the moment when Nikka had started to pull away. If she was finally being honest, the whole *I'm not ready to come out to my parents* was only half the story in that break-up. But tonight she didn't want to run.

Surprising even herself, she perched on the coffee table, facing Maggie, their knees just inches apart. She had been wrong. Maggie's energy was still there. It reached out with a gentle tug. Nikka's heartbeat quickened, and her skin tingled. Who was she kidding? After the day they had, she craved this intimacy too.

"So what happened out there?" She tested the waters.

Maggie sighed and leaned forward to rest her elbows on her knees. "With George?"

Nikka nodded and noted how close they were now. She didn't move away.

"Nothing really. My brother thinks I need to grow up and stop getting people—and myself—in trouble by thinking with my heart, not my head."

"He may have a point."

Maggie raised an eyebrow.

"Even you have to admit this was one crazy, messed-up day."

Maggie jerked as her elbow slid off her leg.

Nikka grabbed her forearm to steady her. Having a contact point, Maggie's energy found her. Nikka quickly let go; it was almost too much.

"Well, it was," Nikka said. "But look where the day ended up. You were right. Beth's now safe. She and Josie found each other." She glanced down at her fingers. They tingled at the tips where she had made contact with Maggie's arm. Actually, the after-feeling was quite nice.

"Yes, but what about you? My brother may be right. I pull everyone in after me with crazy schemes."

"Like I said, Beth and Josie are happy that you did. "

"Are you?"

Nikka pulled back a little. What exactly was Maggie asking?

"I mean what about your job?"

"Ah...that. Gone, I'm sure." She winced. She couldn't help it. Her plans to make partner had been carefully crafted over years and destroyed in only one afternoon. She studied her fingers to digest that realization and curled them in to transfer the fading current of Maggie's energy into her palm. Her stomach settled with the motion. "But, you know, I realized today standing there in that parking lot with everyone staring at me that, yeah, I want what Lea has, but I don't want to be her. I'm not sure I saw the difference until today."

"Really?"

"Yeah. Thanks to you." Nikka raised her eyebrows.

Maggie sat up straight in response and a shy half smile crept to her lips.

"Yep. Tell your brother that sometimes you got to find crazy ways to pull fish out of a pond."

Maggie's smile turned into a laugh. "Where on earth did that come from?"

"The man who judges me. My father."

"You've got a family member who critiques you too?"

"In a big way." She was holding back a laugh now as well. There was definitely something about this woman. "But I'm not sure I handle him half as well as you handle your brother."

"I could give you some pointers."

"When this is all over, I might just take you up on that."

The left-over tingle swept up the back of Nikka's neck. What would it be like if it were everywhere...at once?

"We should probably get to bed. Who knows what tomorrow will bring?" Nikka said, trying to drive that image from her head.

"Yes. Yes." A flush crept across Maggie's cheeks.

They both stood at the same time, their bodies brushing as they rose. So close, Nikka felt the heat coming off of Maggie's skin. She took a step back to fight the dizziness that had abruptly hit her.

"I'll show you your room." Maggie rubbed the back of her neck as she moved away. She headed to the stairs, leaving Nikka to wonder what might have happened if they both had stayed put.

The next morning, Nikka awoke with a start. She had a lot of work ahead of her these next two days. Luckily, she had her work briefcase and computer with her. Well, it wasn't luck. She took them everywhere. She had left nothing important at the Riverside Inn except clothes. Maybe she could get Maggie to call over there at some point.

Trotting down the stairs in athletic clothes she had found by her door, she felt surprisingly refreshed and good all things considered. She told herself it had nothing to do with the fact that Maggie was right around the corner.

Maggie and Josie stood by a percolating old-school coffee pot as the morning sun streamed in through an open window. They were talking softly, and Maggie's shaggy hair hung around her face in an I-just-got-up-look. It totally worked on her.

"Morning." Maggie gave her a small, happy smile.

Nikka let out a breath she didn't even know she was holding and joined them in their huddle.

"Josie was just filling me in on Beth."

"She had a rough night. Tossing and turning. I don't know whether she was having a nightmare or if it's part of the detoxing or if they're one and the same..."

"And I told Josie that hopefully we'll get some answers. My brother just called. The doctor is supposed to come out here around ten to examine Beth. He's a family friend, so we don't have to worry about him giving away where we are."

Josie poured herself a cup of coffee. "I'd better get back in there. She drifted off around four or so. I don't want her to wake up alone."

"She's unbelievable." Maggie eyed Josie as she walked down the hall. "We're so lucky she fell into our laps."

"I don't think luck has anything to do with it. Your brother last night? A doctor this morning? This all sounds suspiciously like a plan."

"And the good doctor's even bringing you gas and us food. How's them apples?" After a crisp nod, Maggie added softly, "So, that means if you want to go this morning, you can. I mean, when we're ready, I can call George or a friend, and they can come get us."

It made a lot of sense. She should drive back to town as soon as she could. Everything would be simpler down the hill. Her father's voice, loud and clear and thick with his Russian accent, jumped into her head. "If you want to control future, drag into present, and strike."

But did she? In trying to control her future, she had left Beth in a horrible situation longer than she should have for her own potential gain. Maybe it was time to give up on her stranglehold on the future.

"Thank you for thinking of that. The gas, I mean."

Maggie's face fell, so Nikka quickly added, "But I, or we rather, need to talk to Beth and see exactly how far she wants to go with all this. Maybe we should come up with a plan together and see where it takes us." She took another flying leap. "That's how you do it, right?"

Maggie rolled her eyes and scoffed. Not at all the reaction Nikka had been expecting.

"You're as bad as George. I don't know why everyone thinks I just wing it all the time." Maggie reached out and grabbed Nikka's hand. "Come on. I want to show you something."

She led her through a small mudroom to a back door, where she paused and gestured to a pair of old garden clogs by the washing machine. "Put those on."

Nikka had barely slid into the second one before Maggie flung the back door open. Nikka had to trot to catch up.

"Look." Maggie slid to a stop by a narrow trail next to a rock wall a hundred yards from the house.

Nikka swiveled her head to look down the empty path. "At what?"

"At that." Maggie gestured to the granite boulder right in front of them. Filled with cracks and jutting bits, it rose up at nearly a ninety-degree angle for about twenty feet.

"I'm sorry, what is this?" She glanced at Maggie, whose eyes were shining with excitement.

"This is who I am."

"A rock wall?" Nikka laughed.

"Not surprisingly, a lot of people would say I'm just as stubborn and as unmovable. But no. We're talking philosophically." She gently bumped Nikka's shoulder. "Watch."

She leapt onto the wall as if on a spring and grabbed it with outstretched hands and feet. Swinging wildly from one foothold to another handhold, she climbed nimbly up its face until she pulled herself onto the lip.

"See?" she called down to Nikka.

"Not in the least." Admittedly, she had been busy watching Maggie's lithe body dangle right in front of her. When Maggie had switched her center of gravity, her muscles stretched and flexed across her entire body. Maggie had given her a full-body picture of who she was, and she had to admit, that was pretty nice. Nikka would bet hard money, though, that wasn't what she was talking about.

"Hold on." Maggie darted back from the ledge and in a few moments came down the path to join Nikka. "Tell me what you saw?"

"You scampering up that rock. Pretty impressive."

"Thanks. That's what everyone sees, though. Me jumping in, willy-nilly, just hoping that I'll get to the top one way or another. But it's really like this."

She leapt back onto the wall.

"Everyone looks at the hands, but really it's all about the feet. See how I'm clutching the rock with my pinkie toes? Well, you can't see since they're in my sneakers, but I am. It's called a back step, and it forces my hip to hug the wall, so I don't fall off. Excellent footwork is the foundation that makes the climb look easy. It will free up your hands. That way, you can test holds before you commit. See?"

"I'm beginning to."

"Right." Maggie patted a round rock that jutted out from the face. "From the ground, this looks great. A jug, a kind of handhold that you can totally get your fingers around. But now that I'm up here, I see it's not and this little guy over here is a much better choice." She swung over to grab something with her fingertips that was so small Nikka couldn't even see it.

"Wow," Nikka said, but she wasn't sure if she was talking about the move or the fact that it put Maggie's sexy ass on display again.

"See? That's why I get such a kick out of bouldering. It's all about mental strength. You need to find the best possible solution on the fly." She bounded off the rock back to Nikka's side and found her gaze. "There's no way to truly plan your route from the bottom, so why even try?"

"I get it." She did. She just didn't know if she could live that way. Up to now, if she didn't have a plan, she would much rather stay on the ground and not climb anywhere.

"I know it's not the way most people do things. They think its rash or impulsive. But I think figuring out things as you go along is a gift that life gives you. Does that make any sense?"

"Is that why they call it the present?"

"Ha!" Maggie punched her shoulder playfully. "You do get it."

Maggie laughed, low and gentle, and Nikka loved how easily it came to her. She smiled back as that warm, fuzzy feeling from the night before spread throughout her again. Their gazes met, and Nikka pressed a hand to her chest. Her heart was beating a mile a minute, her breath coming a little faster than it should.

For a moment, she was tempted to take that step forward, right into Maggie's space. But even as her foot shuffled, the fear about what would come afterward checked her movement. Figuring it out as she went along? Must be nice, but, no, it just wasn't in her DNA. They were too different. Forget what she felt last night...and right now.

"We should probably get back." She took a step back.

When Maggie said nothing, she added, "I need to start the paperwork for Beth's case. I'm afraid there aren't going to be many footholds on the rocks we're going to have to climb these next two days."

Maggie watched Nikka turn and head back to the house in silence. Her mother's plastic clogs made squishing noises as Nikka walked. This wasn't the way she had hoped to end that particular climb. While she had only brought Nikka out to explain who she was, she had thought that Nikka felt something just then, at the end. She knew she had. She swallowed hard and pushed down the butterflies that were still fluttering in her stomach.

A pattern, and not a good one, was clearly developing between them. Every time they were alone together, things were going along swimmingly at first. There were stolen looks, enamored laughs, touches that tested the waters...and then...

Bam, they lost their foothold and dangled helplessly by the rock face on ropes.

She couldn't figure it out. What was she doing wrong? She had never had trouble getting started with any of the women she had been interested in before.

She sighed deeply. Maybe solving Beth's problems was just putting too much pressure on them, or maybe she was more interested in this one than in all the women combined.

The sound of tires skimming over the dirt driveway cut into her thoughts. Dr. Harvey was here.

With his kind face and three-piece suit, he looked as if he had stepped out of a Norman Rockwell painting to make this house call. He held out his arms for a big hug. "You've caused quite a stir, young lady." He squeezed her tight.

"Just you wait. I'm not done yet."

"It's the talk of the town. But I, for one, never thought you had kidnapped our local treasure."

"Thank you for that and for coming all this way. I'm not sure Beth is up, but we can wake her."

She filled him in on the little she knew about Beth's condition as they entered the cabin. Nikka was just setting up her computer at the kitchen table, pushing up her sleeves as she prepared for work.

"Dr. Harvey, this is Nikka Vaskin, Beth's lawyer." Why had she chosen this way to present Nikka and not "my friend" or even "one of the Steelhead Spring's outlaws"? Admittedly, that last one was dumb, but "Beth's lawyer" certainly made it clear what they were to each other.

After they exchanged pleasantries, Maggie led the doctor to Beth's room. When Josie opened the door, Beth was awake, sitting up in her bed, pillows bunched behind her. She looked tired; her eyes, puffy and swollen, held that haunted look that Maggie had seen off and on.

"Beth," Josie said, "here's the doctor I was telling you about. No need to worry. He's just going to examine you. I can go or stay. Whatever you want."

"Stay."

"Good morning, Ms. Walker. My name is Bernard Harvey." He crossed to the bed and offered her his hand.

"I'll just wait in the kitchen." Maggie withdrew.

Hunched over her computer, Nikka was already tapping on the keyboard with a fierce focus that Maggie had rarely seen. No wonder why Lea had hired her.

Suddenly shy in the face of so much concentration, she retrieved the groceries from the front seat of Dr. Harvey's car and put them away. She tried to be as quiet as possible, but Nikka had eyes only for the computer.

Maggie had poured herself a second cup of coffee and retired with an old copy of *Heartwood* to an overstuffed chair when Dr. Harvey made his way down the hall.

"Well?" Maggie asked.

"Good and bad news."

Nikka tapped out a few last words and joined them.

"The good news is that physically she seems fine. She's done most of the withdrawal on her own, and she could stop taking the opiates right now with little consequence. I drew blood, and my hope is that the tests will come back within normal range."

"And the bad news?" Maggie asked.

"Clearly, there has been elder abuse. That'll be a nasty bruise on her upper arm, and there're older ones in other places. They'll fade over time, of course, and luckily, there doesn't seem to be any deeper critical damage."

Nikka sighed as Maggie closed her eyes for a moment, trying to block the image of Beth being hurt by Vivienne. It didn't work.

"I also think the reason she started taking those pills isn't merely physical. Her ankle is weak and probably still hurts her, but aggressive physical therapy and Advil should help. No, there's something much deeper in that woman that's the cause of all this, and until you solve that mystery, our patient won't be truly cured."

"Sounds like we need a different kind of doctor." Maggie shared a long look with Nikka. Neither let their gazes drop.

When it came to Beth, good to know that they were still on the same page.

They had retrieved the gas can out of his trunk and said their good-byes to Dr. Harvey when Maggie's phone yodel-ay-hee-hooed.

Nikka jumped and looked around the driveway. "What the hell is that?"

"Me." Maggie pulled her cell phone out of her pocket.

"You take that rock-climbing metaphor everywhere, don't you?"

"It's my brother." She tapped the screen. "Hey, George, you're on speaker."

"Who else is there?" he asked.

"Nikka," she said and then quickly added, "My friend."

Nikka, who had been scuffing the dirt with one foot, stilled at the word *friend.*

Good? Bad? Maggie didn't know.

"Excellent." They both returned their focus to the phone. "You both need to hear this. We drove out to Fern House, and the place is completely empty. No sign of Vivienne. It's like she's never been there. And we didn't find any medication with Beth's name on it anywhere."

"Nothing?" Maggie's voice quivered.

"That was quick." Nikka shook her head, but she didn't seem at all surprised.

"So what's your next move?" Maggie asked.

"Nothing," George said. "All we can do is hand the case over to the DA. If they want to pursue it, they can file charges, and then we can get into it more."

"Wait a sec—"

"There's no evidence. Come on, Mags, you got to see—"

"Did you talk to Lea Truman?" Nikka brought composure back to the conversation.

"We did. But she claims that she had no idea what was really going on out there. And there's no evidence to suggest otherwise. She's back in the City now."

"Of course she knew." Maggie looked at Nikka for confirmation. Shockingly, she just shrugged.

"Not as far as the law is concerned." Her brother's voice drifted out of the speaker. "She's kept her hands very clean in all this. I've got to go. I'll let you know if I find out anything else."

George ended the call on his end and left Maggie glaring at the phone in her hand. She slammed it against her leg as she scowled at Nikka. "Surely, you aren't going to let it go as easily as my brother?"

Nikka stood in front of her, apparently deep in thought, the model of a Zen meditation: quiet breathing, relaxed muscles, serene eyes.

"No," Nikka said so quietly Maggie had to still her own mind to make sure she heard her right.

"No?"

Nikka reached out to cup her arm. Her touch was light, but just her fingers brushing her elbow made Maggie relax and take a deep breath.

"No, of course not. Lea had Vivienne wrapped around her little finger, and that woman definitely would've done whatever it took to not disappoint her. Either they had a thing, or Lea made it seem like a thing. She's ruthless, for sure. But we need to prove she's a criminal, not just suspect it. That's a million times harder."

Maggie rolled back on her heels. "So what do we do?"

"We need to get Lea out of Beth's life once and for all."

Maggie nodded. "How?"

"First, Beth needs to officially fire Lea as her attorney. Then we'll be in court first thing Monday morning to break the conservatorship. Let's see how that all turns out, and then we can talk to the DA about criminal charges."

"Sounds like a plan."

Nikka smiled. "What? Maggie Chalon following a plan?"

"I'm not the only one who is trying something new. You started it when you said, 'Let's see how that all turns out.'"

Nikka laughed. "I guess I did, didn't I?"

"Another page?" Josie asked.

Beth opened one eye to look at her.

Josie held up a well-loved copy of *Heartwood* she had found on the coffee table in the main room.

She was curled up in the chair next to her bed in such a familiar way; Beth screwed her eyes shut in response. *Concentrate on the words. They'll get you through.*

"Yes, please."

"Okay, where was I? Bonnie had just found the memo that her boss had written, framing Daisy. That was clever the way she found it. Is this what's going to bring them together?"

"Read and find out."

Josie read well. No surprise there. She had a lot of her grandmother's talents. It was so strange, though—listening to a book she knew intimately but hadn't read in over fifty years. She remembered vividly sitting down at the desk in her writing room to create that scene. The horror that Bonnie had felt and the overwhelming desire to protect Daisy at any cost. Even now she could still see the pencil sliding over the composition book in a rhythm inspired by the clicking of Dawn's crochet needles behind her. And yet, nothing about it was recognizable—not the words, the phrases, the feelings. How could that be?

Her mind drifted to the doctor. He had been very nice. Another thing to thank Maggie for. It had been a long, long time since anyone had looked her in the eye and seen her strength. Almost a lifetime, in fact. True, the purple bruise on her arm still throbbed where he had probed it, but maybe that pain was more about the fact she hadn't taken action earlier against Vivienne and less about the bruise itself. She rubbed the spot and hoped that both feelings would eventually fade away.

Right now, all she had to do was listen to Josie, whose voice drifted to her a like a soothing melody. The warm sun streamed in through the open window and covered her like a blanket. Pretty soon, she couldn't keep her eyes open.

The dream played out as it always had.

Beth stood on the stoop outside of Fern House next to Dawn on a beautiful, fresh morning. The redwoods rustled in the early breeze; the sun peeked out from behind the trees—a few delicate rays stretched out to bathe them in a golden glow. Everything was all right. Dawn was standing right next to her, telling her favorite joke about the Hollywood agent, laughing hard before she got to the punch line. All Beth had to do was reach out and encircle her, and they could move forward into the future that should have been theirs for the taking.

She lifted her arms, fingers already trembling as they were just inches away from Dawn's body.

"Don't do it. You'll be sorry," a man's disembodied voice called out, shattering the calm.

Beth frantically looked around. Jimmy, dark as the morning was light, popped up between them, forcing Beth to move back.

"You foolish girl. She's not going to throw her career away for you." His mouth opened wide as if it were on a hinge, and black tendrils of night spun out, darkening the rosy sky.

When the shadowy wisps had almost reached Dawn, Beth shouted, "Get the hell away from her."

Anger and indignation welled up in her; she grabbed Jimmy, hit him with her fists, and then with superhuman strength flung him to the ground.

As his hip hit the stone of the stoop, he shattered into a thousand pieces. With a deafening crash, brittle shards of what had been James Montgomery spilled onto the driveway and scattered into the brush at its edge.

She hadn't run or frozen at the first sign of trouble. She had acted, shown Jimmy exactly what she had thought of him, and saved Dawn, who had never been able to save herself, from the monster. Jimmy was gone. She turned to Dawn; her body tingled with energy. She had stood up for herself. She had done it!

Dawn's laugh, full of sharp edges, cut through the air. "You didn't really think it would be that easy, did you?"

All the Jimmy pieces on the stoop and in the driveway skittered across the ground and came together, building one upon the other to form a new Jimmy.

"I think she did." His laugh was deeper than his wife's, but just as harsh. "Tell her, sweetheart. Tell her why it didn't work."

"I never loved you," Dawn said to Beth. "It was all a game. I never loved you... I never loved you..."

A hand shook her awake. Beth jolted back from the big green eyes only inches from her. "Stop...saying...that." She reached out to push Dawn away.

The face that had been mocking her was now only full of concern.

Beth stilled, and the girl who was so like Dawn and not at all like her pulled her back into reality—a reality where Dawn didn't have a chance to love her or scorn her since she was long gone.

That pain hit her like the first time she had heard the news at the local hospital where they had treated her ankle. A nurse had run into her room to tell the doctor the incredible news that Dawn Montgomery had just died after giving birth to a daughter in their little hospital. Yes, right down the hall. They were going to be famous! The doctor's face had glowed with excitement.

Only a few feet away, shock and denial had closed in around Beth, threatening to suffocate her. All these years later, she was still fighting to take a breath that would finally fill her lungs. She lurched to the side table next to her bed and fumbled over a bottle of water and around the clock.

Josie moved to the side of the bed and pulled the napkin of pills out of her jeans pocket. "Are you looking for these?"

Beth froze. What was in that napkin tugged and yanked at her. "I... I..." She fixated on luminous green eyes so full of hope and optimism. There was no doubt at all swirling in their depths.

"No." She let the girl's belief carry her over the chasm of her longing. "I need to get up." With small jerks, she swung each foot to the floor. Her body tingled with need.

Her fingers fluttered as they searched for a pill that wasn't there. "Get my mind off it. Let's go out and watch Nikka and Maggie circle around each other. They put on a good show." The last sentence came through clenched teeth.

"I know. They should just get a room already." Josie helped her up.

She could feel the girl's gaze on her. Slowly, she met the look. Again no judgment, no demand for explanations, just good will.

"I'm proud of you, Beth."

"Don't be. It's just one *no* when I've already said *yes* a million times. One small step."

"Take a lot of steps, and you're walking down a road."

"Let's just start with the hallway."

"Hello!" Maggie said brightly as they appeared in the kitchen. "You're up. Right in time for supper."

"I've slept the day away."

"I can think of worse things to do."

Not with the dreams I have. She kept that thought to herself as she slid into the chair that Maggie pulled over for her. "It smells delicious."

"It should." Nikka joined them from the living room. "She's been working most of the afternoon."

"So have you. I didn't want you to toil alone." Maggie ran an appreciative gaze up Nikka's body to her face.

The flirting show had begun right on cue. Beth tried to focus on that and on the wonderful garlic smell that permeated the kitchen.

"Wow, this is really good," Beth said. The chicken melted in her mouth. "I can't believe you spent all that time in my house and only made me soup and sandwiches."

Both Nikka and Josie nodded, their mouths full.

"Well, those were Vivienne's orders, not mine, and—" Maggie bit her lip and cringed. "Sorry."

Maggie glanced at Nikka, who shook her head slightly.

Not very subtle. There was something they weren't telling her. It could wait. She was safe. That was all that mattered. No need to ruin the dinner. Besides, her nerves felt like live wires; she wasn't sure she could take much more. "Where did you learn to cook?"

"Cordon Bleu."

"In Paris?" Nikka asked.

"I won a cooking contest and got a scholarship. Don't look so surprised."

"It's just that…"

"I know. How could I end up back in the Springs, making cupcakes?"

"Well, I mean…"

"Have you ever tasted one of my Lemon Lovers?"

"No, and—"

"Relax. I'm just messing with you. I was there for just a semester. My Cordon Bleu was in the City." Maggie grinned, and Nikka rolled her eyes in response. The push-and-pull between them was so strong that Beth could almost see a thick, corded rope stretching out across the table as if they were playing some amorous game of tug-of-war. Was that the way she and Dawn had been?

"It's not what you do that's important," Maggie said. "It's how you feel when you do it that really matters."

Beth nodded. Maggie, for sure, wore her heart on her sleeve, but the intensity behind her words spoke to something else. People had told her, just like they had told Beth, that her life choices weren't correct.

"Is that why you made those little flowers on my plate? And the happy faces?" Beth asked.

"I didn't know you noticed."

"Sometimes they were the best part of my day. The only thing that would get me through. Seeing what little surprise you'd send up."

They shared a smile.

"What about intellectual property law? Is that fun?" Josie paused from shoveling in forkfuls of chicken only long enough to ask Nikka the question.

"It is. I love it."

"Really?" Maggie spooned another thigh onto Josie's plate.

"Now who's being closed-minded? It's a very exciting field."

Maggie raised her eyebrows, but Beth had the distinct feeling that it was just an excuse to look at Nikka, who was, admittedly, extraordinarily good-looking. She wished Dawn could have seen this world where two women could openly flirt with one another.

"IP law is all about ideas and how new ones are created. We encourage innovation in the world and facilitate the free flow of information. Thanks to us, you can sing 'Happy Birthday' right here at this table for free. No synchronization license needed."

"We already sang it all the time." Josie grabbed another piece of bread.

"True," Nikka said, "but what about the monkey that took a selfie? The courts are battling whether the monkey or the photographer owns the rights. You got to admit that's one fun case."

Maggie chuckled. "Okay now, you're just making things up."

"Want to bet? Josie, search for *grinning monkey selfies*."

Josie pulled a phone from her lap and, after a few taps, turned the screen around and showed them a crested macaque monkey with amber eyes and huge white teeth, grinning from ear to ear.

"No way. The monkey took that?" Maggie motioned for the phone and took a closer look.

"Yeah, he did," Nikka said. "This nature photographer was in Indonesia, and allegedly, the monkey just grabbed his camera and started shooting. And therein lies the problem. Does this photograph belong to the monkey or the nature photographer, or does no one own the copyright and it should fall into the public domain for the public to use however it wants? There are valid arguments for all three results."

"That's what you do?" Maggie asked.

"Well, it's not all birthday songs and monkey selfies, but yeah, we try to fight for self-expression and creativity. And I like to fight for the people who need help protecting their ideas."

This last comment she directed at Beth, who met her gaze briefly before looking down at her lap. Her hands were clenched together so tightly her knuckles were white. How could she have not noticed? She pulled them apart to rub one palm with her other thumb.

"Thank you," Beth said softly. "All of you. I..." She faltered and looked around, not knowing where to rest her gaze. She didn't want to meet any scrutiny, which, if she were being honest, she had always run from her whole life.

Josie reached out to pat her arm. In this light she was, once again, the spitting image of her grandmother. Her face, however, was open and unguarded as if she had no secrets to hide. The difference between them hit Beth like a jolt.

"You don't care what other people think, do you?" Beth asked.

"No." Josie shook her head. "I don't. Never have."

Was that what their problem had been? Beth cared only what Dawn had thought about her, and Dawn had cared about what everyone thought. The reason, though, was the same. Neither she nor Dawn had had faith in themselves. Even after every critic had praised *Heartwood* to the skies, and every lesbian she met had told her how it had changed her life. Even then, she had never written another adult book. She didn't have any faith in her talent, in her love for Dawn, in herself.

Three sets of eyes, all different colors, gazed at her with the same look. They all believed in her.

She took a leap. "I...don't know what would've happened if you all hadn't shown up yesterday. I don't even want to think about it. Just the future. You can get my rights back?"

"I don't want to make any promises, but yes, I think so," Nikka said. "To the short story and the memoir."

"The what?" Had she heard Nikka correctly?

Nikka licked her lips and paused as if choosing her words very carefully. "The letters...to Dawn Montgomery...after she died."

Beth reached for Josie's hand, and it was there instantly. She grasped it and held it hard. "That's what the press conference was about? The letters? Not about 'The Tarot Card'?" The truth fanned out around her. Beth took in a ragged breath. "The letters... I never meant for anyone... They're just angry musings about life."

"Don't worry, Beth." Nikka leaned in. "I really think I can stop it. You were coerced into signing that contract when you weren't really competent to give consent."

A dark shadow fell over the table. Beth dropped her fork on her plate and placed a hand on her stomach. Dinner was careening around inside as if she were on a roller coaster.

"What's in the letters?" Maggie jerked as if someone, probably Nikka, had kicked her beneath the table.

"Nothing. Everything. I really only asked one question and created a thousand answers. I just... I've always wondered if Dawn really loved me."

"Of course she did," Josie said.

Beth let go of her hand as if it had become red hot.

Nikka raised her eyebrows in reprimand. Only Maggie voiced her outrage. "Josie!"

"Well, she did."

"How do you know?" Beth swallowed hard. Her mouth had gone completely dry.

Josie's gaze darted back and forth. Finally, she shrugged. "She told me."

Beth closed her eyes, waiting for the pain to subside. She had trusted this girl. Once again, she had been sucker punched. When she opened her eyes, Josie was gone from the table.

A few moments later, she came back, holding a black composition book—a twin to every book that had sat in the writing room at Fern House.

"What is that?" Beth's question was barely more than a whisper.

"Her diary...when she was with you."

"Shut the front door." Maggie's eyes widened into round circles.

277

Nikka hit her on the shoulder and threw a pointed glance.

Beth studied the tattered notebook that Josie offered to her. Could it be true? Had Dawn kept a diary? The white faceplate was blank and gave nothing away. If there was anything inside, it was as if Dawn hadn't really acknowledged it.

Beth wanted to grab it with both hands, pore over every word, and finally, after all this time, find out what Dawn had really been thinking. She raised a hand only to drop it. "How? Where did you find this?"

"With her sketchbooks. At my grandfather's. I was going to tell you earlier. I don't know why I didn't. Sorry, it just didn't seem like the right time."

Josie slid the book onto to the table and pushed it with one finger closer to Beth. "Maybe right now isn't the best time either. Here it is, though, if you want it."

She did, desperately. She just didn't know if she was strong enough to actually open it. After all, she had been burned by Dawn before.

Chapter 14

"I TOTALLY WANT TO READ it." Maggie spun Nikka away from the sink, where she was just finishing the dishes, and pointed to the table.

Dawn's composition book lay like a tempting morsel on the table. When she and Josie had retired to the bedroom, Beth had left it behind.

"Don't you want to read it?" Maggie wagged her head back and forth and sent her a hopeful look.

"Of course, I do," Nikka said. And she did. She would gladly give her right arm to sneak a peek.

"Maybe just a page or two?" Maggie's fingers snaked out to the notebook.

"You're terrible." Nikka darted close to playfully slap her hand away.

In a move perfected on the rock wall right outside, Maggie twisted her hand to catch Nikka's before it dropped.

"I told you, I look for the best handhold." Maggie interlaced their fingers one by one. "And then when I get it, I don't let go."

Maggie's hand was calloused, not unpleasantly so, and her fingers curled around Nikka's with a tensile strength that made all other hands lifeless by comparison. She marveled how strong yet soft her touch was and the how a current of energy flowed up her arm.

Maggie squeezed her hand tighter and, like an angler with a fish on a line, started to pull Nikka closer until their bodies were almost touching. Maggie's energy swirled around her. It was so strong it was almost humming. Then their gazes met.

Oh God, she's going to kiss me. Nikka didn't move.

"Oh, I'm so sorry."

Nikka jumped back at the voice.

Josie stood at the end of the hallway, hand to her mouth, eyes shining with amusement.

The heat which had been smoldering in Nikka rose to her cheeks.

"Um…" Josie danced in place. "Beth decided she wanted the book after all. She says she's not going to read it, but I think she's working up to it." She slid between the two and grabbed the notebook off the table. "Carry on."

Nikka took another step back. What the hell was she doing? Josie had come in just in time. She seemed to be rescuing everyone this weekend.

"Look." Nikka waited until Josie had left. "I'm sorry. I…I… This is really fast for me." She rubbed her neck. "Especially with all that's going on."

"Okay." The gleam that had been in Maggie's eyes faded fast.

"You're not mad?"

Maggie shook her head.

Yes, I'm mad! But not at you.

Maggie listened to Nikka move around the bedroom next door, most likely getting ready for bed. Sleep for her was still hours away. Too much energy. She paced around the small room so fast that static electricity crackled in the 1970s shag carpet.

Shit on a brick! She knew better.

In the cooler, which seemed like a lifetime ago, she had understood how to handle Nikka. Slow and steady. Nikka needed to roll things around in her head for a long while before she would feel comfortable with any action. That had only been reconfirmed at the rock wall. Yep. She had heard her loud and clear. Let her make the first move.

So what did she do? Grab her hand in the stupidest way. God help her. If Josie hadn't come in, she would have tried to kiss her.

Suddenly, her mind exploded with clarity. For the first time in her life, she wasn't running the show. She always attacked life as if she were climbing a mountain: finding her route as she went, only looking up to the top, not waiting for others to catch up. Forging ahead was exciting, for sure, but in the long run, climbing up with someone would be better.

Dammit! Her brother *was* right.

Everybody climbed her mountain differently. Some even approached it the way Nikka did: deliberately, cautiously, with plans. Was this what George meant when he had told her to grow up? She needed to downshift and try Nikka's pace.

Only one problem, though. Moving slower gave her more time to look around...and down. Often, the bottom was a long way off, and she didn't need to be reminded that a horrible fall could happen. That fact made the climb a million times harder...and scarier.

Nikka punched the pillow into a ball and turned onto her side. Impossible to find a comfortable position in an unfamiliar bed. Especially with Maggie right next door.

What on earth was she doing? Running a marathon? All that energy had to go somewhere, she guessed.

Nikka scrunched up the pillow even tighter and pulled herself into a sitting position. Why even pretend sleep was near? She rubbed her chin with her forefinger and thumb as she fell into her familiar routine of cataloging the day.

Despite the way it ended, her day had been productive. Several almost finished motions sat on her computer desktop downstairs; they still needed little tweaks, but for the most part, she was ready to file on Monday. Beth seemed to be making progress in that two-steps-forward-one-step-back kind of way. Nikka had big hopes for the diary. If it was even half of what Josie said it was, it could give Beth the closure she so desperately needed.

Then there was Maggie. Nikka had enjoyed that moment out at the rock wall. No, it was more than just fun. Maggie had been eloquent, passionate, and sexy—all the things that Nikka was looking for in a woman. She had definitely felt something there and in the kitchen, too. She couldn't deny that anymore. Her fingers moved from her chin to her lips, running a nail across the sensitive skin. Why, then, hadn't she stayed around to finish what they had started?

One, it was stupid to start something when her life was already in upheaval. Two, they didn't even live in the same town. Three, she was going to have to work like a dog to find new employment. Four...she was scared.

Of what exactly?

All that energy, for one. Maggie was a fireball wrapped inside an explosion. But Nikka was also afraid of opening herself up, of the raw intimacy that Maggie offered.

Her last real relationship had ended in disaster when Nikka made law review and Gemma didn't. Since then, there had been a week here and a month there, but no one really.... until now.

Five... Shit, there was no five. One through three were all conquerable. Just four—she was scared shitless.

One point didn't make a list. How was she supposed to constructively build a case for or against Maggie if there was no list?

Maybe she would just have to take a leap to the next handhold and make her way up this mountain.

Beth got out of bed and crossed to where Josie had made up her pallet for the second night in a row. A backpackers' pad and a sleeping bag didn't seem all that comfortable, but Josie was sound asleep, curled on her side the way Dawn used to sleep. She was wearing a tank top for pajamas, and its thin strap exposed the cherry tree on her shoulder and chest in all its glory. She really was an exquisite artist.

Stiffly, Beth bent down to pull the sleeping bag up an inch. That was better. She didn't want Josie to be cold. When she grabbed the dresser to pull herself back up, she froze. There on its top, waiting quietly, biding its time, was Dawn's diary. She knew Josie had gone back to get it, but not where she had put it.

Like a siren's song, it called to her. *Take me. Read me. I can fill that empty space in your heart.* A hand that wasn't entirely under control reached out for it. Fingers brushed its surface and then froze.

Why was she so sacred? Josie had said Dawn had written that she loved her. It could so easily be a lie. After all, it was just as common to fool yourself as someone else. She could certainly attest to that fact.

She swung back to the bed empty-handed...and empty-hearted.

The next morning, the same three women sat around the kitchen table, nursing their second cups of coffee. Maggie had thrown a dollop of vanilla ice cream into the mugs with the first and second go-around. One look at everyone stumbling into the kitchen and she had declared that they all needed a sweet beginning to the day.

"This is really good." Nikka licked her top lip. "It's like dessert all dressed up as a breakfast necessity."

God. She was pretty even with an ice cream mustache. Maggie forced herself to stop ogling and looked away.

Beth smiled too, at Nikka or catching her staring at Nikka—Maggie wasn't sure.

She seemed better. She wasn't clenching her hands or rubbing them obsessively anymore. Instead, they lightly gripped the mug in front of her.

Nikka's phone pinged, and she picked it up with an apologetic glance in their direction. "Sorry, I'm trying to keep track of what's going on in the outside world."

"Well?" Beth asked.

"Truman and Steinbrecker has finally released a statement."

"What is it?"

Nikka flicked at the screen. "It says that you aren't well and that in deference to one of their most cherished clients, when it all proved to be too much, they arranged for you to leave. Oh, and apparently you're very grateful."

Beth almost choked on her coffee.

Nikka bit her lip as she looked up from her phone. "This is Lea's first move. We definitely need to be at the courthouse at nine o'clock sharp to get the ball rolling. How long will it take us to drive down the hill?"

"An hour and a half," Maggie said.

"Okay, now add whatever else you need to make me feel comfortable."

"Two hours, then."

"We'll leave here at five thirty."

"That's crazy—" Maggie bit her lip. Nikka wasn't messing around.

"This has to work. Those letters can't be published." Beth pursed her lips. "Nikka, when this is all over, will you stay with me? I'll need someone to take care of this kind of stuff if it ever comes up again."

Maggie's heartbeat quickened. Nikka might stay!

"Let's just get through tomorrow. You may want bigger guns than I have. But I'll do everything I can to help you right now."

Now Maggie's heart pounded even faster. Nikka hadn't said yes, but she hadn't said no either.

"Hey, you guys." Josie shuffled into the kitchen, rubbing her eyes. "Why didn't anyone wake me?"

"Because I didn't need to." Beth couldn't keep the quiet triumph out of her voice.

"That's fantastic!" Josie's smile lit up the room, and despite her agitation, Maggie made a mental note to put a few of Dawn Montgomery's films on her Netflix queue.

"So what are we going to do to celebrate?" Josie asked.

"What if we go on a picnic?" Maggie jumped up to get Josie her coffee. "There's a meadow just down the path outside that puts Yosemite to shame this time of year. It's not far, Beth. You can make it. We'll all help. Ice cream in your coffee?"

"Oh yes." Josie held up two fingers. "Can I have two scoops?"

"Absolutely. I've a feeling that this is going to be a two-scoops-of-ice-cream kind of day." Maggie looked at the women in front of her. A week ago she hadn't really known any of them, and now she felt as if she was in the bosom of a brand-new family. Her glance lingered on Nikka. Head down, she was still tapping on her phone, still monitoring the outside world. Her hair hung in front of her face, giving her the tousled look that made Maggie's insides melt.

Tomorrow, she'd put back on her silk blouse and A-line skirt to drive down the hill, become Beth's knight in shining corporate armor, and possibly never come back.

She would if she wanted to. It was up to Nikka now.

"Excuse me." She gave Nikka one last look and headed out to the front porch. The sun hit it straight on in the morning, and the cell reception had always been better there.

Lauren answered on the fourth ring. Maggie could see her with her finger poised over both red and green buttons, jerking back and forth.

"Yes," she said.

"Lauren. I'm glad you picked up."

"I almost didn't."

"Yeah, I know, and I wouldn't have blamed you. Look." Her words came out fast. "I called to say I'm sorry for stealing your keys and for everything else over the last few days. I could tell you I did it for Beth. And I did. And I'm not sorry for that. But…"

Lauren said nothing; her breathing filtered through the line, though. She was still there.

"Okay. I did it for myself too. I know I do that a lot. I'm sure it was part of the problem between us, and for that I am sorry."

"You know you caused me a shitload of trouble. When they found out you were my employee... Well, let's just say a whole truckload of Lemon Lovers isn't going to fix this."

Maggie took a deep breath. Here was another woman who would have to find her own way back to her side.

"I get that. I didn't call for forgiveness...although that would be nice." She chuckled. Lauren didn't. "I called to tell you that I get why you were so pissed at the station with George and everything else. And I'm going to try to make it up to you whether you're offering forgiveness or not."

The silence stretched out over the phone line. "Maggie, I can't have you back at the bakery."

"I know," she said. "Just tell me you'll keep an open mind and let me try to show you that I value our friendship and not just what you can do for me."

Lauren sighed deeply. "Okay. But I'm no longer going to be a pushover where you're concerned."

"I know that too."

They hung up, and the tightness in Maggie's chest loosened. She almost called her brother. This was the adult she wanted to be.

Beth chuckled. The meadow was everything that Maggie had promised and more. Open and sunny, the picturesque grassland sat below rugged mountain peaks still dotted with snow in the distance. Purple, yellow, and red wildflowers carpeted the far side in a smorgasbord of color. Josie squealed as she rounded the corner. Her ever-present backpack flapping at her side, she scooted right to a patch of graceful red blossoms at the base of a pine tree. She had her sketchbook out even before she hit the ground.

Beth stopped as the path ran into the grassy field and rolled and stretched her ankle. It hurt. Nothing she couldn't handle, though. They had taken the walk slow and steady, and the brace that Maggie had talked her into wearing had helped.

"It's infused with copper." She had dangled the black ankle brace in front of her before they had left.

Beth had taken it to be nice and because she didn't want to kill the ready smile that always seemed to be on Maggie's lips, but after walking with it for five minutes, she was ready to buy stock in the company. Or maybe her ankle had never really been that bad to begin with...

"Here, let me help you." Nikka slid a hand under her arm and helped her off the path. Maggie was already spreading a quilt in the shade of a large tree, and soon more food than they could possibly eat covered its patchworks.

After lunch, the afternoon became lazy. The day was just warm enough to be comfortable; puffy clouds dotted the sky, and hummingbirds darted in and out of the wildflowers at the edge of the meadow. Resting on her elbows, Beth closed her eyes and took stock of her own body. The craving for comfort was still there, but it was muted and buried. The war might never be over, but this particular battle, she believed...she hoped, was won.

Buoyed by relief, she opened her eyes to find Josie a few feet away sketching intently, colored pencils littered all around. Her green eyes studied something far off in the distance, and blonde curls bobbed as she bent her head back to the page on her lap. Beth waited for the sharp stab of pain that always accompanied a glance at Josie. Nothing. It didn't come. Beth finally only saw Josie—not some strange version of Dawn with reshuffled features. For the first time, she considered the girl in front of her.

Lovely, for sure, but her looks weren't her best quality. She radiated a confidence in herself, and that was far better than beauty. Dawn would have been very proud of this poised, courageous young woman at the edge of the blanket. Actually, now that she was thinking about it more clearly, Dawn might have been a little envious of her as well. No matter. Beth was proud enough for the both of them.

"Beth, why didn't you ever write a sequel to *Heartwood*?" Nikka's question cut into her thoughts. Her smile must have turned into a frown, for Nikka quickly added, "Sorry, am I prying?"

"No. No. Their story was over. Bonnie and Daisy had nothing more to say."

Nikka nodded, generously accepting the answer that Beth had given for decades.

"The truth, though," she surprised herself by adding, "is a little more complicated."

The air around them stilled. Nikka leaned in; Maggie stopped repacking the picnic basket, and even Josie flipped closed her sketchbook to give Beth her full attention.

Was she ready for this?

"Before Kerry and Collier, *Heartwood* was published by Titanium Pages as a pulp lesbian novel. You should have seen that cover. A woman—I guess it was Bonnie—takes a chainsaw to a freshly fallen tree. She's busting out of her flimsy blouse as she leans over. As if anyone would work in that kind of shirt. Daisy stands on the other side of the tree, looking at her with such longing, it's as if she invented the feeling. God, I hated the cover when I first saw it, but I was really in no position or mood to argue. And I guess Titanium knew what they were doing. It did well as pulp. Just enough moments to fuel straight men's fantasies, I guess."

Beth ran a hand through her cropped hair. "But then something amazing happened. Somehow it reached small towns, and lesbians, isolated from themselves, each other, and the world, believed that here was a book that told their story. Maybe they didn't live in California or work in a sawmill, but I guess they identified with Bonnie. Coming of age all rolled up in coming out. I was, at the same time, cranking out volume after volume of *Don't Waste Your Wishes* because it paid the bills and numbed my mind, since writing anything real had become unthinkable. For a long time, Kerry and Collier tried to hide the fact that the same woman who had written about wishes and mythical creatures for kids had also written about the forbidden love between women. So any time the idea of a sequel came up, they cut it off at the knees. It's been so long. Honestly, I can't believe anyone is still asking."

"Oh my God, Beth," Nikka said. "Your book made all the difference for me. I had a hard time accepting who I was until I read that book. Bonnie spoke for me when I couldn't." She looked at Maggie and blushed.

"I love it more every time I read it," Maggie said. "Daisy's so full of life."

"And I want to finish it. I mean, that's saying a lot for me."

They all laughed at Josie, who went cross-eyed in a mock scowl.

"You know, there were times I thought about a sequel. Scenes or moments would pop in my head. Then I told myself that I was done with real writing. But the truth, and I know that I've denied this for years, is that everyone's right. Bonnie is me and Daisy is Dawn, and to go back and tell a story that could only exist in fiction is just too hurtful."

"You never found anyone else?" Maggie asked.

"No."

Beth rubbed her eyes under her glasses. A hummingbird whizzed past her. They all turned to look at it. No one was going to bite.

Except Josie. "My grandmother hoped you would," she said softly.

"Would what?" Beth wanted to know and didn't all at the same time.

"Write more. She wanted a whole slew of *Heartwood* books. She even had an idea about Bonnie and Daisy living out their golden years in some exotic locale."

"Is that in the diary, too?" Beth's voice grew shaky.

"It is." Josie grabbed her backpack, pulled out the tattered composition book, and held it out to Beth for the second time. "Why don't you take a look?"

Beth froze and studied the blank cover. A thousand thoughts whirled through her mind—so many she was having a hard time sorting them all out.

The girl was right. She was going to read it sooner or later; everyone here knew that, including herself, and whatever was in it, good or bad, wasn't going to change. Fear could only hold her back for so long.

Beth swallowed hard and reached out a hand for the book. It was lighter than she remembered. It took her a minute, but eventually she cracked open the cover. The first page was yellowed, and the ink faded into its seams. In her memory, she could so clearly see Dawn sitting at the kitchen table filling her black-and-gold fountain pen, a gift from the studio, with ink every other week. When she had asked why, Dawn had shrugged and had mumbled something about autographs.

Maggie pulled first Josie and then Nikka up and off the blanket. "Let's give her some privacy."

Beth ran a finger down the first page. Her world narrowed to just her and the composition book.

> *B doesn't know I took one of her books last night. She won't miss it, and it's comforting to have a secret that I don't share with her. I know that having her here and making her fall in love with me is necessary to my plan, my future, and, more importantly, my child's future. But it feels like she is everywhere all at once. I created that writing room so I would have some time to myself every day. It's hard to take, the way she looks at me, her brown eyes so full of hope and adoration. This whole scheme is almost too easy. Like taking candy from a baby.*

Alone on the blanket, Beth gasped, and dread spread from her heart to the tips of her fingers. This was everything that she had feared. No, it was worse. She was all but admitting that their whole relationship was a means to her end. Dawn's voice, low and rich, had reached across the years to hiss *like taking candy from a baby* right into her ear and into her soul.

She snapped the book shut, and her shoulders tensed as she tried to build up her defenses against those words and what they could do. *Take a breath. Take a breath.* Beth looked out to the meadow as fresh air filled her lungs. The green grass, the blue sky, Josie studying something thin and purple in her hand. She cocked her head. Josie wouldn't steer her wrong. She wasn't sure of much these days, but she was sure of that.

She flipped through the pages, and the book opened almost of its own accord. A crease in the spine maybe or Dawn's hand from the grave. Who knew?

I'm in trouble. Deep, deep trouble. B read me her story today. I was expecting something immature and childish that I could easily dismiss. It was on some level, but I could see the glimpses of the writer she will become. Not that I'm any real judge, but I've read enough bad material from writers to know when I am in the hands of someone good. God help me. I felt like I was in that tent. The heat from an Indian summer surrounded me. All I had to do was reach out, and I could run my fingers down the rich brocade of the curtains. I saw tarot cards in front of me as sure as I see my hand right now. But they weren't Karen's cards. They were mine—and they sure as hell weren't blank. They were full of dark images of Jimmy and fighting him for a child he doesn't want. Images of me old and ugly in a world that celebrates youth. Certainly, nothing good there. And then as Karen's future began to fill with those wild adventures, mine began to change too. To a different future, a better one. Every time that Madame Valentini flipped a card over for Karen, she flipped one over for me too. And I couldn't believe it! B was in every single one of them!

I just looked back at the beginning, what I wrote there. B looking at me with hope and adoration. I thought it weak then. But now I know there is power in such a look. She's the only person I have ever met who looks at me with rose-colored glasses and at the same time loves me for exactly who I am, warts and all. The first person where I can be myself and not have to act all the time. She makes me feel really and truly safe. For the first time in my life.

When the story was over, I got up and went to her and kissed her. She's wanted it from the moment we saw each other in that odious man's real estate office and my plan took root. I knew that I would have to kiss her eventually, but what I didn't know is that I would want to. It's inexplicable, but when our lips touched and she jumped into us with everything she was, my tarot cards were suddenly in indelible ink. I panicked and withdrew from her lips. This is not the future I had planned. But now, it is the only one I can imagine. I am terrified. God help us both.

The words blurred as tears flooded into Beth's eyes. If only Dawn had told her half of this and not kept her feelings a secret. If she had, Beth would have stood up to Jimmy that fateful day and their future would have been so very different. She ran her fingers over the diary's cover. At least she knew the truth now. Dawn loved her as much as she had loved Dawn.

Nikka followed Maggie down a tiny dirt path that ran from the edge of the meadow into the pine forest. "This is gorgeous."

"Isn't it? I used to pretend it was Ameliah's forest in *Don't Waste Your Wishes*. I even had my wishing tree."

"Oh my God. So did I." Nikka laughed. "In a park right by our house. Mine was nothing like these. I think only dogs and I ever paid it any attention."

"It's not the tree, though, right? It's the belief that wishes can come true." Maggie stopped at a sugar pine that soared upwards.

Nikka reached up to touch a long pine cone that hung from its branches and then dropped her hand to the trunk. "I think I might have believed that once. Somewhere, along the line, though, it turned into a belief in hard work."

"I still believe. This is my tree." Maggie patted its rough bark and slid her finger down close to where Nikka's was.

They both glanced at their hands and then at each other. They were almost exactly the same height. Strange, Nikka had never noticed that before. All either of them had to do was lean in and twist her head ever so slightly, and their lips would meet. That warm, fuzzy feeling that she had been nursing all day turned positively scalding. Would the kiss be soft or hard...or, God help her, maybe both?

"We should wish for something now." Nikka's voice was low and cracked with emotion. "If you'll share your tree with me..."

"Yes." The word was little more than a breath.

They both leaned in to opposite sides of the tree.

Nikka whispered the only desire that leapt to mind, "A kiss."

"A kiss."

Maggie closed her eyes as her lips brushed the bark on her side of the tree. Visions of grabbing Nikka and swinging her around until their bodies pressed together materialized as soon as she said the words. She would take her in her arms and kiss her long and deep until they both gasped for breath. She tingled all over with excitement seeped in doubt. No. Nikka would have to make the first move.

They came around the tree at almost the same moment, their hands still inches apart on the trunk. All Nikka had to do was slide her pinkie finger down an inch, and they would be touching.

"Son of a bitch. Do I have the worst timing or what?" Josie materialized two trees down, grinning from ear to ear. The teasing was unmistakable in her voice. "Beth wants to show you something. Or should I tell her that I threw down some breadcrumbs, and you'll make your own way out?"

"No, we're coming," Maggie said.

"Did she read the diary? Did it go well?" Nikka asked.

Maggie gave the tree one last pat. The wishes didn't have to come true immediately. They never did in the books. They were always granted at a time when you least expected it.

Beth waved them over as soon as they cleared the trees.

"Look!" She held out the composition book open to a page filled to the edges with ink.

From far away, Maggie thought it illegible scribbling, but as she got closer, she realized the same three words were written over and over until there wasn't a blank space on the page.

I love her, I love her, I love her.

Beth had her answer. And then some.

"Oh, Beth. I'm so happy for you." Nikka bounced on the tips of her toes.

Maggie blinked hard and looked at her again. There was something softer about Nikka, around her eyes and her mouth. Maggie couldn't put a finger on it. Something had changed, but what? Something good, she hoped.

Josie poked her playfully and gave her a glance as if she knew exactly what she was thinking.

"What about you? You got someone special?" Maggie had wanted to ask for ages. It had just never come up. Her gaydar, which was usually so accurate, just couldn't get a read on Josie.

"Oh God, no. I'm way too young to settle down. Besides, I'll tell you, slinging the ink is practically foreplay. Men, women, and everything in between throw themselves at me. All you got to do is pound some skin if you want to pound some skin, if you know what I mean."

"Not in the least." Nikka laughed.

"I think it's tattoo slang, and she's telling us that no grass grows under her feet in the relationship department," Maggie said.

"Pretty much. I'm fluid in my life: my partners and my sexuality."

"Now you sound exactly like your grandmother." Beth hugged the diary to her chest.

"Thank you. I can only hope my someone special is as great as you someday."

They continued to chat until everything was packed away into the basket.

Maggie went over to help Beth up. "You good?"

"Yes. Actually, better than I've been in a long time." Beth's gaze flicked down to the book still in her hands. "You?"

Maggie's gaze drifted off to Nikka, who stood at the edge of the meadow, laughing at something Josie had just said. Just looking at her made her insides melt. She had it bad. "I hope so. We'll see."

Nikka punched the down arrow key on her laptop repeatedly until she had scanned all the motions she would file first thing tomorrow. One stated that Lea had abused her conservatorship in every way possible. Another claimed that the contract for "The Tarot Card" had been signed under duress. A third made a case to throw out all the contracts Lea had signed just days before. Yes, a very productive afternoon and a good omen for tomorrow.

She reached for her briefcase to find her to-do list so she could slash these jobs off the paper. Her hand froze in mid-air. She hadn't started one! Probably the most important moment of her career and she hadn't even started a checklist? What the...?

"Hey, I thought you might need a pick-me-up." Maggie placed a mug of something hot and steamy on the coffee table by her computer. "It's tea. Not caffeinated, so you can sleep, but it's supposed to make you alert. I don't know how that works, but it's on the box, so it must be true."

Maggie looked down at her on the couch and smiled. Not her ready grin, but something more timid and cautious.

They hadn't said much to each other since they all got back to the cabin. Beth, fooling no one, had announced that she was going to take a nap and had disappeared with the book and her memories. Josie had escaped to the front porch to make a series of phone calls. Maggie had taken off for a run, and Nikka had sat down in the living room at her computer to put the finishing touches on her work.

Truth be told, the touch-ups had taken her so long because she kept replaying that moment out by the tree. Not the way Maggie's energy had reached for her, although that sure was something. She'd never felt anything like that before, and she was beginning to miss the current when it wasn't there. No, the moment she had kept replaying was leaning in to the tree and whispering for a kiss. Putting her desire into words gave it reality, somehow.

"You ready for tomorrow?" Maggie asked.

"I am. At least I think I am."

"You'll be great." She gave a long look and then moved to the stairs. "Six thirty sharp. Right?"

"No, we said—"

"I know. I'm just messing with you. Good night."

"Night," Nikka said, already regretting Maggie's absence. It would be foolish to go after her. Wouldn't it?

A shrill ring was her answer—an old-fashioned telephone ring reverberated around the room. It took her a moment to realize that it was her father's ringtone coming from her briefcase.

"Papa? Is everything all right?" She couldn't remember the last time he had called her.

"You tell me. Sasha heard about client of yours. Beth Walker. Tell me you aren't mixed up in this nonsense?"

Nikka forced herself to take a deep breath. This was the one call she was dreading most of all. Talking to her father was another thing she had intended to push off until tomorrow, when she knew how to spin it, but her father had always had an impeccable sense of timing—upstairs, Maggie's bedroom door clicked shut.

"Well, Papa…" Better rip the Band-Aid off fast. "I am."

He groaned deeply. "I would expect this of Sasha, but not you, Jenikka."

Nikka cringed. Using her full name was never a good sign.

"Look, Papa…" She needed time to think. "I… I…" Inspiration struck. "You know how you always say that a problem is often an opportunity dressed up in an old tolstovka shirt full of holes?"

"Da."

"And that you need to take the shirt off to really see what is underneath?"

"Da."

"Well, that's what I'm doing, Papa. I've got something that looks like a problem to everyone else, but I think, I hope, that when we undress it, we'll see a huge opportunity."

Silence stretched out between them. Her father was almost never at a loss for words. The last time he had been so quiet was when she had told him that she liked women. Then, it had taken him a full ten minutes to reply, and it hadn't been favorable. Her heart began to pound. She needed her father behind her if she was going to make a real go of this in the morning.

"How big?" He finally broke the silence.

"Pretty big." Superstition took hold of her, and she whispered, "It could make my career. Or kill it. It's unclear. But, Papa, it's the right thing to do whatever happens."

More silence. This time she could almost hear the wheels in her father's head turning.

"Then go for it."

Nikka let out the breath she had been holding.

"You know, I always say if opportunity doesn't knock, build door and do knocking yourself."

That was a new one. Sound advice and, more important, her father was in her corner. A warm feeling washed over her.

"Thanks, Papa."

At five thirty sharp the next morning, all four of Nikka's Subaru doors popped open right on cue. Nikka glanced at her watch and smiled at Maggie over the car's roof. "Good omen. We're perfectly on time."

Maggie choked back a cough. It wasn't fate at all. She had set the alarm by the side of her bed, arranged for her brother to call her five minutes after that, and only Josie's pre-arranged knocking had finally gotten her out of bed. Still half asleep, she studied Nikka through eyes that were almost slits.

She had called it. The silk blouse and straight skirt were back. She looked the part, but her voice was brittle and that smile hadn't spread to her eyes. Maggie could tell that she was nervous.

Who wasn't? Butterflies, and not the good kind, circled in her own stomach. So much rode on this morning. Beth's future, Nikka's, and her own probably too.

"Would there be time to stop for coffee?" Beth asked from the backseat. She looked tired, but calm as she pulled the seat belt over her shoulder.

"When we get gas, we can also get coffee." Maggie needed some herself.

Only Josie seemed unfazed by the early morning wake-up call, but even her shoulders tightened when the Subaru slid into the empty parking lot of the courthouse.

Nikka parked right up front, killed the engine, and swiveled around to pat Beth on the arm. "It won't all happen right now, but rest assured *Beth Walker Revealed* will never see the light of day. I won't stop until it's dead and buried."

"Gruesome," Josie said.

"Just do your best." Beth squeezed Nikka's hand. "Thank you, dear."

Nikka swung back and already had the door half opened when her gaze found Maggie's. "Come with me?"

The butterflies in her stomach landed. "Yes, I would love to."

After jumping out of the car, they met on the sidewalk.

When they were just about to enter the courthouse, its doors swung wide open with a bang. Standing there on the threshold, like the Wicked Witch of the Springs, was Lea Truman.

Tall, sexy, and very, very angry.

"What do you think you're doing?"

"What Beth wants, Lea," Nikka said calmly, but the tremor in her voice betrayed her. "I could ask you the same thing."

"Oh please. It doesn't take a genius to figure out where you'd be first thing this morning." Maggie felt the temperature drop by at least ten degrees. "I just didn't know you'd bring the whole Scooby gang. Which one is she? Fred or Velma?"

Heat flooding her face, Maggie took a step toward Lea.

Nikka quickly threw up a hand to halt her progress. "No. She's not why we are here," Nikka said, and with the truth of those words, Maggie backed down.

"Good to see you haven't lost your good head on those pretty shoulders. Listen carefully because I'm only going to offer this once. Come back to the firm. Your job's still there. Bring Beth. Tell her whatever you need to get her to come back. Surely you can see it's in both our best interests to bury this as deep as we can. The press will buy it. You can take the lead on this case. I'll make you rich, and eventually, I'll name you partner."

Maggie almost choked right there on the spot. What the fuck was Lea thinking? They hadn't gone to hell and back in the last forty-eight hours to hand Beth back to Lea. Had they? Nikka wasn't saying anything, and her eyes had gone all steely. Was she actually considering it?

"Think of your career, Nikka. You might have Beth Walker as a client right now, but as soon as this is over, she'll want an established firm, bigger than you. The door will be hitting you on the backside before she can say 'I terminate your services.' Then where will you be? Unemployed and unhireable.'"

Still Nikka said nothing. Maggie tensed. Why wasn't she getting in her face?

"I can bury you." Lea's voice was cold as steel.

"But I will bury you." Finally. The reply was perfect, but it came from the last person Maggie had expected.

Nikka and Maggie both jumped back as Beth, who barely came up to Lea's chest, slid in between them. Her eyes blazed behind her black glasses, and her body shimmered with strength.

"Ms. Walker." Lea's voice turned silky smooth. "I'm so glad you're here. There seems to have been a terrible misunderstanding, which we can rectify at once. Just meet with me—"

"A long time ago, I knew another bully. Worse than you even. I let him convince me of things that weren't true. And I'll be damned if I'm going to let that happen again. I've no idea what's going to develop from here on in, only that I withdraw my business from your firm. You'll be hearing from my one and only lawyer."

She wound her arm first through Nikka's and then Maggie's before they walked through the door to the courthouse. Josie jumped out of the car to hurry after them.

"What are you looking at?" Lea lashed out at Josie when she passed.

"Nobody."

Maggie squeezed Beth's arm. No truer words had ever been spoken.

The late afternoon sun sparkled off the river at the Riverside Inn and Resort like a band of diamonds. When they stepped inside the empty lobby, Germaine, the handsome concierge, waved to them with both hands.

Looks like I'm back in grace, Nikka thought. All it took was a kidnapping, a weekend on the run, several hours in court, and a new attitude.

Her gaze drifted to Maggie, who walked one step ahead of her. With her long legs, floppy hair, and energy that knew no bounds, she was the reason that Germaine and the business owners in the Springs no longer hated Nikka. Maggie had also been ready to bite Lea's head off earlier just to protect her. A warmth that was beginning to feel familiar seeped through her.

Nikka grinned. The morning couldn't have gone better. Everything was filed; Kerry and Collier had been notified and had given assurances that the website for *Beth Walker Revealed* and the book itself would be pulled down as soon as humanly possible. Beth had returned triumphantly to Fern House to find it hers again. Josie had danced around the room, pointing to things and places that she had read about in Dawn's diary.

Why, then, had Maggie been so quiet since the courthouse? She of all people should be walking on air. Both Josie and she had their roles, but Maggie had been the one from the start who had figured out what was going on and had never given up—she was able to make the hard choices when everyone was against her.

"Well, hello, you two," Germaine said. "I hear congratulations are in order."

"Who called you from the courthouse, Jane or Manny?" Maggie asked.

"Both." Germaine laughed. "Within minutes of each other. So it went well?"

"It did." Nikka smiled.

Maggie still wasn't looking at her.

"Here, let me get your stuff." Germaine opened a door to a side office and darted inside while she continued talking. "When Maggie called this weekend, we cleared out your room. I hope we got everything. Oh wait, your little suitcase isn't here. I'll just run upstairs for it."

As soon as Germaine had left, Nikka reached out to Maggie. Every other time they had touched, Maggie's arm had tensed with excitement, but now it just lay limp in her grasp.

"Hey, is there something wrong?"

Maggie shook her head.

"Come on. I know you well enough by now. You say whatever is on your mind. What's stopping you now?"

"I'm not sure I want to know the answer." Her tone was strangely serious.

"To what?"

"Okay, so when Lea asked you about coming back and making you partner, you didn't say no. In fact, you didn't say anything. Beth was the one who said no, and I was just wondering..." She searched for her next words and finally just shrugged.

"If I was considering it?"

"Yeah."

"How could you think that? I told you that I didn't want what she was offering anymore."

"I know, but—"

Nikka squeezed her arm. "You want to know why I didn't answer. One, I was too busy thinking you were right. You had Lea pegged from the start. She's a flat-out criminal."

Maggie slid her hand up and grasped Nikka's arm. The connection was electric.

"Two, I was making a to-do list in my head of all the things that I can pass on to the DA so he can write up an indictment against Lea."

"A to-do list?" A little smile formed at the edge of her lips. "Seriously?"

"Yeah, I do it all the time. I thought I had broken the habit, but apparently I was wrong." Nikka glanced around the still-empty lobby and pulled Maggie away from the open space by the front desk to a more protected one by the fireplace. "And crazily, three, I was thinking about when I would do this."

She dropped a hand to Maggie's hip and pushed slightly. Maggie groaned and took a step back.

Nikka slid into the space. The push-and-pull continued until Maggie was pinned against the fireplace with no escape. Not that Maggie seemed to be looking for one. Nikka slid in so close that they were just inches apart, eye to eye, nose to nose, mouth to...

Her lips were soft and yielding and parted instantly as Nikka found them. Maggie moaned, and Nikka trembled in response. Desire rippled through her and dug in deep below her belly. A tongue darted across her lips. Maggie's touch was exquisite, and the kiss leapt to new heights.

Nikka slid her hands up Maggie's back and crushed them even closer. Maggie's breasts were full and firm and promised a thousand other pleasures. Still Nikka couldn't get enough, and she slipped a leg between Maggie's, bringing them even closer. Every part of them melted into each other. She had no idea where she ended and Maggie began.

Finally, after what seemed like an eternity locked in each other's arms, they pulled away. Their breaths came in gasps, and Nikka licked her swollen lips.

"I got my wish," Maggie said simply.

"I didn't."

Maggie's eyebrows raised in an unspoken question.

"I didn't know a kiss like that existed. So how could I wish for it? I—"

Maggie grabbed her face with both hands and crushed their lips together again. Hard and soft all at the same time. Nikka melted in her arms.

When they finally broke apart, Germaine was back by the desk, Nikka's little case on its slick surface.

"See? I told you." Germaine stared at them with wide-eyed amusement. "The Springs changes everything. You just got to know when to grab it."

Epilogue

When I was nearly twenty-two, I tore all the
ligaments in my right ankle. Looking back at it
now, I believe it all started when Mr. Thompson,
the dentist from the City, insisted that he wanted
a showstopper of a house, and my boss—

BETH'S FINGERS FROZE ON THE keys of the computer;
the blinking cursor sat there by the last *s*, not moving. No
reader would want to hear about her and Dawn that way.
They didn't want old Beth looking back at events that had
happened so long ago they could have happened to someone
else.

Readers wanted young Beth, before the ankle injury,
before she knew who she was. When love was shiny and new,
and the future was still a mystery.

Beth snapped the laptop closed and riffled through a shelf
above the desk. She pulled out one of the new composition
books that Josie had brought up on her last visit. The cover
was a baby-blue. She ran a finger across the smooth surface.
Dawn would have loved the color.

She grabbed a shiny mechanical pencil out of a Citrine
pencil holder that *Home at Heartwood* had sent her when
Nikka had renegotiated the contracts with the town. She
clicked the bottom, and lead magically popped out of the

point. After all these years, she finally had her enchanted pencil.

Yes, much better.

Maggie had just left for her run in the woods. Training for another crazy climb, she'd be gone for a while and then be back to make her dinner, complete with pineapple happy faces. Maggie had branched out to poodles made from broccoli and penguins from tiny eggplants. Now Beth chuckled every time they sat down to dinner.

Rehiring Maggie had been her first act when she got her life back. And it had proved to be her best move—laughter everywhere. Even if the scale ticked upwards every time she got on it. Dr. Harvey had congratulated her on her good health, but she couldn't button any of her pants anymore.

Beth rubbed a hand down her new pajama jeans—looked like jeans, felt like pajamas and no button. Easy answer to the problem, if Maggie stayed, that was. She was making noises about moving to the City so she and Nikka could be together full-time.

"Grab love when you can," she had told the girls when they had cautiously brought the scenario up. "You never know how long it will last."

They nodded and smiled, but so far nothing at all had happened. The logistics of what Maggie would do down in the City and how Nikka would run a business and a relationship out of a small condo had loomed too large. They were electric when they were together, but Beth had firsthand knowledge of what could happen to true love when logistics got in the way.

So, when the building that used to house Hank's real estate office came up for sale, she had snapped it up. What had Nikka's father said when he came out to help repair the deck? *It pays to plan ahead. It wasn't raining when Noah built the ark.*

She could give Nikka an office in town, and Maggie could stay on at Fern House. Their lives would go into overdrive once Nikka added the negotiations for the Hollywood movie deal for *Don't Waste Your Wishes* to her plate. And then there was that Broadway producer who was sniffing around, talking about turning *Heartwood* into a musical. So many reasons to bring Nikka to the Springs...for good.

The pencil felt cool and heavy in her hand. She positioned it right above the paper, and excitement ran through her. The tingling that surged from the tip of her finger to her toes felt exactly like falling in love. This was her way back to Dawn...and to herself. The pencil flew across the page as the words poured out of her.

A small bell jingled as the front door of the Good Neighbor real estate office swung open. I cringed at my desk. The bell was a happy sound, but its tingling reminded me that my life was not my own...

About Catherine Lane

Catherine Lane started to write fiction on a dare from her wife. She's thrilled to be a published author, even though she had to admit her wife was right. They live happily in Southern California with their son and a very mischievous pound puppy.

Catherine spends most of her time these days working, mothering, or writing. But when she finds herself at loose ends, she enjoys experimenting with recipes in the kitchen, paddling on long stretches of flat water, and browsing the stacks at libraries and bookstores. Oh, and trying unsuccessfully to outwit her dog.

She has published several short stories and novels.

CONNECT WITH CATHERINE:
Website: www.catherinelanefiction.wordpress.com
Facebook: www.facebook.com/profile.
php?id=100004577749399
E-Mail: claneauthor01@gmail.com

Other Books from Ylva Publishing

www.ylva-publishing.com

The Set Piece

Catherine Lane

ISBN: 978-3-95533-376-8
Length: 284 pages (64,000 words)

Amy gets an irresistible offer: Become engaged to soccer star Diego Torres to hide that he's gay and in return get a life of luxury. The simple decision soon becomes complicated. Diego is being blackmailed, and Amy needs to find the culprit. It doesn't help that Casey, his pretty assistant, is a major distraction. Will Amy watch her from the sidelines or find the courage to get back into the game?

Popcorn Love

KL Hughes

ISBN: 978-3-95533-265-5
Length: 347 pages (113,000 words)

Her love-life lacking, wealthy fashion exec Elena Vega agrees to a string of blind dates set up by her best friend Vivian in exchange for Vivian finding a suitable babysitter for her son, Lucas. Free-spirited college student Allison Sawyer fits the bill perfectly.

Bitter Fruit

Lois Claorec Hart

ISBN: 978-3-95533-216-7
Length: 244 pages (50,000 words)

Jac accepts an unusual wager from her best friend. Jac has one month to seduce a young woman she's never met. Though Lauren is straight and engaged, Jac begins her campaign confident that she'll win the bet. But Jac's forgotten that if you sow an onion seed, you won't harvest a peach. When her plan goes awry, will she reap the bitter fruit of her deception? Or will Lauren turn the tables on her?

Bunny Finds a Friend

Hazel Yeats

ISBN: 978-3-95533-499-4
Length: 204 pages (55,000 words)

Cara Jong's bad day doesn't improve after a run-in with Jude Donovan, who's playing Santa in a department store in Amsterdam. When Cara finds out that the woman beneath the Santa suit is a children's book writer, she's intrigued. But she doesn't trust her luck in love. Can Cara's meddling sisters and a hilarious road trip convince her to go after her happily-ever-after with the writer?

Coming from Ylva Publishing

www.ylva-publishing.com

Flinging It

G Benson

Frazer, head midwife at a hospital in Perth, Australia, is trying to make her corner of the world a little better by starting up a programme for at-risk parents. Not everyone is excited about her ideas. Surrounded by red tape, she finally has to team up with Cora, a social worker who is married to Frazer's boss.

Cora is starting to think her marriage is beyond saving, even if she wants to. Feeling smothered by a domineering spouse, she grabs hold of the programme and the distraction Frazer offers with both hands. Soon the two women get a little too close and find themselves in a situation they never dreamed themselves capable of: an affair.

As the two fall deeper, both are torn between their taboo romance and their morals. But walking away from each other may not be as simple as they thought.

Not-So-Straight Sue

Cheyenne Blue

Lawyer Sue Brent has buried her queerness deep within, until a disastrous date forces her to confront the truth. She returns to her native Australia and an outback law practice. When Sue's friend, Moni, arrives to work as an outback doctor, Sue sees a new path to happiness with her. But Sue's first love, Denise, appears begging a favor, and Sue and Moni's burgeoning relationship is put to the test.

Heartwood
© 2016 by Catherine Lane

ISBN: 978-3-95533-674-5

Also available as e-book.

Published by Ylva Publishing, legal entity of Ylva Verlag, e.Kfr.

Ylva Verlag, e.Kfr.
Owner: Astrid Ohletz
Am Kirschgarten 2
65830 Kriftel
Germany

www.ylva-publishing.com

First edition: 2016

Credits
Edited by Sandra Gerth
Proofread by Jacqui McCarthy
Cover Design & Print Layout by Streetlight Graphics

Printed in Great Britain
by Amazon